THE HOTEL MAID

MICHELLE DUNNE

Storm
PUBLISHING

To request permissions, contact the publisher at rights@stormpublishing.co

Ebook ISBN: 978-1-80508-525-6
Paperback ISBN: 978-1-80508-527-0

Cover design: Blacksheep
Cover images: Shutterstock

Published by Storm Publishing.
For further information, visit:
www.stormpublishing.co

For Emily

PROLOGUE

JUNE

Just inside the door of room 208, the maid stood uncharacteristically still. Her cleaning bucket rested on the floor near her feet. She glanced up, but only briefly, before her hands started busying themselves. She smoothed down her pin-sharp waistcoat, turning each of its buttons so the hotel crests lined up perfectly. Then she took a shaky breath as she tugged on the cuffs of her heavily starched white blouse, noticing a tiny splash of bright red blood. She frowned and checked her wounds, but the bandages were pristine.

'Damn it,' she whispered, ignoring the chill that came over her.

It probably wasn't as noticeable as she imagined. But June liked things to be just so. That's what made her one of the best maids the Cedarwood Manor Hotel had ever had.

She'd been in the room for more than a minute now, but she still hadn't gone past the short entrance hall. The plush, hand-tufted carpet felt like a cloud under her feet and the bespoke Egyptian cotton bed cover with the hotel's crest hand-sewn into it was pulled tightly and smoothly across the bed. It looked like it either hadn't been slept in, or that someone had got there before her. To the left of the enormous bed, the bathroom door was ajar. Through it she could see the gold taps shining in the morning sunlight. For the most part, the room appeared not to need her services. Which would have been highly unusual given its current occupant.

Erica Kelly was not the kind of guest who tidied as she went. She also loved to complain. But not today. She was too busy being dead in a pool of blood, on the floor beside her bed. Only she couldn't be dead, could she? Not Mrs Kelly.

The dead silence that was beginning to settle on the room was broken by the shrill ringing of the antique rotary dial phone on the bedside table. The sudden noise shocked June into action and she hurried across the room to answer it. She didn't immediately notice the pair of bloody footprints she left in her wake, which was just as well. June could become distracted by something like that. And she couldn't afford to be distracted now. Not from this.

'Hello!' Her voice was almost as shrill as the ringing had been.

'Mrs K... June? Is that you?' the receptionist, Lauren, asked.

'She's...'

'Is Mrs Kelly's daughter, Mia, there?' Lauren asked anxiously. 'Mrs Kelly called the police and they're on the way up! She reported Mia missing from *here*, June!'

June's breath caught in her chest.

'Put Mrs Kelly on the phone. June? Will you bloody answer me!'

'She's dead,' June said, but the words hardly came out at all.

'What? No, she... oh my God, Mia's dead!' Lauren cried.

The line went dead. June slowly lowered the receiver back into its cradle. She glanced down at the bloody mess on the floor, which only vaguely resembled the formidable woman she once was. Mrs Kelly was dead, alright. But more importantly, ten-year-old Mia Kelly was missing and the police were on their way. June could hear them hurrying along the hall now.

She glanced breathlessly between Mrs Kelly and the door, as she waited for their arrival. And with it, a world that existed only within the walls of the Cedarwood Manor Hotel would be razed to the ground.

ONE

JUNE

Six weeks earlier...

June Calloway has been cleaning rooms at the luxurious Cedarwood Manor Hotel for exactly six years. Every day she dons the crisp maid's uniform and makes her way from bedroom to bedroom, glimpsing at how the other half live. She takes care to do a good job, discreetly and quietly. Even if the guests are still in the room while she's there, they hardly notice her moving among their anti-fungal creams and soiled underwear that they've discarded on the floor. All the little things that would make them die of shame if an actual *person* were to see them. But June never discusses what she sees. And the guests' utter indifference to her doesn't bother her in the slightest. Truth be told, she likes it. There's a certain comfort in being invisible and June doesn't mind the work. This hotel took a chance on her when many others wouldn't have. She repays them by being the best maid they've ever had. *They* might never admit to that. But *she* knows it and that's what matters.

Like she did every day, June arrived early at the service entrance. She wore black leggings and a black sweatshirt, of which she had two. She'd never been the type of girl that people noticed. This, she realised, was a valuable trait to have. Despite being only twenty-two years old, she kept her dark hair in a short, cropped style and wore minimal make-up. June was always careful not to be seen by any of the guests until she was decked out in the sharply pressed navy trousers, crisp white blouse and buttoned-up waistcoat of the Cedarwood Manor Hotel, whose crest was proudly emblazoned upon it.

She made her way through the bowels of the hotel to the locker room, combed back her short brown hair again, scrubbed her hands and removed her fresh uniform from its garment bag. June liked the uniform. Every time she put it on, she felt transformed, from nobody, to somebody. She felt important when she was wearing it, because it was designed to look like a suit. And people in suits always tend to look important, regardless of what they're doing. But her favourite thing about it were the shoes. Soft, black leather lace-ups, with cushioned insoles. Wearing them felt like walking around on soft springs and June always did a little bounce when she put them on.

'Christ, I hate this bloody waistcoat,' one of the other maids complained, yanking it around her narrow frame. Two of them were fighting for space in front of the long mirror.

'I hate this whole ridiculous uniform,' the other retorted. 'Wouldn't it make more sense to let us clean in our stretchy pants and runners? I mean, who do they think will be looking at us?'

June shook her head. She couldn't remember either of their names because they'd only been working at the Manor for a few weeks. That seemed to be the case with most hotel staff these days. But they'd started on the same day, which forged an alliance between them. So as soon as one started complaining about the establishment, which never took more than a week or two, the other felt safe joining in. They'd leave soon, she was certain of it. They all did. That's why June made no effort to get to know them. Truth be told, she avoided them as much as she could. They had no sense of this place. No appreciation for it. So, she ignored them *and* the mirror. Like she always did.

Instead, she closed her locker and went about loading up her trolley. The other two weren't far behind her, but they had yet to acknowledge her presence. Or to stop talking and take a breath.

'My mouth is as dry as a nun's fanny,' the skinny one said, making a clucking sound.

'Good night so?' the other one asked, with a knowing grin.

'Ugh. Too good. This shift might actually kill me.'

Trudging behind June, they made their way to the store-room, which was located between the locker room and the laundry. As June took stock of what she needed, she half listened in relative silence. They emptied every thought in their heads out into the room and then waited for each other's approval. Or something like it. Still she listened in on their conversation. She liked to do that sometimes.

'...so Malcolm let me stay till after closing,' the skinny one continued with a grin.

June perked up at the mention of Malcolm's name.

'Oh, yeah?' giggled the other one. 'Is that all he let you do?'

The skinny one who had stayed somewhere until after closing glanced in June's direction and her smirk vanished. She looked to her taller counterpart and they both returned to loading up their trollies. They were probably the same age as June, but they were wary of her. Perhaps they thought she would snitch on them.

But that wasn't why June liked to listen in. She never gossiped or told tales. She just liked to listen in on stories about Malcolm Levy. He was the hotel security guard, and he had a finger in just about every pie. He pulled all sorts of strokes on the side. The kind of strokes that earned him money from people who could least afford to give it. And, as Heather in laundry often said, he'd get up on a gale of wind. Despite the fact that his long-time girlfriend was also his boss. She was the boss of *all* of them.

June didn't understand what anyone could possibly see in him. He was a middle-aged egomaniac, who managed to charm his way into the pants of every new staff member, in minimal time.

'Six years today, June,' Liz Sheehy announced sternly, as she strode in through the swinging door leading from the laundry room to the large, windowless storeroom.

'Wow,' the hungover maid muttered. 'She could be waving a sparkler in the air and singing happy birthday and she'd still make me feel like I was in trouble.'

'Thanks, Liz,' June replied, knowing that her statement was meant as a verbal pat on the back.

Liz stopped walking. She ignored June's reply and glared at the other two maids. 'You can start on the lobby toilets. I'll want to see my reflection in the porcelain, Annie. And when you're done there, the front steps need to be washed.'

'It's raining,' skinny maid, Annie, drawled.

The taller one busied herself stocking up her trolley.

'Last time I checked, there was no soap in that rain,' Liz replied with a tight smile, which wasn't really a smile at all. 'But maybe the rain is different where you come from.'

Liz had a prickly demeanour, but June was used to it. She was just that kind of boss. But she was alright in the grand scheme of things. Behind her back, everyone called her Luscious Liz on account of her addiction to injectable cosmetics. Some shortened it to just Luscious. Her face had been frozen, filled and plumped, and it was no longer capable of expressing her mood. But no matter what Liz had 'done', that mood never seemed to lift. Neither did her self-esteem, but no one saw that except June. There was some truth in what Annie had said. About the sparklers and the feeling of being in trouble. But June thought she was a silly girl to say it.

Liz was holding a small bundle of little brown envelopes containing their payslips. June's envelope also contained her actual pay, though none of the others knew that. There'd be uproar if they ever found out that she was paid in cash, while their hours all went through the books. That was the chance the hotel took on her when others wouldn't have.

June had no choice but to live below the radar. She gave Liz her reasons when they first met, and Liz agreed to keep June off the books. To keep her safe. In return, June helped keep hotel standards up where they belonged and never gave her boss anything to worry about.

'Let me know anytime you want me to put your P45 in one of these envelopes, Annie.' She was looking directly at the hungover maid, as she handed them out.

June wondered if she knew about her and Malcolm. If there even *was* a her and Malcolm. Either way, Liz had definitely taken against the girl. June could tell.

They each took their envelope and slipped it in their pocket. None of them was trusting enough to place it in their locker and walk out the door.

'What are you all still doing here? Chop-chop!' She clapped her hands loudly and walked away.

The new girls glanced at each other as Liz left the room through the other door. The one that led to the lifts and up to the hotel proper. When they were sure they were safe, they rolled their eyes in unison and laughed.

They all knew that Liz would never follow through and actually fire any of them. Hospitality staff were too hard to come by and Liz wasn't in the business of cutting off her nose to spite her face. Metaphorically speaking, at least. But she would make their lives infinitely less pleasant, despite herself.

'I honestly can't believe that you've been working here for

six whole years!' Skinny Annie was aghast, like this was a fate worse than death. 'I'll tell you what: if I'm still here after six years, you all have my permission to take me out and shoot me.'

'Do we have to wait the full six years?' June asked, only half-joking.

'Seriously, though, shouldn't there be a cake or something for that?' the tall one grumbled, and looked to Skinny Annie for agreement.

'Cake?!' Skinny Annie guffawed. 'Girl, she counts the nuts each squirrel gets, out in those woods. If she ever feeds us cake, you may be sure it's because she's checking to see if it's poisonous.'

The tall one laughed and nodded. 'You're right. You couldn't trust it.'

'She'll be back any minute,' June mumbled, just to shut them up. 'Maybe we should get a move on.'

'Do you actually like working here, or something?' the tall one asked, her nose scrunched up like there was a bad smell in the air.

'It's a job,' June replied, running through her trolley contents for a final time. She returned a few items to the shelves that she didn't require. 'I need some towels from the laundry.'

'As you're there, can you grab some for us, too?' the tall one asked. 'You need a few towels, don't you, Annie?'

'Yeah, thanks, June,' Skinny Annie replied, as she opened a miniature bottle of body lotion and began smearing it up her arms.

'Oh, is that nice?' The tall one leaned over to sniff Skinny Annie's arm.

June just stared at them for a minute, but they were oblivious. And lazy. Always waiting for someone else to do their work for them. She should say no, but she didn't. Truth be told, she was glad to go anywhere they wouldn't be.

One of the things she liked about her job, was the solitude it provided for a good portion of the day. Aside from early mornings in the storeroom and break times when they all herded themselves into the depressing staff canteen. But even then, June usually managed to avoid them. She very rarely had to spend time with her colleagues, and that suited her just fine.

'There she is now,' Heather said, as June went into the laundry. This was her standard hello. Heather was the long-suffering laundry worker who was heavily addicted to cigarettes, among other things. June liked her.

'Did you hear about that other dope?' Heather sidled up and half whispered, as she folded some sheets.

'Which dope?'

She bobbed her head towards the door. 'That scrawny maid in there.'

June shook her head, picking up a stack of towels.

'Well, Malcolm Levy is going around telling everyone that she was throwing herself at him, and some other bouncers, in a club in town last night.'

'Oh.' June nodded.

'He actually said to that lad, Simon—'

'Who's Simon?'

'The new boy in the bar. So, he says to Simon that she was "gagging" for it.' She rolled her eyes. 'But wait, wait.' She laughed then. 'Malcolm said that *he* wouldn't touch her with a bargepole, so he left her with one of his bouncer friends.'

'Sounds like Malcolm is the dope,' June muttered, still focusing on the towels, calculating how many she needed.

'Ah, well, we all know *he's* a dope. But I mean, talk about asking for trouble. What kind of an eejit goes on the prowl with their boss's boyfriend?'

They were quiet for a minute, while June picked up another bundle of towels for her lazy colleagues and Heather snapped another sheet open.

'Mind you,' she said, 'I don't think there's a woman alive

who Malcolm wouldn't touch. Bargepole or not.' Her mouth turned down and she shook her head. 'Nah. He's lying through his arse.'

June nodded, but Heather probably didn't notice. She was hidden from the waist up, behind a large pile of neatly folded, Turkish cotton towels.

'Anyway. See you at lunch.' Heather's gravelly voice hacked its way back around the bank of washing machines.

Built sometime in the 1800s as a private mansion, most of the Cedarwood Manor Hotel's old features had somehow been protected, but with every modern convenience and luxurious touch you could imagine. Everything from the plush, mono-chrome carpet to the gold bathroom taps and even each indi-vidual piece of furniture was bespoke. So much thought had gone into every single detail, down to the ice cubes served in the bar with the Cedarwood Manor crest moulded into them. There were two floors and only ten bedrooms in total. But a small family could live comfortably in each one. The Cedar-wood Manor was exclusively for the rich and powerful, with its mile-long, tree-lined driveway leading to a gated entrance and the main road. The grounds and the surrounding woodland were vast and provided total seclusion for the hotel and those who stayed in it. The nearest town was six miles away in one direction, and Cork City was ten miles in the other. But locals rarely went beyond the imposing entrance for fear that even the journey up the driveway might somehow drain their bank accounts. It gave June a certain level of pride to say that she worked there.

For the next half hour, she watched the guests as they moved through the lobby, hardly noticing her as she polished the huge hand-carved cedarwood table that dominated the space. This was her favourite piece in the whole building. She loved this table and gave it as much of her attention as she could each day. She watched the new receptionist, Lauren, preening at a male guest. He was stood at the desk studying the map she'd given him and every so often glancing up to smile at her. He was a regular visitor to the Cedarwood Manor and June could have told Lauren that he no more needed a map than she did. But Lauren was young and very pretty, and that particular man did like pretty girls. It was her first week, in her first job, so she didn't know how to spot that yet. But, like everything else, it would come with time. June moved on to polishing the brass until it shone, while she listened to the concierges talking among themselves.

'Watch out for the honeymooners,' John, the older one, mumbled. He was imparting his wisdom to the new guy, who did a poor impression of someone who cared.

'Yeah. Why's that?' he asked, looking at something on the tip of his finger.

'The fella will always be mad to impress.' He rubbed his thumb and fingers together.

'Oh yeah?' The new guy perked up a bit now. Tips on how to get tips were universally welcome. 'What about the billion-aires who come here all the time?'

'Tight as a badger's arse, the lot of them. How do you think they became billionaires?'

June smiled to herself and moved along. Even they hadn't really noticed her as she stood not six feet from them, polishing.

Once finished inside, she headed out into the cool autumn air and took a very brief moment to breathe it in. Then she hunkered down on the step and began cleaning the brass kicker plate at the bottom of the heavy entrance door. As she did, a short, sharp pain shot down her leg and she lost her balance. Her hand waved involuntarily and splashed Brasso up the sleeve of her blouse. The pain vanished as quickly as it had assailed her.

'Damn it,' she hissed, pulling herself upright and wiping herself down with a buffing cloth. Then she hunkered down again to clean up the small spill on the granite step. As she did, the skinny maid stepped out the door with a bucket of soapy water.

'Trying to make me look bad, are you?' She towered over June.

'Just cleaning up my own mess.'

'Yeah, well, be sure you do.' She trudged down the steps, sloshing water around as she went.

June got back up and went inside.

'Back so soon, madam.' John smiled at her as she passed, after only going outside a few minutes earlier. John allowed no one to pass without letting them hear his voice. He, and he alone, was very fond of it. The young lad was back to examining his fingertip.

June returned a half smile in acknowledgment and gestured to the unsightly stain on her sleeve. Maintaining her decorum, she walked as quickly as she could through the lobby, with her sights fixed on the service elevator that would take her back down to the locker room to get cleaned up.

Hotel staff didn't have personal lockers in the staff locker room. There was simply a bank of lockers to choose from, into which you deposited a token and chose a four-digit code. Not exactly Fort Knox, but they all knew not to bring valuables to work. June was always first to arrive and so she always had her choice of lockers. She picked the same one every time. Right in the corner, furthest from the doors. She was certain she had locked it that morning, using the same code she always did. But when she arrived back with her Brasso-soaked blouse and opened it up, her bag was not how she'd left it. Or at least, she didn't think it was. Not that she paid too much attention to the positioning of her bag when she shoved it in there each day. But she'd hardly have left it gaping open and she certainly would have noticed the neatly folded sheet of paper poking out the top. She looked around the empty room, her brow furrowed. She slipped the paper out slowly and opened it up.

I know what you did.
Keep your mouth shut.

TWO

JUNE

That was it. Nine little words. Each one innocent enough on its own, but strung together they chilled her to the bone. All four walls of the windowless room crept in on her. She sat down slowly and deliberately, steadying herself with one hand on the slatted bench. She gripped the note in her other hand and read it again. A familiar dread crawled through her.

The fingers on her left hand wound themselves around what little hair she had, while her right hand gripped the page tightly. She'd taken to pulling strands of hair out of her head at some point in her life. This was one of the reasons why she kept it so short now. *Too* short for her fingers to find purchase. If she couldn't grip it, then she couldn't pull it out by its root. Tess had taught her that much. Still, it was a subconscious act, so her fingers twisted and tugged of their own accord while she read that little string of words, over and over again.

'You're getting awfully comfortable there, June.' Liz's voice wafted over the bank of lockers.

June froze. There hadn't been a sound in the room until then, which meant that Liz hadn't just come in. She'd been there the whole time. But what was she doing, loitering in silence in the staff locker room?

'I had a spill.' She stuffed the note back in her bag and shoved it in her locker. Getting to her feet, she peeled off her waistcoat and shirt, careful not to smudge the Brasso onto any other part of her uniform. Then she pulled some wet wipes from the bottom of her bag, scrunching the note to the side as she did. She quickly cleaned the back of her hand and up along her arm. Her skin tingled and itched, but not because of the Brasso. June's skin was the most uncomfortable part of her. She had ways of quietening it down that usually worked. But for now, with Liz less than six feet away, she had to try to ignore it. She put on a freshly starched and pressed shirt, of which there was no shortage. Perfect uniforms were high up on Liz's list of what was important. Like everyone else, June always had a spare in her locker.

Her locker. That someone had interfered with. How many of her trusted colleagues could have been in there since she left to begin her shift? Aside from Liz. She caught herself, as she began rummaging in her hair again and forced her restless hands to smooth down her trousers instead.

'What kind of a spill?' Liz strolled around to June's side of the locker wall.

'I got Brasso on my shirt,' she said, turning her back to Liz as she buttoned up.

Liz stood there with her arms folded across her enhanced chest while June tucked in her blouse and put on her waistcoat. Unable to raise her eyebrows, Liz looked pointedly at her watch instead. June locked her locker and left, but Liz stayed close behind her. 'Go straight up to the second floor and get started on those rooms. You'll be lucky if you get a lunch break at this rate.' The pair stepped into the lift.

'I'll get them done, don't worry.'

'Properly.'

'Of course.' June's response was clipped.

June glanced at her out the side of her eye, while Liz stared straight ahead. She was in a mood, as she so often was, so the ride upwards seemed so much longer than the ride down. Eventually the elevator doors pinged open on the ground floor. Liz walked out and towards reception, while June stepped back and let the doors slide shut again.

She wasn't feeling very well suddenly. Like there wasn't enough air in the ascending box. She pressed her knuckles against her chest as the elevator doors slid open again. She pinned herself to the wall, allowing the happy couple from room 202 to enter the lift before she eased herself out past them. She gave them a muttered *good morning* and a polite smile, which only the man returned. The woman was busy checking her teeth for lipstick stains in one of the three streak-free mirrored walls. The doors slid shut, taking them away and letting June's face slide back to its neutral position.

'Housekeeping!' she called out, while simultaneously knocking, swiping her key card and wondering what Liz might have been up to in the locker room. She grabbed her bucket of supplies off the trolley and shouldered open the door with more bluster than usual.

'You come through the door like some kind of farm girl.' Erica Kelly's judgmental voice snapped June out of her own thoughts. She was standing by the window with her back to June.

Mrs Kelly had the kind of silhouette that was instantly recognisable. She had square shoulders for one thing. They made her look like she was always braced for something. But the rest of her was long and lean. Her legs seemed to go on for miles in her tight leather trousers and four-inch heels. Even her neck was elongated by the elegant blonde chignon that she always wore. She could easily be mistaken for a woman in her thirties. From behind, at least. But inevitably, one of two things would happen. Either she'd turn around, in which case any decent lighting would show up the age spot on her left cheek. She used heavy make-up to disguise it, but the creases around her ice blue eyes weren't so easy to hide. Or she'd speak. Her voice held the type of bitterness that only came with age.

But standing as she was just now, straight-backed with one hand on her hip, Erica Kelly was a striking woman.

June was annoyed with herself, because Mrs Kelly was right. Her entrance was all wrong. Cedarwood Manor staff were ghosts, floating around and getting things done, unseen. Not blustering into a room, slapping bucketloads of cleaning supplies off the doorjamb. That might be acceptable in another hotel, where guests left their rooms early and stayed out all day. But not in the Cedarwood Manor. Their VIPs, in particular, hardly left the hotel grounds during their stays. Most spent considerable time in their rooms because they craved the kind of solitude that they could never get in their real lives. Now June had encroached upon that.

'Terribly sorry, Mrs Kelly,' June mumbled in the soft suburban accent she'd perfected over the years. A gift for acting was another job requirement of the Manor.

'Look at this.' Erica beckoned June over to the picture window, which was framed by heavy velvet blackout curtains. 'Just look.'

June lowered her bucket to the floor and went to stand near, but not too near, her. She was in full make-up and wearing a designer silk blouse that looked intimidatingly delicate.

She pulled back the curtains and gestured out the window. Erica's room overlooked the front lawn and carefully land-scaped Chinese Garden. Behind which was the vast cedarwood forest and woodland trails. On the path, headed towards the woods, was a young woman struggling along with a twin buggy. The buggy was weighed down with bulging changing bags and other paraphernalia, while its intended occupants, two toddlers dressed in puddle suits, were running riot around her.

'Do you think any of the guests who actually pay to stay here, want to be listening to that racket at this hour of the morning?'

The triple-glazed windows, when closed, were pretty much soundproof. June certainly couldn't hear much more than a distant high-pitched laugh. Or perhaps it was a scream. But whatever it was, there was joy in it, she was sure. She moved behind the curtain and reached up to close the window. As she did, her eyes met those of the young mother. She looked so tired and depressed that it made June want to offer her a small smile. Or maybe a wave. But she didn't.

'I didn't say I wanted my window closed!' Mrs Kelly slapped June's hand away from the window. 'Why should I have to suffocate in my very expensive room so that her rug rats can run riot out there? Is she paying to be here? Only she doesn't look like someone who could.'

June didn't need to come up with an alternative to closing the windows and suffocating Mrs Kelly in her air-conditioned room. John appeared outside, just in the nick of time. The dutiful concierge made his way quickly towards the woman.

The mother's face seemed to slump a little further as he spoke to her. He then proceeded to try to herd her toddler boys back towards their buggy. It would have been funny to watch, if it weren't for Erica Kelly's voice trilling in her ear. And the young mother's face. It seemed to cry out for help with her two boisterous boys. Would it have been so terrible to allow her to show her children the squirrels and other woodland creatures? To let them ramble in the wildflowers for a while. To let a mother rest her tired mind and breathe.

But this was not June's argument. Mrs Kelly's dislike of the little family was more about herself than the laughing toddlers in question. It wasn't personal, June knew that. She also knew why. The woman had alluded to her own family tragedy more than once. Usually after several glasses of wine in place of food. Her mood could darken the whole room when she spoke about them. Their end was catastrophic. But even though she carried it with her everywhere she went, no one else saw it. June did, though. She could feel it in the room with them, even now. So, no. She wasn't going to argue about the family outside her window.

Of course, she didn't always speak of her family in terms of tragedy. There were other times when Mrs Kelly would spit venom about her husband. A pig of a man. Her words. There was also his son. That's what she always called him. *His* son, never *their* son, whom she seemed to despise at times. They had a daughter, too. Mia. She rarely spoke of her, but whenever she did, it was with an undertone of melancholy.

There were lots of rumours, of course, and they hinted at the dark truth. Some spoke of a drunken argument gone wrong, of a husband's rage and a mother's despair. Others whispered of a grisly murder-suicide. A family torn apart by secrets and lies. But June never added what she knew to what the rumour mill *thought* it knew. She never talked about the times when Mrs Kelly's hands trembled, and her voice wavered while she spoke of her terrifying past. June let everyone go on thinking that the woman was unshakeable. But she, the maid, knew differently. Which was why she never took the woman personally.

'Finally!' Mrs Kelly threw her hands up, snapping June out of her daydream. 'I called him ten minutes ago!' She walked away from the window, but soon turned back. She pulled the curtain aside again and watched. 'He was obviously busy with his Facebook or whatever until now. Open that window all the way, June,' she barked.

June did as she was told without speaking.

'I remember when this place had standards.'

With her head down, June returned to get her bucket from

inside the door and she brought it with her to the bathroom. Mrs Kelly went back to reading her newspaper. She sat in the armchair in the corner of the room, but her eyes were still on the window.

'Parents these days seem to think it's perfectly fine to bring screaming children into the adult world,' she continued. 'Especially those young girls who probably never wanted children in the first place.'

June didn't respond, because she knew better.

She continued to clean in silence, breaking from time to time to drive her knuckles deep into her thighs. She got to her knees and scrubbed the spotlessly clean claw-foot bath.

'Of course, what do they expect? Kids are brought up to think there are no consequences in life, nowadays,' Mrs Kelly said. 'She's no different. I bet her mammy kept telling her how special she was. How she could do anything.' She laughed a cruel laugh then. 'Not feeling so special now, is she?'

June reluctantly finished in the bathroom and came back into the room.

'You know that's the most damaging style of parenting. You keep filling a child's head with notions and *that's* how they end up. Children need to know how the real world works from an early age. They need to know that the world around them doesn't give a damn about them. Why would it? Kids need resilience. They need work ethic. They need...'

The internal phone rang, interrupting her flow. Depending who was on the other end and why they were disturbing her, they might well be very sorry about that. But June wasn't.

Erica Kelly was a VIP guest, of which there were several. Regular visitors who left a lot of money behind whenever they stayed. Unfortunately for June, Erica insisted that June was the only maid to be allowed to work on her room during her frequent stays.

'Yes?' she brusquely answered the vintage copper rotary

dial phone beside her bed. 'Fine. But that Alexandria girl had better not come near me this time.' She ended the call abruptly.

'I'm going to the spa for a massage,' Erica then said, as she picked up her bag and headed for the door. 'Don't forget my Nespresso pods. I want more Cosi this time. Anyone would think there was a shortage.'

June nodded with a small, obedient smile.

'You know, you're one of the few people around here who doesn't feel the need to pollute the air with your voice all day.' With her thin lips pursed, she let her cold, assessing gaze roam over June. She nodded then, in something like approval. 'Very well trained,' she mumbled. Then she left, letting the door slam shut behind her.

THREE

JUNE

On the train home that evening, June sat with her head resting against the cold window. She stared at the landscape whizzing past outside, but she saw none of it. She was caught up in a tangled web of dark thoughts, all woven together by that note. Mentally she'd already compared the handwriting to that of all the people she knew. But anyone could disguise their writing with block letters, so that detail wouldn't help her. She read and re-read the words.

I know what you did. Those particular words implied that they were written by someone who knew June very well. But that theory was contradicted by the order to *keep your mouth shut.* Anyone who felt the need to tell June that didn't know her at all.

June Calloway had been keeping her mouth shut all her life. She kept her own secrets, and those of so many others, locked away in the vault of her memory. She wouldn't be sitting here now, rumbling towards the city on a commuter train if she wasn't predisposed to staying quiet. So how could someone claim to know what she'd done, if they didn't also know that about her? The more she thought about that note and those words, the more tangled her thoughts became.

By the time she realised the train had stopped, its carriages were already empty. Kent Station, Cork, was its final destination, and passengers for the return journey had started to board. If June hadn't been unintentionally battered by someone's shopping bags, she might have found herself continuing her journey, back the way she had come.

By that time the sun was sinking low in the evening sky. She usually enjoyed the twenty-minute walk to her home on Wellington Road, regardless of the weather. The houses in her area were old and big. Three or four stories most of them, and mostly broken up into multiple rental spaces. June's home was nothing fancy, but it had everything she needed. She let herself into the basement flat at just after five in the evening.

'I'm home,' she called. There was no reply, but she didn't expect one. She passed the door to the room that was their kitchen, dining and living rooms combined. She paused outside the door to the slightly larger of the two bedrooms. She knocked gently and pushed open the door.

'Oh, hello, my love. I didn't hear you come in.' Tess's snow-white hair ran wild across her pillow and her face broke into a wrinkly grin. 'Wait till I get up and make you something to eat.' She made a show of pushing herself up in the bed, knowing full well what would come next.

'Stay where you are, Tess. I'll make the tea.'

'Are you sure?'

'Of course.' June smiled and nodded.

'Ah, you're a good girl, June, you know that? The best girl in the world, you are. I'll come and help you in a sec.'

June gave her a small smile and pulled the door closed again, to keep the heat in her room.

They lived in a draughty old building that had been hastily divided into flats sometime in the sixties. Now none of the building's tenants could afford to heat the place properly. The landlords didn't care to do anything about it, but June and Tess made do.

Before going to the kitchen to get started on putting a meal together, June went to her own room first and closed the door. Hers was a box room, which was probably never intended to be used for anything other than storage. Her bed had to be specially built to fit in between the two walls. It had accommodated so many bodies before hers, that there was a dip in the middle of it – one she rolled into each night. There was no space for a wardrobe or a chest of drawers in the room. But June didn't need much space. She had a rail on which to hang her three pairs of black leggings, her two sweatshirts and her four T-shirts, most of which were currently in her laundry pile. She took her pay packet out of her pocket and placed it on the bed. She always undressed as soon as she got home. Partly to close off the workday, and partly to save her clothes from any late spillages or stains. Those clothes were good for a few more days, all being well. But a tedious trip to the laundrette was looming. She hated laundry nights. The nearest public machines were a fifteen-minute walk away. She had to stand there waiting for the washer and dryer cycles to finish before facing the walk back home again. She made the odd sneaky trip to the hotel laundry, but not often enough to create an obvious pattern. She didn't want to risk getting caught.

June didn't mind people knowing that she was poor. But she would mind someone thinking she was indebted to them. Especially Malcolm Levy. Certain people could smell vulnerability in the air like a shark smells blood in the water. So, yes. Clothes off and kept clean enough for another day.

Even though she was alone in her room, she undressed and dressed again quickly. By design, there were no long mirrors in her home. She did have a face mirror hanging over the bathroom sink, put there at Tess's insistence. But just like at work, June didn't look at it much. Nor did she need to see reflections of the scars that crisscrossed her body, some of which never quite got the opportunity to heal. There were other marks on her body, too, but she rarely saw them and always tried not to think about them. She shoved on her fleece pyjamas. The grey ones that were dotted all over with big red love hearts.

Next, she pulled open the drawer beneath her bed. When it was almost all the way out, she jiggled it so that it slid out completely. She set the awkward drawer aside and crawled in under the bed unit. Then, using the tips of her fingers, she pulled at a small section of skirting board. It came away in her hand and she took out the padded brown envelope that lived behind it. She kept a small pocket torch under the bed as well. She felt around until it was in her hand, switched it on and shone its light at the envelope. Inside was a small stack of money. She added more money to it and then she counted it, as she did on payday each week. Three thousand, two hundred Euro. Her life savings and the most money she'd ever had in her whole life. Looking at it regularly helped her to keep going.

There were times when, out of nowhere, she... no, that's not true. When June was assailed with dark thoughts about bringing her life to an end, it was never *out of nowhere*. It built and built and built until she found herself thinking about all the different ways she could do it. Down to the last detail. That's why she often pulled out the envelope to look inside. It was a reminder of why she needed to keep going. A reminder that she couldn't give up. That light was coming.

She replaced the envelope and the skirting board and crawled out backwards, inserting the drawer behind her. When the room looked exactly as it had, June sat up on her bed with both palms pressing down on her thighs. Sometimes doing that helped calm things down, though never for long and it never relieved the pressure in her chest. But she still did it.

Aside from her life savings, she also kept a shoebox under the bed. She let her foot rest on the shoebox as she reached into her bag. She unfolded the crumpled note, laid it flat on her lap and carefully smoothed it out. Then she brought the shoebox up onto the bed. There wasn't much inside it. Just a book given to her by Tess and an old letter, neatly folded inside its envelope.

'I think I'd like some dinner,' she said to herself, her voice at a higher pitch than usual. She lifted the lid on the shoebox just enough that she could slip the note inside. She closed it quickly and hurried out of the room, as if the innocent-looking box on the bed were about to chase her. She pulled the door shut behind her and headed for the kitchenette.

The area where they cooked was as basic as everything else in their flat. One short counter running under a small window with a sink in the middle. They didn't have a cooker or a washing machine. But they did have a small, undercounter fridge, a hotplate, a deep fat fryer and a microwave. She could buy a cooker if she really wanted to, but she didn't. At least not badly enough to compromise her savings. God knows it took her long enough to gather that money and she needed every penny of it. Opposite the kitchenette was a two-seater couch and an armchair, both facing an old television set, which rested on a cheap corner table. Jammed against the back of the couch, was a very small dining table with two chairs. They never had visitors, so they had no need for more. June would have been happy to balance her plate on her lap in front of the TV. But Tess insisted that meals should be eaten at a table and June didn't care enough to argue.

June switched on the deep fat fryer and then opened the fridge. Inside was a pint of milk, half full, a small carton of spreadable butter and two zip-locked bags. One bag contained four chicken goujons, while the other one had most of a block of cheddar cheese in it. She fished out the bags and emptied the goujons into the fryer basket. They'd have the same dinner as yesterday just to use up the goujons before they went off. Tomorrow she'd buy something that would do them for the next two, if not three, dinners. Probably jumbo sausages. They were the tastiest of all the cheap meats. They always had a bag of potatoes under the counter, and they almost always had pasta.

While she worked on their meal, the little white bag in her bedroom called out to her. She did her best to ignore it by humming some unknown tune in her head, as she pulled the ring tab on a tin of own-brand baked beans, which were every bit as good as the posh ones. But she needed more of a distraction and as such, she was looking forward to her meal with Tess. She stopped short of pouring the beans into a bowl and exhaled loudly, trying to expel the demons that lived within her. She never really expected to succeed. How could she win against them? They taunted her from the minute she opened her eyes in the morning, and they only got louder as the day went on. By the time evening came around, it was impossible to see, hear or feel anything else. 'Okay!' She brought her hands to her temples and went back to her room, closing the door quietly behind her.

She got to her knees and pulled the drawer open. She took the shoebox down from the bed and found her little white leatherette washbag in the drawer. She placed both on the floor beside her and looked from one to the other. Her heart thumped in her chest and her breathing was suddenly loud enough to kill the silence. She reached out and upturned the shoebox with one finger. It was a memory box of sorts, but June had very few happy memories. Still, she kept it to remind her how far she'd come. But it could also drag her violently back to the dark times.

June sat there staring at the contents as they settled themselves on her threadbare rug. Her whole body shook with each breath. She swept her hand gently over the hard cover of the book, the letter and the latest note.

There was one other that she'd stuck between the pages of her book. One she'd all but forgotten about until this new note arrived.

Dirty, dirty, dirty!

The *dirty* note arrived the day after she'd had sex with the hotel groundskeeper at the end of her first week at the Cedarwood Manor. She'd let him do what he wanted to do with her, in the shed where he kept the ride-on lawnmower and the rest of his tools. She needed a place to stay, and he wanted to be awkward about it. Sex meant very little to June. But to some people it was valuable currency. The God-awful groundskeeper at the time accepted it in exchange for a very temporary roof over her head. That note was accurate and left her in no doubt about the fact that someone had been watching her. She assumed it was one of her new work colleagues. But that was six years ago and there'd been nothing since. Until now. Now whoever it was was back, and they wanted her to keep her mouth shut. But about what?

She reached for her small washbag and pulled it alongside her. One hand smoothed down today's note and placed it in line with the other mementos on her rug. Her other hand slid open the zip on her bag. She leaned sideways against the bed, not taking her eyes off the page. Her fingers had no trouble finding the ball of tissue at the bottom of the bag. She placed the tissue in her lap and unwrapped it, then she raised her hips and lowered her pyjama bottoms. Finally, she pulled her eyes away from the threatening words that screamed up at her from the rug and she looked at her bare thigh. She used her fingers to trace the hardened lumps of scar tissue there. A neat row of short, bumpy roads leading nowhere. She brought the bare razor blade to an older scar and let it hover there for a time. Then as a single tear rolled off her chin, she sliced it slowly back open. The sharp sting of pain took her breath away momentarily, as tears poured more freely from her eyes. But she didn't make a sound. She felt elation in the agony of it. Like a weight that had been bearing down upon her chest was lifted and she was free. If only for a moment.

FOUR

JUNE

By the time she returned to the dining room, Tess was already there. She'd set the table with two plates, some cutlery and two glasses of water. She was sitting with her hands in her lap, patiently waiting for June to join her. Both plates had a neat arrangement of chicken goujons, two each, a scoop of beans and a small pile of grated cheese. Tess smiled when she walked in and picked up her knife and fork.

'A feast fit for a pair of queens.' She grinned.

'You should have started without me.' June went and sat down opposite her.

'Oh, I'm far too polite for that.' She winked mischievously. 'Besides, I like to hear the news while I eat.'

'Then maybe you should turn on the TV.' June looked at the old and rarely used television in the corner.

'*Your* news, my love. I like to hear *your* news.'

There were times when June wondered if she really knew Tess at all. She was in her eighties and spent a lot of time in bed seeming impossibly frail. But then she could just as easily jump up, get dressed and take over the household chores, like she'd just done.

'So, tell me,' she said, taking a tiny nibble of a goujon.

'What would you like to know?' All June could think about was that note. But Tess wouldn't hear about that.

'Is my little Henry back?'

Hearing about the goings on at the hotel was the highlight of Tess's day. Tess had a fascination with the wealthy VIPs. She'd taken to calling the elderly Henry Lovell *my little Henry*. She liked that he attended tea dances in a three-piece suit with a dicky bow. Not to mention that he was incredibly wealthy and was estranged from a very large family. Without actually knowing the man at all, Tess was of the opinion that when Mr Lovell died, he'd leave all his money to the society for injured bats.

June shook her head. 'Not yet. But he'll probably come next weekend. It's been more than four weeks since his last stay.'

'How's Luscious Liz? Has she had any more *jobs* done since I saw her last?'

'You've never seen Liz!' June replied with a chuckle.

Tess tapped the side of her head. 'I know exactly what she looks like.'

June shoved some beans into her mouth and shook her head again. 'Nope. No more jobs.' She never talked about any of the guests to anyone. But Tess wasn't just anyone. She never left the house and had no other human interaction that June knew of. So, she didn't see the harm in sharing her days with her.

They were quiet for a while then, while June ate hungrily. Tess nibbled like a baby bird opposite her. When June's plate was nearly cleared, Tess asked, 'So? Is she there?'

June stopped chewing for a second and looked at her. She didn't need to ask *who* Tess meant. Tess had venom in her voice when she spoke about Erica Kelly. A woman she'd never met. But ever since Erica had shouted at June on her first week in the job, Tess's dislike for the woman seemed to grow and grow.

'She's there.' June nodded and picked at her grated cheese,

one strand at a time. She wanted to fill her mouth with cheese. But more than that, she wanted to make it last.

'Well? What kind of mood is she in?'

'She's okay.'

Tess looked expectantly at her.

June sighed and decided to give Tess what she wanted. 'I mean, Mrs Kelly wasn't happy with a young mother today. Would you believe she had the audacity to bring her baby twins for a walk around the grounds? She even let them laugh too close to Mrs Kelly's second-floor window.' June grinned at Tess's incensed expression. 'But other than that, she's fine. Same old, same old.' She was glad suddenly that she'd told her. She did enjoy Tess's outrage at times. It was a nice distraction.

'What kind of a woman would begrudge a poor mother a bit of time out of the house?'

June shrugged.

'One who clearly never had the kind of cabin fever that only a new mother can have.' Tess answered her own question.

'She has kids.'

'Does she indeed?'

'You know she does. A son...'

'Not biologically hers. And she gave out socks about him to you on more than one occasion!'

She was drunk on each of those occasions, but June didn't remind Tess of that. 'And a daughter.'

'Who she leaves at home every time she goes to your hotel. What kind of a woman...'

'Begrudges a mother some time out of the house...' June laughed quietly.

'Ah, feck off and don't be throwing my own words back at me.'

June laughed and so did Tess. Then Tess did what she always did.

'I can't eat another bite. Here.' She shoved one of her goujons onto June's plate.

'No, Tess, I don't want it. I'm full, too.' Her stomach rumbled quietly.

'June, I lay in bed all day and have a wrinkly old woman's constitution. You're a hard-working woman. You need the sustenance. Now eat it, or bin it. But if you bin it, I'll get the wooden spoon to your arse.'

Tess stood up and brought her plate to the sink, while June watched her go. She had quite a strong gait for a woman of her age and a stubborn streak to match. She felt terrible eating Tess's food, but it was pointless to argue. If June didn't eat the goujon, then it would still be there come morning. They couldn't afford to waste food, but Tess would do it, just to get her way.

'You're a stubborn old goat, Tess.'

'Yes, and I must take myself out to pasture now.' She patted her stomach and walked towards the door. 'Wait.' She turned around. 'That sounded like I was going off to die or something. But I'm just going back to bed. All that talking and eating really took it out of me.' She grinned and turned towards the door again. But she paused, with her hand on the door handle and half turned her head. 'Have you not been using the little rubber band, June?' Her lowered voice had lost all its humour now.

June's small smile vanished, but she didn't respond.

'Remember that trick I taught you? Snap the elastic band on your skin. It can stop you from...'

'Goodnight, Tess,' June replied in a sharper tone than she intended.

'Indeed it is, June. And when I close my eyes tonight, I'll dream of all those forms they like to fill out in hospitals. You know the ones? They have all those questions on them. Questions that lead to more questions, that lead to people in suits, and even uniforms, knocking on our door. *Those* ones. That's what I'll dream of tonight.'

June kept her eyes on the one remaining goujon and worked to steady her breathing. She was deeply uncomfortable now.

'Where would we be then, I wonder?' Tess sounded almost wistful, but a quick shake of the head brought her smile back with it. 'Anyway. Think about those elastic bands. They worked when you were twelve and they can work now.' She glanced over her shoulder at June, who was still sitting with her back to the door and her palms flat on the table. 'Goodnight, June. And sweet dreams.' She left finally, closing the door gently behind her.

June let out a long, slow breath. Tess's intuition had got them far in life. But it was beginning to make June feel that privacy was an illusion. She hated Tess knowing that she couldn't control the urge to cut. She hated that Tess could no longer help her the way she once could. But most of all, she hated that Tess was right in what she'd said. June's impulsive behaviour was putting them both at risk and she needed to get a handle on it. Her thigh started to throb just thinking about it and the image of a man in uniform, knocking on their door, formed in her mind.

She picked up her plate and pushed her chair back from the table. She quickly ate the last goujon on her way to the sink and then dropped the dirty plate in noisily. When she looked up, her reflection was staring back from the darkened window. 'Good fucking night, June,' she said through clenched teeth.

The woman in the window said nothing. But even she seemed to judge June with her blackened eyes. June stared defiantly back at her. Then she blinked slowly, turned away and went to bed.

FIVE

JUNE

It was five to eight when June arrived at the staff entrance the following morning. She'd barely slept and yet somehow, she was later than she'd ever been for work. She felt stressed by this, but strangely, no one seemed to notice. This was unusual.

Liz was always lurking somewhere in the basement, referring to her watch with each staff member's arrival. She should be there now. *You're lucky you still have your day's pay intact, June.* She heard her disapproving voice in her mind. But there was no sign of her. The other maids must have already loaded their trollies and started their work, too. She couldn't hear so much as an echo of them. But something heavy hung in the air and June felt it as soon as she stepped inside. She was convinced that this ancient manor had a personality of its own. It could sense when a day was going to go badly, and it would warn her as best it could. It seemed depressed today and this, combined with Liz's absence, gave June a sudden sense of foreboding.

She changed into her uniform quickly and hurried to stock her trolley. But while the whole process was rushed, June still made sure she was perfectly turned out and had everything she'd need for the day. Then she hauled her trolley through the basement and shoved it into the lift.

June was about to get started on the lobby but decided to go to Liz's office instead. All night she'd been seeing images of Liz creeping around the locker room, slipping notes into her bag and watching June while she worked. Her absence now was disconcerting. It bothered June that she hadn't been there to admonish her when she arrived. She should have because June was very nearly late. *Was* she actually watching her? If Liz felt the need to threaten June like that, then why would she suddenly stop keeping tabs?

She brought her bucket containing polish and cloths with her. Liz's office was beside the reception desk and the door was nearly always closed. June knocked twice and waited with her ear to the door. She heard an abrupt movement inside. Rather than waiting to be invited, June opened the door and stepped in.

'Morning, Liz.'

She'd been crying. Her face looked even worse than usual whenever she cried. Her inflated lips appeared lumpy. Her filled cheeks were blotchy. Her fake eyelashes were like wet mops and her frozen features looked like they ached for movement.

June didn't comment on any of it. Nor did she allow her expression to give away the fact that she'd noticed the woman's upset. Instead, she started polishing the cedarwood desk, lifting things up and replacing them exactly as they were. Out of the corner of her eye she saw Liz glancing up at the clock, but she didn't say anything. Neither of them did, for the whole time June was in there.

. . .

By the time she got to the second floor, it was almost ten. She parked her trolley and took a walk along the length of the hall, as she often did. This was how she decided which room to start with. It might seem logical to begin at the first room and work your way along. And June did that sometimes. But on other days she liked to change things up, and as she passed room 208, she paused. She could hear Erica Kelly's voice through the door. She was speaking to someone.

'Housekeeping,' she called, as she swiped her card and let herself in.

Mrs Kelly ignored her and continued with her call. Normally, she'd never allow anyone to be privy to her private conversations. But luckily for June, she was the maid. And maids were not considered to be people of consequence. At least, not in this room.

June brought her supplies with her and closed the door quietly. She headed for the bathroom and cleaned with the door open.

'It's not my home,' Mrs Kelly hissed. There was a hint of desperation to her voice, which was one of the strangest things June had ever heard. 'I don't care what he wrote on a piece of paper, and I don't care what I signed a hundred fucking years ago. Are you not listening to anything that I'm saying?'

The other person tried to speak. June could hear the tinny male voice from where she stood behind the bathroom door with the toilet brush hovering just above the bowl.

'Ah ah ah ah! I don't want to hear it. You're supposed to be *my* solicitor. Not his. You're supposed to work for *me*. I want you to get me out of it. Do you hear me? If I have to spend one more night under that roof, I'll...'

The man on the other end was brave enough to cut her off mid-sentence and June wished she could hear what he had to say.

'What am I paying you for?' she asked, like it was a genuine question. 'Please tell me. What the fuck am I paying you for?' She roared the last bit and then she threw her phone at the bed, abruptly ending the call.

June flushed the toilet and got started on her work.

SIX

MIA

'I didn't steal it. I didn't!' Mia Kelly called out. But no one was listening. Her mother was standing on the doorstep talking to a woman who looked to be very distressed. The house was identical to all the other rundown houses around it.

You're in for it now! A boy's voice coming from behind her was low and dripping with excitement. Two more came towards her from across the green. They were squared up, trying to look bigger than they were, but to Mia they were giants. One of them was shouting, *Think you can nick my bike, you stupid retard?*

Mia's stomach fizzed and popped as fear rose, along with the instinct to run. She looked from the boys to her mother, but her back was still turned. She hadn't seen them. She didn't sense the same danger as Mia yet. *Run!* she thought. But she couldn't. Her feet were stuck under a crashed bike.

Finally, her mother turned her head. She looked from Mia to the boys, but she didn't move. She showed no signs that she might be worried for Mia's safety, although the other woman looked terrified. Mia wondered what her mother was threatening her with. Erica Kelly, in all her fine clothes and high heels, was always threatening someone. In direct contrast, everything about the other woman looked worn down. Her shabby clothes, her unkempt hair, her tired face. But as danger loomed over her, Mia's instinct wasn't to run to her own mother for protection. Instead, she was drawn to the other woman.

Mia glanced down at the crashed bike with the buckled front wheel. The toe of her shoe was wedged through the spokes. Her own fear started to rise further, but it battled with so many other emotions. Elation being one. The thrill of cycling a bike at speed with the wind blowing her long red hair out behind her like a fan. The delight of being chased. The sheer exhilaration of knowing that she *might* just get away. Or she *might* get caught. Her mother turned and walked towards her while the other woman brought her hands to her face and cried. Everything had switched to slow motion and...

Mia inhaled sharply as she bolted upright. Her stomach was a ball of tension, and her hands gripped the sheet under her in tight fists. She breathed heavily and looked frantically around the room. Slowly, she returned from the dream world to her real world. Mia rarely dreamed. Most nights she entered a black void and stayed there until it was time to get up again. But when she did dream, it was always a version of the same one. Some nights she stole the bike. Other nights someone on a bike stole her. There was always a bike and there was always a chase. Some nights the worn-out woman was laughing, other nights she was crying.

She was awake now. Hers was the coldest room in the house by far. It was also the biggest, but it was completely bare. Green-and-yellow linoleum covered the concrete floor, and the painted cinderblock walls retained no trace of heat from the day before. Not that much heat made it down here to begin with. There was a single bed, a bedside locker with a small lamp on top and an old chest of drawers that once resided in her mammy's room. On the other side of the stairs behind a partition wall, was a toilet, a shower and a sink with a little shelf above it. Her room didn't have any windows, so it was only the tick-tick-ticking clock on the wall that let Mia know whether it was day or night. Whether she was early or late. It was daytime now. Or at least, it was getting there fast. Five forty-seven am, so she was early. Her body clock usually went off at six sharp.

Her breath clung to the cold air around her and she rubbed her arms brusquely, in a vain attempt to warm up. She got out of bed and hurried into her clothes. Thick woollen socks which she knew she'd regret before the morning was out. And her ankle-length brown dress with the long sleeves and white belt. On her feet she wore black sliders. Only when fully dressed did she make her way to the toilet. Normally she relished this part of the day, when she could just be. Sit there and do her business in her own time. Wash her face and teeth. Brush her hair into a tight ponytail. Do all those little things that were for no one else, but herself. But even the toilet seat was too cold to enjoy today, so she rushed through her morning routine. The wee, the wash and the brush. Without pause, she walked up the old wooden stairs and opened the door at the top.

During the summer months, opening that door could be blinding. The morning sun would stream in through the kitchen window. It bounced off the chrome taps and appliances before attacking Mia's corneas as she entered from her room below. But it was winter now and the sun had yet to show its face, so Mia turned on the overhead lights before closing and locking her bedroom door. That was one of the many house rules. The key was to be hung on a hook in the pantry. Another rule said that breakfast was to be served in three sittings. The first was at seven for Dr Evan Kelly and his son, Kevin. Not to be mistaken for Mia's dad and brother. Doctor Kelly had another life before and nineteen-year-old Kevin was his son who lived with them. His real mother was never mentioned by anyone, ever. Mia's mother must have had another life before, too, but she never talked about it. And she didn't actually have any children. But seeing as the doctor had Kevin, she decided she wanted a baby of her own. So, because not all mammies can have their own babies, she adopted little baby Mia whose own mammy didn't want her, and she had no daddy at all. They both took Dr Kelly's name and Mia called him Daddy. That was another of the house rules. Everyone knew who was and wasn't related by blood, but that they were a family, nonetheless. She called him Daddy and Kevin called Erica Mammy. A mammy, a daddy, a big boy, and a small girl. The perfect family.

The second breakfast sitting was for Mammy at half past eight, after the previous one had been cleared away. When she was finished and they'd all gone about their business, Mia would clean the place up again. Then she'd go about preparing the third breakfast of the day. That one was for herself, and it consisted of porridge. Always porridge. They had scrambled eggs, bacon, and sometimes a weird smelly fish. But it was always something hot and tasty. Aside from the smelly fish, that is. Kippers they were called, and they were sent up from hell weekly to assault Mia's senses for an entire day.

This was Mia's job within the family. They all had one. Daddy was a vet and so he looked after animals for farmers all over the county. Kevin was like his assistant. Sometimes he went with Daddy, but other times he stayed home to look after their own animals. They had horses. Mammy used to ride them, but she didn't anymore. These days she just sent them off to races and she got all dressed up in fancy clothes and hats to go with them. Those days were very important and would determine the mood in the house for the week that followed. Mia's job was to cook and keep the house clean. After breakfast and clean-up, Mia had school. This consisted of one hour at the kitchen table, reading Daddy's newspapers from the day before. It was vital that she knew how to read. Mammy said that even imbeciles should be able to read, and Mia was very good at it. She was also very good at remembering. She remembered every headline, from every paper, and most of the stories that went with them. She looked forward to school each day. She liked reading about all the things that happened in the world. Sometimes Mammy would circle the stories she wanted Mia to read. They were always frightening ones and she'd quiz Mia on them in the evening.

Mia hated those quizzes. Mammy would come into the kitchen when she was just finishing up her evening chores. She'd have a glass of red wine with her, and she'd make a bit of a show of pulling out a chair to sit on. Even late in the evening, Mammy would still have her high-heeled boots on. She seemed as comfortable in them as Mia was in her socks. 'See?' she'd say, slapping the folded newspaper down on the table and tapping the circled story with her painted fingernail. '*That's* the kind of thing that goes on out there, Mia. And that happened to a normal person. Imagine if *you'd* been there.' Mammy's eyes were the same colour blue that sometimes shone through in ice. They could chill you just as easily and when she tested Mia on those stories, her eyes did more talking than she did. *That could be you*, they'd say, while Mammy's pink lips stayed in a tight, straight line. But the white bits of her eyes could be just as pink on quiz nights.

Mammy kept Mia safe from the world, though. She made sure that no one could ever hurt her, so Mia always listened to her and did what she was told.

Luckily, today was Tuesday. Kippers were Friday so it was just a normal scrambled eggs and bacon kind of a day, followed as always by porridge made with water. She opened the fridge and took out the eggs. Before she had a chance to get started, the door leading to the hall, and the rest of the house, flew open and Kevin came barrelling in. He was the kind of person who managed to fill whatever space he was in. Mia stiffened with his arrival and checked the clock on the wall. She was still ten minutes ahead of schedule and she hadn't done anything wrong yet. He had no reason to be mad at her. Not that he needed one.

'Come here,' he said, tugging on her arm. Kevin smelled like poo and onions. Onions because he required them to be in every meal he ate. And poo because he spent so much time working in it.

She said nothing as he pulled her towards the back door. Outside he dragged her down the two steps and over to where they kept the bins. He released her elbow and shoved her against them.

'Well?' he snarled.

Mia looked around, her stomach fizzing and popping again, but for real this time. Her chest tightened when she saw what he was cribbing about. A black bag of rubbish on the ground beside the bin. She'd put it *in* the bin the night before, but the bin was full so the lid wouldn't close properly. It had been picked open by hungry wildlife and they'd made a right mess.

'I... I didn't...'

'Don't I know you bloody well didn't!' He grabbed her by the back of the neck and shoved her downwards until she was on her knees. He kept shoving until her face was pressed into the stinking bag of rubbish. Something soggy squished against her nose and mouth and suddenly she couldn't breathe very well. She tried to shout at him, her arms flailing at her sides. But when she tried to move her head, he just pressed down harder. She breathed in the foul smell and taste, but little air alongside it. Her muffled voice cried out and eventually he did let her go.

She pulled herself upright and gulped down the clean, country air. Banana peels. The one thing the kitchen's waste disposal unit struggled to devour. It just shredded them into strings that got tangled around the blades. And now the stinking, rotting skins were a part of her face and she knew that she'd smell them for the rest of the day. This was almost worse than the kippers.

'I need a piss,' Kevin said, like nothing had happened. 'My breakfast better be on the table by the time I get back.' He walked away towards the house but turned back before going inside. 'Oh, and Mammy wouldn't want to see that mess, would she?'

She blamed the dream for this because a bad day followed it everywhere. And when they started bad, they only ever tended to get worse. That had always been her experience and at ten years of age, she'd had a long time to come to this conclusion. By the time she'd cleaned up the rubbish and trudged back into the kitchen, Mammy was already there. Mia froze inside the door. It was too early for her. Kevin and Daddy hadn't even had their breakfast yet and Mia was still wearing banana peel on her face. Her hands were filthy as well.

Mammy just stood in the doorway looking at Mia with a stern expression on her face. She was already dressed in her leathery black trousers and the softest-looking white jumper you've ever seen. Her fake blonde hair was in a French roll, which Mammy liked to call a chignon. She wasn't happy.

'I was just...'

Mammy held her hand palm up towards her. Her pointy high-heeled boots were loud on the shiny cream floor tiles as she walked slowly towards Mia. But rather than a happy, click-clacking sound, they made a dull thud-thud.

She stopped in front of her and looked her over from head to toe. Mia tried not to think about what bin juices might be smeared on her dress, or what her face must look like. Mammy took her face in one of her hands and bent down to look at her. Her thumb was digging into Mia's cheek, and her fingers were squeezing her jaw. It hurt, but Mia didn't say anything. No one likes whingers.

She turned Mia's head this way and that. Then she caught her by the shoulders and turned her around. 'When did you last wash your hair?'

Mia thought. It was either yesterday or the day before, but she couldn't tell her that. Mammy didn't like guesses, so she needed to get it right. Otherwise, she'd say Mia was lying.

She got a slap in the side of the head before she could answer. 'If you have to think that hard about it, then it was too long ago.' She sniffed. 'You're disgusting, Mia.'

'I fell outside and I...' She glanced at Kevin.

'She didn't fall. She let the rubbish out for the birds to destroy the place with, so I stuck her head in it.'

Mammy didn't look at him, nor did she respond. But she did listen. Her top lip curled ever so slightly while she and Mia locked eyes with one another.

'Get down those stairs and wash yourself, you filthy little beast.'

'Hang on,' Kevin protested. 'What about my breakfast?'

'You should have thought of that before you put her out with the bins, shouldn't you? You know she's too dumb to wash of her own accord, and I, for one, don't feel like being poisoned today.' She turned to face him then. 'But you're right. Maybe I should let her go ahead and feed you. A dose of the shits might do you some good.' She thud-thudded back towards the door, leaving Kevin standing there, fuming in her wake.

Mia didn't like it when Mammy talked about poisoning. Especially as she thought she might have been poisoned herself once. By Kevin. He'd fooled her into drinking a hot chocolate, right after dinner one night. She remembered taking it from him. But she never remembered finishing it. The next thing she knew, Mammy was dragging her up the stairs and into the kitchen and it was morning. The dinner mess from the night before was still where everyone had left it and there was no sign of Kevin. Or the hot chocolate cups.

The day all that happened, Mia had been cleaning upstairs in the house. Mammy was out, Daddy was at work and Kevin was supposed to be down in the paddock looking after the horses. Mia had no idea that he was in his room when she walked in to retrieve his laundry. Yet he was. He was in his bed, under the covers with another boy. They were kissing when Mia opened the door. But then they stopped, and they both just stared at her. It was as if someone had hit pause on all three of them, just for a few seconds. Then Kevin roared at her to get out and she did. She got such a fright that she stumbled backwards and fell, right at the top of the stairs. As she tried to right herself, he roared again, and she went bumping downwards. Bump, bump, bump. It was such an awkward fall that by the time she landed halfway down, her ankles were over her head and there was dirty laundry scattered everywhere.

She wasn't sure when the other boy left, only that he wasn't there by the time she was serving dinner that night. Afterwards, when she'd eaten hers, Kevin came back into the kitchen. He went to the counter and stood with his back to her as he prepared the drink.

'Listen, I'm sorry for shouting at you, okay?' he'd said, handing her the cup.

She should have known because he'd never been nice to her before. He certainly never apologised. Now here he was, handing her a steaming cup of foamy hot chocolate.

'So, I won't tell on you for having this, *if* you forget all about today?'

It hadn't even crossed her mind to tell on him, but she agreed anyway. She was a fool for falling for it. But she nodded and took the cup. Then all the lights went out.

The morning after the hot chocolate was the sickest she'd ever felt. And dizzy, too. She couldn't think, and every single part of her hurt. Her legs, her arms, her ribs. Like she'd been kicked and rolled down the stairs and into her bed. She vowed not to take so much as a sip of water from him ever again. But she never mentioned the boy in his bed. Not because he'd poisoned her, but because she had no one to mention it to. She often did wonder what kind of poison he'd used, though, and where he got it from. Daddy used all sorts of medicine on the animals, so maybe he got his hands on some of that. She wondered, too, what might happen if *she* could do the same. Mia had never known a world without Kevin in it. But she wondered all the time what it might be like.

Before she left the kitchen, Mammy turned back to Mia. 'Daddy's left already, so I'll have breakfast in fifteen minutes. It had better be hot and you'd better be clean.' She turned to Kevin again. 'And you had better be gone.'

As she thud-thudded out the door, Kevin looked at Mia with such hatred in his eyes. He'd never liked her. Nowhere near it, in fact. But since the day of the hot chocolate, his hatred for her grew its own profile. It made its presence felt before Kevin even entered the same room as her.

Mia hurried to retrieve her key from the pantry. She unlocked the door to her basement room and, even though she wasn't allowed to, she locked it again behind her. Every day she wished that she wasn't the keeper of Kevin's secret. But she was. For this reason, she couldn't trust him. The fizzing and popping in her belly told her time and time again that he spent his days thinking of ways to hurt her. One day, maybe, when he got his chance, he'd even go ahead and kill her.

SEVEN

JUNE

'Well, Malcolm's gone missing again,' Heather whispered conspiratorially, as she pulled a plastic chair out through the emergency exit door for June to sit on.

'Where's he gone this time?' June asked, handing a toasted cheese sandwich to Heather on a plate.

She accepted it with a curled lip. 'Would it break them to give us a bit of ham in these things? Or maybe even cheese that isn't as plastic as the wrapper it comes in? You wouldn't catch them serving this tripe to the crowd upstairs, I can tell you that much!'

June nodded and took a bite. Heather had this gripe every day. Personally, she was glad of the free toastie. It saved her ever having to think about what to have for lunch. They could order a *staff lunch* from the kitchen if they really wanted to. But they'd have to pay for it so none of them did. Except for the concierge, John, who liked to appear more important and well-off than the rest of them.

'He's not answering calls and they checked his house. He's not there. He didn't turn up for his shift last night and no one's seen him.'

'Who are *they* that checked his house?'

'Who do you think? Liz's lapdog, John. She could hardly go looking for him herself, could she? No. She sends John with an *urgent message* to deliver to him. She always does that when he disappears.'

June nodded.

Heather talked on about Malcolm and Liz, covering old ground at times as she was prone to doing. But June was tuning out. She was thinking about Mrs Kelly's phone call and was coming up with her own theories as to what it might have been about. People held very black-and-white opinions about their esteemed VIP guests. Mostly black in the case of Mrs Kelly. But June saw nothing but grey in the woman. Over the years she'd been given glimpses into her real life, and it was far from the fairy tale people assumed it was.

'...He's like one of them fellas who holds all the strings on the dancing puppets. What are they called?' Heather nudged her.

June shook her head and shrugged.

'It was him who made her get all those implants and bloody...' She waved her hand over her face. 'The state of her! And there he is, still off shagging anyone who'll...' Heather rambled on.

Erica Kelly was looking for a way out of her home and June could think of several reasons why that might be. She wondered if she might be able to get back into room 208 in the afternoon. Perhaps if she checked in with the spa staff, she could find out if Mrs Kelly was booked in, then she could...

'Are you even listening to me?' Heather poked her, jolting June back to her lunch break.

'I'm listening.'

'I was just saying, he offered me a cheap basement flat once.' She inhaled sharply on little more than the butt of her second cigarette. 'I'd rather live in my old dump than have him as my landlord. I wouldn't give that yoke any kind of power over me.'

'Doesn't it worry you, living there?' June asked, a little more interested now because she was curious about Heather sometimes. There were few worse places to live than in one of Malcolm's flats, but Heather had managed to find one.

'What, you mean my neighbours, the methadone clinic?' She smiled and shrugged. 'I've been mugged on my doorstep three fucking times. So no, it's not ideal, is it? But...' She stubbed out the cigarette and broke into a rendition of 'That's Life'.

June stood up, eager to get back to work now.

'Right, so our next job is to find out who his bit on the side is this time.'

'You done?' June nodded towards Heather's plate. There was still half a sandwich left on it.

Heather looked at it and curled her lip again. 'In more ways than one, girl.'

June took the plate off her lap and stacked it on top of her own.

'See you tomorrow.' Heather smiled, as June went to leave. 'It is, after all, another fucking day.'

'Bye.' June left the laundry room and then proceeded to eat the second half of Heather's sandwich on the walk back to the canteen.

'You're wanted in the lobby,' John said, as soon as she stepped through the door. His mouth was bulging with soup-soaked soda bread.

By the time she got there, the signature serenity of the lobby had been lost. Or rather, it had been stolen. By Mrs Erica Kelly. The enormous Venetian glass vase, which always sat around three feet from where Lauren was perched, was shattered on the marble tile floor. It contained an arrangement of lilies today. Or at least, it had. Now those lilies were scattered miserably among the shattered glass, while all the water ran for cover.

'I demand to see that ridiculous woman you call boss. Right now!' Erica shouted at Lauren, who looked like she'd mentally checked out.

June didn't need to ask why she'd been summoned. She was there to clean up the spill and dispose of the vase that probably cost more than her entire life savings. And she would. But her attention was drawn momentarily to the Cedarwood Lounge bar. Or rather, to Liz who'd just gone skulking through its entrance. She couldn't have *not* heard the demand for her presence. Usually, Liz relished the opportunity to solve the problems of her wealthy guests. Even the irate ones. It's what she did best. But not today, it seemed. Her current pit of despair must be a deep one, if she was passing up an opportunity to shine.

Lauren picked up the phone and made a show of dialling Liz's extension, probably not for the first time. This didn't look like a situation that had just started. After a few seconds Lauren said, 'I'm sorry, Mrs Kelly, but Miss Sheehy isn't at her desk at the moment. I'll pass on your...'

'Child, the only thing you can pass is wind.' Erica slapped the counter with both hands.

June brought her whole trolley with her, rather than just a bucket of supplies. She parked it between Mrs Kelly and the Cedarwood Lounge. Then she hunkered down and started cleaning. Just as the woman was about to start shouting again, June interrupted her.

'Mrs Kelly?' She stood up again and placed a bunch of battered lilies in the bin on her trolley. 'I couldn't help overhearing that you're looking for Miss Sheehy, but I'm afraid she's off-site this afternoon. I believe she's meeting with one of our suppliers.'

'Is the maid the only person who knows what's going on around here?' She directed this at Lauren again. Then she turned to June, leaning her elbow on the reception desk. She looked like she was about to tear strips off June, too. 'Well, seeing as you know so much, maybe you can tell me' – she pointed a limp finger at Lauren – 'why she is so fucking dumb?'

She was drunk. June glanced at Lauren who, to her credit, just rolled her eyes.

June gave her half a smile. 'It's because she's so pretty, I think. People often mistake the two.' She glanced at Lauren again. 'And she smiles a lot, I suppose.' June pulled the mop out of its clip and started on the pool of water. 'Now, me, on the other hand, I only happen to know about Miss Sheehy's meeting because she almost forgot about it. She went running out the door not long ago. She told me to let Lauren know, but naturally enough, I forgot. Until just now.'

Mrs Kelly squinted and gave a cynical sneer. 'Well, maybe you, the all-knowing maid, can give her a message from me.' She stepped closer to June and stabbed a finger towards her face. 'You tell that bitch not to get in my way.' Her teeth were clenched, and each word was spat at June. 'Do you hear me? I'll roll right over her. You tell her that.'

June nodded, wide-eyed, but she didn't dare speak. She glanced from Mrs Kelly to Lauren, who looked like she was straining to hear the words being hissed.

Mrs Kelly's face changed then, as if June had told her something earth-shattering, even though she hadn't opened her mouth. Frowning at her, Mrs Kelly brought her hand to her chest and took a small step back.

'Are you okay, Mrs Kelly?' June asked quietly.

She shook her head. 'I... I'm, you just...' She squinted then, looking more quizzically at June. 'You just reminded me of...' She shook her head again. 'Nothing. Forget it.' She regained her composure. 'You pass that message on to your boss,' she said, a little less sure of herself suddenly. Then she turned and walked away, balancing perfectly on her high-heeled boots, despite the wine.

June frowned and watched her go. Then she remembered

something. 'Eh, Mrs Kelly?' She reached into the middle shelf of her trolley. She pulled out a sleeve of Nespresso pods, knocking her stack of clean cloths onto the floor in the process. She ignored the cloths for now and waved the coffee at her. For some reason June felt the need to cheer the woman up. She'd looked genuinely shook there at the end. She walked over and handed her the coffee. 'They're a limited edition. Dharkan, they're called. Apparently, it's George Clooney's favourite one.'

Mrs Kelly snatched the packet out of June's hand, without looking at her. Then she walked away towards the lifts.

'Ugh. What the hell was all that about?' Lauren drawled. 'It's early in the day even for her, isn't it?'

June got back to rounding up the shattered glass with the mop.

'Seriously, though, what did she say?'

June shook her head and shrugged her shoulders. She wasn't listening to Lauren.

'Thanks for the dig out, June,' Lauren said anyway, leaning over the counter.

June shrugged again and watched Erica Kelly standing straight-backed, hand on hip, facing the closed elevator doors. Another silk blouse. Another pair of black pants. And her signature high-heeled boots. Anyone who didn't know her would think she was a picture of elegance and grace.

When Mrs Kelly was safely ensconced in the lift, June bent to retrieve her cloths from the floor. She lifted the black canvas flap on her trolley and slipped them back on the middle shelf. She was just about to lower the flap when she spotted a folded piece of paper, sticking out from underneath a stack of pillowcases. June's breath caught in her chest. She glanced up at Lauren, but she was pretending to be busy. She looked all around the lobby. It was bustling quietly with guests going to and from the restaurant, and the concierge who was doling out more unwanted advice. But none of them appeared to notice

June, hunkering awkwardly beneath her trolley. She touched the paper with the tips of her fingers. It looked every bit as harmless as the one she'd found in her locker. But June already knew that it was anything but. She was cold all of a sudden and her body started to tremble in a way that felt almost painful.

Slowly she lowered the flap and forced her weakened knees to straighten. Then she shoved the trolley towards the lifts. Once there, she parked up and reached into the shelf again. She slid the page onto her bundle of cloths and stacked some pillow-cases on top. She slid the nonsensical bundle out and brought it with her into the lift and down to the basement.

She held the bundle tight to her chest until the doors slid open and the darkened hall greeted her. She hurried along it, past the locker room, past the laundry and into the stone stair-case. She pulled the door shut behind her, slid the paper out and dropped the rest of the bundle onto the steps. She squinted to read in the dim light, but there was only one word. And it was crystal clear.

Killer

EIGHT

JUNE

When June got home that evening, Tess was up and about and dressed in her Sunday best. That's what she called clothes that were clean, relatively well matched and less than ten years old. She'd been cooking and was humming to herself in the kitchen.

'Ah! There you are. It's good old-fashioned bacon and cabbage for us tonight.' Tess smiled, placing two plates, piled high with food, on the table.

June nodded, then turned back towards her bedroom.

'June.' Tess's tone changed from dithery old woman to stern headmistress. 'Don't do that just now. Come and sit. Let's eat while it's hot. It's not every day we have a dinner like this.'

June hesitated for too long, and Tess moved to pull out her chair for her. She went and sat down, feeling like she was moving around under water. Her thoughts would not line up and she didn't have it in her to make small talk tonight. But Tess wouldn't give up. June knew that much for a fact.

Tess sat down opposite her, smiling again. She plopped some extra butter on her potatoes before shoving the dish towards June.

'Have you been shopping or something?' June asked. She

tried to ignore the dull ache in her stomach for now and register the amount of food on the table.

'Pension day.' Tess grinned.

Technically it wasn't pension day. Pensions got paid on Fridays. But Tess had been picking hers up on a Tuesday for as long as June'd known her. At bang on nine am. According to Tess's calculations, that was the exact time of the week when she was least likely to meet other people at the post office. But June just nodded again.

Tess rolled her eyes and sighed. 'Oh, for heaven's sake, what is it?'

'Nothing.' June glanced at Tess. Her hands desperately needed something to do, so she began mashing her potato, cabbage, and butter into a gloopy heap in the centre of the plate.

'Well, obviously it's something, June. You haven't said more than two words since you got home. It's like you're functioning in slow motion or something.'

'It's nothing.' Tess did not need to know about any of this. She worried too much already.

'Oh. Okay. And I'm just supposed to believe that, am I?'

June dropped her fork and brought her hands to her head. She'd been feeling nauseous since she found that new note and now the room was starting to spin.

Tess reached across the table and caught June by the hand, concern finally making its way across her face. 'What is it, June? And please don't say nothing.' She squeezed her hand and lowered her voice. 'Did you hurt yourself? Too much, I mean? Are you alright?'

June was shaking her head. She pulled her hand back from Tess and grabbed a hold of her hair.

'June, you're scaring me! I...'

'Someone knows!' June blurted, dropping her hands onto the table.

Tess just stared at her for a minute, her eyes searching June's face for answers. 'Wh...?'

'They know.'

Tess closed her eyes and shook her head. 'Wait. Who knows?'

'I don't know who!' June shouted back.

'You're not making sense, June.'

June clenched her jaw shut and shoved back her chair.

'Don't you dare leave this table.'

'I need the toilet.'

'You need to stay where you are.'

June shoved her plate away in frustration.

'Just slow down for a minute, okay? Now, tell me, what does anyone know?'

June placed her palms on the table, fingers splayed. Slowly she looked up at Tess, but it was taking everything she had to control her movements. To slow them all down, as Tess had demanded. She had to tell her. She had to tell *someone* and there was no one else. 'Someone left me a note.' The words barely came out.

Tess closed her eyes and her shoulders sagged. 'Is that all?'

June straightened up and looked more sharply at her. 'Is that all? Did you hear what I said? I'm not talking about a love note, Tess. It wasn't someone asking me out to the movies.'

'That might have been more shocking,' Tess mumbled.

'More shocking than what? I haven't told you what the note said.'

'More shocking than someone messing with you, June. What could anyone at that place possibly know about you?'

'It said: *Killer*.'

At last, Tess was silent.

June's chair scraped loudly away from the table, and she hurried from the room. Seconds later she was in her bedroom with the door closed. She cried as she fell to her knees on the cold floor and pulled open her washbag. She lowered her leggings and found a smooth, unblemished patch of skin on her upper thigh. She stroked the skin gently with her thumb, knowing that it would never feel like that again.

'Hang on!' Tess barged into her room and her eyes immediately went to the blade in June's hand. She looked like she'd been slapped.

June yanked her leggings up around herself. 'Get out!'

But Tess didn't get out. Instead, she lowered herself slowly onto her hands and knees and crawled to June's side. She placed her hand over June's, but June would not relinquish the blade to her.

'They know nothing, June,' she said softly.

'But they said...'

'They *know* nothing.' With one hand still on June's, she tapped the side of her head with the other. 'Think. This is someone trying to manipulate you. Someone intuitive. Someone who's figured out a way to shake the unshakable June Calloway. You hear me? That's all this is. Now, look at me, June.' Tess leaned her head forward, making it harder for June to ignore her.

June turned her head slightly, her face wet with tears. She'd rather die than have this conversation at all. But to be having it in her most vulnerable moment, with her blade in her hand, was utterly mortifying. If only the ground would open up and let her fall into the flames below, it would be far less torturous than this.

'Are you listening?' Tess's gaze was impenetrable. 'They. Know. Nothing.'

June nodded. 'I need you to go,' she whispered.

Tess glanced down at the blade.

'Please, June.'

'Go. Please.'

Tess rubbed her face. 'June?'

June shook her head. Tess struggled to her feet and walked slowly to the door. She turned back before leaving and if June could have brought herself to look at her then, the sadness in Tess's eyes would have broken her heart.

As the door closed softly, June sobbed. Her thoughts echoed Tess's and she begged herself not to do it. To control it. But her blade had already begun to glide gracefully along that smooth patch of skin. In its wake, a bright red river flowed, while June chased a feeling that only existed in her memory.

NINE

MIA

Mia shoved the heavy old vacuum cleaner over the thick-pile white carpet in the good sitting room. Mammy was in there reading her paper, which was unusual, because no one ever used that room. Mia was in her socks while she worked because she wasn't allowed to wear shoes inside the house, aside from her sliders, which were only allowed in the kitchen and never on the carpeted floors throughout the rest of the house. Mammy was sitting in the big armchair with her feet up on a footstool. Her face was more or less hidden behind the broadsheets.

Mia worked as quickly as she could, knowing that she'd soon become agitated by the noise. But she'd be equally mad if the room wasn't vacuumed before lunch, which today was a cottage pie. It was already in the oven.

'Christ, do you have to be so slow about it?' She slapped the newspaper down on her lap.

Mia hurriedly went back and forth over the last corner of the room and then turned off the machine.

'Slow. That just about sums you up, doesn't it?'

Mia knew better than to try to come up with an answer.

Instead, she unplugged the vacuum and wrapped the cord up neatly.

Mammy's eyes followed her around the room. 'Let me have a look at you,' she said, before Mia had a chance to leave.

Mia put down the cord and went and stood in front of her. Not too close, but close enough that she could see her properly.

Her eyes roamed all over Mia's body. The more she saw, the more her lips puckered. She didn't like what she was seeing. That was clear even to Mia. She caught her by the arm and turned her around. 'Have you started to bleed yet?'

Mia frowned and her hand instinctively went to her nose. She had nosebleeds from time to time, but she always did her best not to make a mess. She said a silent prayer that she hadn't dripped onto that dreaded white carpet.

Mammy let go of her and rolled her eyes. 'Not your face, you stupid girl.'

Mia had no idea what she was talking about, but her face was the only thing that bled. Unless Kevin caught a hold of her, then it could come from anywhere. Her shins most likely. Or her lip.

Mammy laughed and it wasn't a nice sound. 'I take that as a no, then.'

'Mammy?'

'What?'

'We ran out of eggs.'

'I don't want eggs today.'

'But I thought you might like them for your breakfast tomorrow and I thought maybe...'

'Thought? You *thought*? That must have been very unpleasant for you.'

'I thought maybe I could go to the shop and get the groceries this week.' Mia persevered. She'd been working up the courage to ask this all week. Now that she had Mammy's full attention, it seemed like a good time.

'Did you, now? Is that what you thought?'

'I... well, I thought I could save you the...'

'Well, that was your first mistake, wasn't it? *Thinking*. Some people are cut out for that sort of thing, Mia, and some people aren't. You, my little half-witted girl, are one of the ones who are not cut out for thinking. For example, did you *think* about Daddy's peanut allergies when you imagined yourself buying groceries? Did you *think* about all the cross-contamination that happens where food is concerned? Did you *think* perhaps the reason I personally have to take on that responsibility is so that no one inadvertently kills him? You could live ten lifetimes and still never manage the level of *thinking* required for someone like him, Mia.'

'Okay.' Mia nodded. She was right. She cooked in fear of Daddy's allergies every day, even though Mammy made sure that nuts never slipped into any of the ingredients she used.

'Secondly,' Mammy continued, even though Mia had already agreed, 'if you were to walk into a shop and try to speak to the people who work there' – she paused for a chuckle – 'do you know what would happen?'

Mia nodded. 'I know.'

'They wouldn't understand a word you said, child.' She told her again anyway. She pulled her feet down off her stool and sat forward in her seat. She looked kind of like she was about to say something nice because her face softened.

'Listen, I've tried to tell you this many times over the years. I've thought of all the nicest ways I could word it. But it just doesn't seem to be sinking in.'

'Okay.' She wasn't about to say something nice, and Mia just wanted the conversation to be over.

Mammy sighed with a small shake of her head. 'You're mentally retarded, Mia. That's why the woman who gave birth to you didn't want you. Remember, I told you all this?'

'I know.' Mia kept her voice low, like she always did.

'Right when you were born, the doctor held you up for your mother to see you. The way they do, you know?' She nodded. 'But your mother took one look at you, and it was like she just knew. She wanted to put you in the bin. Remember, Mia? I told you this.' She reached out and took Mia's hand in hers. 'She was such a cruel woman.'

No one ever touched Mia in a way that was soft and gentle, so her mammy's hand around hers now felt strange. She pondered that instead of the words coming out of her mouth.

'Do you understand? That's why we can't let you go out. People would take one look at you and call for the men in white coats. Remember the ones from that film I showed you before?'

Mia nodded. Mammy's hands were very soft. Not like hers. Hers felt more like the lumpy kitchen roll she used to wipe up spills.

'They'd take you away and inject you with all sorts of drugs. Then they'd leave you to drool in the corner of a padded room for the rest of your life. I don't want that for you and I'm sure you don't either. Do you?'

'No.'

'You're safe here, Mia. This is the only place where we can protect you, so please, stop asking such stupid questions. It only hurts me to have to say no.'

She dropped Mia's hand then and got up. She walked out of the room, leaving Mia standing there, staring at the empty armchair. She was still thinking about her mammy's skin against hers. When she finally turned to go herself, Daddy was standing in the doorway, watching her. She hadn't heard him arriving, and judging by the way he was looking at her, he'd been there the whole time, listening.

He coughed and then smiled as he began to walk away. 'I'll have my lunch now, I think. I need to get going soon. There's a herd that urgently needs my attention.'

Mia nodded and followed him towards the kitchen, stopping along the way to stow the vacuum cleaner in the cupboard under the stairs. By the time she caught up, he was sitting at the kitchen table. She said nothing and neither did he, as she went and checked the oven. The food was ready. Carefully she took out the dish and placed it on the marble counter. She took a plate that had been warming in the oven and piled it high with food, the way he liked it. She placed it in front of him on the table, which she'd set earlier.

'Daddy?'

'This is lovely, Mia.' He smiled behind his greying beard.

'Daddy, I was wondering if I could go...'

'Be a good girl now and put that dish back in the oven. Keep it warm for Mammy, eh?'

Mia stood there looking at him for half a second, before doing as he said. Of everyone, Mia wondered about him the most. He was a lovely, kind man who never said cross things. But she thought maybe he was who she got her stupid from. He wasn't her real daddy, but they had been living in the same house forever. Maybe that's how stupid spreads from one person to another. He'd heard what Mia and Mammy were talking about. He often did. He just didn't seem to understand any of it. One time, he even came into the kitchen just after Mia spilled some of Mammy's good red wine on her pink jumper. Mammy got such a fright she jumped up and screeched. Then she slapped Mia so hard with the back of her hand, that her diamond ring opened a hole in Mia's lip. Daddy just stood there inside the door, waiting for Mammy to finish breaking things and go change her clothes. When she did, he handed Mia a shirt that he wanted ironed for the following day. She was bleeding all over herself and there was red wine and smashed glass everywhere. But all Daddy could think about was his shirt. Surely that made him stupid, too. So how come he was allowed out and she wasn't?

She got annoyed about that sometimes. But mostly Mia was

used to her life. Why wouldn't she be when it was all she knew. They lived in the country, in a very big house with a field out the back. It was called a paddock and there were some horses that lived down there. But other than those horses, all she could see for miles were green fields, tall trees and an even taller wall that surrounded their property. The wall had spiky glass mixed into the cement on top, to stop any robbers from getting in. Kevin told her once that it was really there to stop *them* from getting out. But that didn't make sense. Kevin was allowed out whenever he wanted. He just never seemed to go anywhere for very long.

When she thought about it properly, though, Mia reckoned Mammy was probably right. She read the newspapers. She knew what went on out there. And if her dream was anything to go by, the world outside her home was no place for someone like her.

Using her oven gloves, she returned the dish to the oven, and she vowed that from here on, she'd be the best girl she could ever be. She'd keep her mouth shut and, like Daddy, she'd just smile. Then she wouldn't sound mentally retarded or slow or stupid anymore. No more than Daddy did, at least. She'd show Mammy that she could be quiet and normal and then maybe one day, Mammy could take her on one of her trips. Maybe one of the ones where she took a big bag and didn't come back for days. On those trips, she always came home happier than she'd been when she left. Maybe it could be the same for Mia.

She brought Daddy his glass of milk and she matched his smile perfectly, as she placed it in front of him. From this day on, Mia Kelly would be the best little mentally retarded girl anyone had ever seen.

TEN

JUNE

'Oh... what happened to you?' June asked the lobby table as she ran her hand over it. Her fingers traced the circular stains where at least two wine glasses had rested. 'Well, now, they didn't show you much appreciation, did they?'

Luckily June knew how to use oil soap and she wasn't too lazy to use it properly. She used a whisk to blend it with exactly the right amount of water and applied it with only soft cotton cloths for pieces like this. If it took her all day to bring this table back to its glory, so be it. June had caught a new maid spraying Mr Sheen on it once, about three years ago. She went straight to Liz and demanded the girl be fired. She wasn't, of course. But she was taken off lobby duty and June was put on. Permanently. Now no one touched this table except for her.

Her dry cloth followed her oiled cloth, buffing in small circles all around the enormous piece. When she finally finished, just over an hour later, June took a slow walk all around it. She was looking for streaks or any other imperfections when Liz whipped past her, her face like thunder as she headed into her office.

Satisfied that her table was back to its glory, June followed

Liz to her office. She brought her bowl of oil soap and some new cloths with her. She knocked once, went in, and closed the door gently behind her.

'Morning,' June said tentatively.

When Liz didn't respond, June looked at the bowl in her hands and went about cleaning Liz's cedarwood furniture. There was a miniature version of the lobby table taking up the right-hand side of her office. It looked like it had been cut down the middle to make it sit flush against the wall, but it was very beautiful. And even though it was nowhere near as splendid as its parent out front, June showed it the same respect. They were family, after all. This one was adorned with various awards that the hotel, and indeed Liz, had won over the years.

'Everything okay?' she asked, glancing at Liz, who was sitting at her desk pulling on her ear lobe. She looked wretched and had obviously been crying. Again.

Liz nodded, but the action soon turned to a shake of the head. 'Malcolm wasn't feeling well the other night and he, well, he must have gone home or something and now he's not answering his phone and I... well, it just...' She shook her head and started crying again.

June had seen Liz like this a couple of times over the years, but none of the other staff ever had. It was that invisible woman thing again. It made people let their guard down, even when they weren't the type. Perhaps they assumed that once they'd unloaded their problems, June would simply disappear and forget everything she'd heard.

Liz cleared her throat and pulled some tissues from the box on her desk. Without smudging her mascara, she dried her eyes and hauled herself up straighter in her chair. She was gathering herself. 'Anyway. Is the lobby table done? Did you see those stains?'

'I saw them. It's done.' The conversation was over.

June carried on polishing with her back to Liz. Despite her

unnatural appearance and the occasional meltdown, Liz was one of the most intuitive people June knew. That's what made her so good at her job. She knew what their guests needed, before they knew they needed it. Could she really be the one sending the notes and messing with June? Out of necessity, June had to give Liz a reason as to why she couldn't open a bank account and go on the books like the rest of the staff. Liz had agreed and never mentioned it again. So why would she start threatening her now? She glanced over her shoulder at Liz, who was holding a hand mirror in front of her face. June picked up her bowl of oil soap. 'Can I get you a coffee or something before I start on the rooms?'

'That would be lovely. Thanks, June. And, eh... I know you won't say anything about...' She waved her hand over her face. She was back.

'I don't gossip, Liz. You know that.' She opened the door. 'I'll be back in a minute with that coffee.' She left, closing the door gently behind her.

She pushed her trolley away from Liz's office and towards the lifts. She left it there while she went to get the coffee and by the time she delivered it, Liz had fully bounced back. June left her to it. It was time to head up to her VIPs on the second floor.

Starting with room 201, June worked systematically through her workload. Cleaning had always been the best distraction for June. By the time she finished up in 203, she felt somewhat more contented. It was a temporary feeling, of course. Those notes hadn't gone away, but for now, she was managing. As she returned to her trolley and prepared to move on, the door to room 208 opened. A man stopped in the doorway with his back to June. He was chuckling at something. Then he leaned back into the room and while June couldn't *see* Mrs Kelly, it was very clear that this man was giving her a kiss goodbye. Then he stepped out fully and let the door slam shut. June's eyes widened and her mouth dropped open. As he turned to walk away, towards the lifts and where June stood, his smile turned to a grin when he saw her.

'Morning, maid.'

'Morning, Malcolm.' Though her voice could hide her surprise, her face could not.

'Chop-chop. Those rooms won't clean themselves, will they?' he called out as he sauntered towards the lifts.

ELEVEN

JUNE

Daisy, by Marc Jacobs. Never has a scent been less suited to the person wearing it. And yet it permeated the air, as it always did, long after Erica Kelly had left room 208. It was her daytime perfume. Or so she'd told June once. Her nighttime one was far more expensive and deadly to the senses. June brought her cleaning bucket inside and let the door close behind her. She put the bucket on the floor and took a slow walk through the room. This wasn't part of her check-out routine. This was more to do with satisfying her curiosity. Thanks to the lobby table and a crumbling Liz, she was already late finishing her rounds, so what was another few minutes?

She stood with her hands behind her back, looking over the unmade bed. After a minute, she pulled the sheets back further, all the way to the end, and let her eyes roam over them. There was a tell-tale stain, right in the centre of the bed.

'Naughty Mrs Kelly.'

She let her eyes roam again, up towards the pillows. Some very short, dark hairs were scattered on the one nearest her. More like Malcolm Levy's recently buzzed buzzcut than Mrs Kelly's fake blonde strands. June whipped the sheets and pillows off the bed and left them in a pile by the door. The bathroom was her next stop. What followed sex could often be quite undignified, couldn't it? She pulled two bathroom towels off the rails and another two up off the floor. She added them to the pile by the door. Then she spent far longer cleaning that room than she should have. Scouring it from top to bottom.

'Why are you still here?' Liz arrived in the room without warning, just as June was smoothing down the bed. She looked more surprised to see June than June was to see her.

'I'm running behind.' She tried not to let her eyes drift to her laundry bag and the sheets now concealed within them. But she wondered if Liz could smell him from where she was standing. 'Thanks to the spilled wine on the lobby table, I've been playing catch up all day.' June gave the room a final once-over, nodded in approval and moved towards the door. 'I'm done now.'

'Malcolm called,' Liz said, sounding neither happy nor sad.

'Did he? Where's he been?'

'Well, as you know, he manages Isabelle and Frank's property portfolio. There was a leak in one of the Blackpool properties. He's been trying to get it sorted.'

June nodded and squeezed past her through the doorway. She busied herself tidying her trolley and tightening the strings on her laundry bag, sealing it shut.

Liz sniffed. 'You used a lot of product?'

'It needed a good freshen,' June replied, looking her squarely in the eyes. 'So, what brings you up here?' She got behind her trolley and prepared to push the beast away from the scene, while she waited for a response.

Liz shook her head. 'Just felt like a walk around.'

'And there's no better place for that.' June smiled. 'Anyway, I'd better get home. I'm already dead late.'

'Late for what?' Liz asked, sounding surprised that June might actually have a life waiting for her outside of the Manor.

'Ah, you know, I have a hot date with my pyjamas. How about you? Doing anything nice tonight?'

She shook her head. 'Nope. Just a few more hours of paperwork here and then home.'

'To Malcolm?'

'To Malcolm,' Liz replied more quietly. She glanced around room 208 before closing the door as June shoved her trolley towards the lift, in one direction. Liz went in the other.

TWELVE

JUNE

The walk from the train station to June's home on Wellington Road wasn't a particularly long one, but it was a hilly one. So, by the time her front door came into view, she was usually more than ready to go inside. But today she stopped five doors down from her own, on the opposite side of the road and concealed herself in someone else's doorway. She stood there, flat against it, and counted slowly to twenty. Then she leaned forward and peered up the road, to see whether or not she was mistaken. Though really, she knew she wasn't. Malcolm Levy's cobalt blue Subaru wasn't exactly subtle. With its shiny black alloy wheels that looked too big for the equally shiny car, it was hard to miss. Not to mention the ridiculous spoiler sticking out the back. That unmistakable car was currently parked two doors further up from June's. She could see Malcolm sitting in the driver's side. He was slouched down with his chin resting on his chest and his arms folded. It didn't look like he'd seen her yet.

Technically speaking, Malcolm was June's landlord and could easily explain away his loitering. His excuses might even be believable. *If* Malcolm was the type of landlord who responded to problems within the building, that is. Problems like dampness, mould, broken appliances, not to mention the issues with the plumbing. But he wasn't that type of landlord. Malcolm would happily let the place crumble around its tenants, knowing that his wealthy grandparents, the *actual* landlords, were too busy swinging in their Cayman Island hammocks to give a damn. But he made sure that the rent kept coming. Withholding it was not an option.

Granted, some of his tenants, like the single mother in the top flat, paid him less than they would have another landlord for another flat. Which is how he managed to fill the almost-derelict building in the first place. But it was expensive in other ways for her. Malcolm made demands of those tenants that should see him in jail. But if reported, they'd be out on the street. And so the wheel turned and they all kept running to keep up.

June's rent wasn't due for two more weeks, however. So why was he sitting in his car watching her front door? What did he want?

She stayed in the doorway for a few more seconds, just breathing and thinking. Finally, she stepped out. But rather than going up the road towards home, she went down again, staying close to the wall so that he wouldn't see her. She ducked between two buildings and up another short but steep hill. At the top she took a right and carried on, until she could come back down onto the top end of Wellington Road. From there, she could approach the Subaru from behind. She couldn't avoid him if she wanted to go home. Which she did. But why should he get to see her coming? It was a short detour that gave her little advantage. But little advantage was better than no advantage at all.

She approached the car slowly and when she reached it, she didn't knock on the window or wave in. Nor did she attempt to pass by, pretending not to see him. Instead, she opened the passenger door abruptly and slid in. This startled him and he jumped, which made June relatively happy. This little victory wouldn't last, of course. Malcolm Levy always came out on top one way or another. But June allowed herself a solemn moment of contentment.

'What the fuck is wrong with you?' Malcolm was unsettled but quickly tried to regain his composure.

'Plenty,' June responded quietly, looking straight ahead with her hands in her lap. 'You?'

He turned in his seat to face her. 'Plenty?' He huffed out a mean laugh. 'You got that right. There is so much wrong with you, it would take a team of fucking...'

'Were you looking for me? Or are you here because of the broken letterbox?'

He tilted his head to look at her. She kept her gaze straight ahead and refused to meet his eyes. But she could see in her peripheral vision that his expression was one of fake confusion.

'Fuck the broken letterbox.'

'Well then, it's outside of my work hours. My rent is not due for another two weeks and I can't think of any other business you might have with me.'

He moved so quickly then, so suddenly, that June had no time to prepare herself. His giant, meaty hand gripped her throat and pressed the back of her head into the headrest. The pain as his grip tightened and her chest warmed up with the sudden lack of air was excruciating. And exhilarating. His face came within an inch of hers, contorted in anger. He was snarling, but he said nothing. He held her like that for a matter of seconds and when he let go, June was pleased that she hadn't allowed herself to claw at him. Yes, it had hurt. But June was used to pain. And she didn't feel fear like a normal person might. What did she have to fear when she had so little to lose?

She had no family. She had no real friends, aside from Tess. She had no real life to speak of. Men like him took so much power from others, that to fear them was to feed them. But June had power, too. She had the power of not being afraid.

She didn't respond to his outburst and continued to look straight ahead with her hands in her lap, just as she had before. As if nothing had happened. This angered him, she could tell. But because he liked to be in control of those around him, he would not let her see it this time.

'I get it now,' he said, in a soft, calm tone. 'I know what's wrong with you.'

June didn't respond, and she still refused to look at him.

'You're some kind of special needs one, aren't you? No emotions, that kinda thing.' He leaned slightly towards her again. 'Too thick to know when you're in the wrong place at the wrong time.'

June took her phone out of her bag and looked at the time displayed on it. 'It's after six and that's my flat.' She pointed to her front door. Again, she didn't look at him. 'I'm a little late, but I'm definitely in the right place.'

He put his hand on her knee and leaned in so that his breath gave away what he'd had for lunch. Tuna. June hated tuna. 'I think you still owe me for last month.'

She said nothing for a while. June was not one of his sex-for-rent tenants. But he often threatened to make her one, so it made sense that this would be the next box to be ticked on his threat chart.

She turned slightly towards him in her seat. 'I'm all paid up, Mr Levy. But sex means absolutely nothing to me, so if you're here because no one else will give it to you, then okay.' She gave a very small smile and started unbuckling her belt. 'I could do with some time to think before going home anyway. I have a visitor at the moment who likes to talk *a lot*, so a couple of minutes to just tune out would be fine by me.'

His nostrils flared as he glared at her. Then he opened the door and got out so aggressively that the whole car shook. June watched him in the driver's side mirror as he stormed around the back of the car and opened the boot. He retrieved something from it and slammed it shut. He got back in and shut the door. In his hand was a long wooden truncheon. Like the kind used by cops in American TV shows. He held it right up to her face.

'Stay the fuck out of *all* of my business, or I'll shove this so far up inside you... we'll see how much sex means to you then.'

June looked at the dash, then looked back at him. 'So, should I go?'

He slammed the baton into her stomach, knocking the wind out of her and sending pain shooting in all directions. As she doubled over, he leaned across and opened her door. He shoved her out onto the footpath, started up the car, and pulled away from the curb like a lunatic.

'Hey, you fuckwad!' a woman's voice shouted from across the road. 'Jesus Christ, are you alright?' She came running once she managed to right herself. She'd been gliding towards town on her electric scooter and almost crashed thanks to Malcolm's erratic driving.

June was curled up on the cold ground. She rolled onto her side and vomited. Her stomach felt like it had imploded, but she nodded at the woman that, yes, she was alright.

'Can I call someone for you?' She hunkered down beside June, holding her scooter upright with one hand and her phone in the other.

June hugged her middle with one arm and wiped her mouth on the other sleeve. Then she pulled herself into a sitting position. The woman held out her hand with the phone still in it, like it was another appendage. June caught her by the wrist and was pulled to her feet.

'I hope that was because you broke up with him and are

never planning on seeing him again?' she said, her anger as clear
as day.

'I'm fine. Thank you.'

'Seriously, can I call someone? Do you live nearby?'

'Just there.' June pointed to her front door and gave the
woman a small smile. 'Thank you for your help.' She pulled her
bag up on her shoulder, while the woman with the scooter stood
there watching her go, a worried expression on her face.

As June let herself in through the front door, Tess was coming
out of her bedroom. June groaned inwardly. Her fight was gone.
She didn't have the energy that Tess sometimes required and
now more than ever, she wished that she lived alone.

Tess closed the bedroom door gently behind her. 'Why are
you so late?' She frowned then. 'What happened? Look at you!'
She reached out and touched June's arm.

June brushed her hand away. 'I'm fine. I just got behind on
my work today, that's all.' She walked away towards the kitchen,
with one arm wrapped tightly around her stomach. She'd never
intentionally snap at Tess and even now, she felt bad. But she
would *not* tell her what had just happened with Malcolm.

'Clearly that's *not* all. You're in pain, June. Even I can see
that and I'm halfway blind.'

'I said, I'm fine.'

'Tell me what happened! Did you get another note?'

June shook her head and exhaled resignedly. 'You were
right. It's just someone messing with me.'

Tess looked suspiciously at her. She didn't believe her, but
she dropped it anyway. For now. Instead, she went about
putting four sausages in the fryer basket, glancing at June out of
the corner of her eye from time to time.

Ignoring her looks as best she could, June washed her hands
and took a bowl of leftover potatoes out of the fridge. She

started cutting them into thin slices to be fried on the pan. Her belly was still reeling, and she couldn't imagine putting food inside it just now. But she knew she would. Food was important to June, and she never skipped meals if she could help it.

'So, you'll all have a nice, quiet few days now that Mrs Kelly has gone home.' Tess broke the silence, which was on its way to becoming loaded. 'And that nice honeymoon couple, too. But sure, they were no bother at all, were they?' Tess smiled as she worked, talking as if she was a long-suffering member of the Cedarwood Manor staff herself. Normality was restored.

'She's having an affair with Malcolm,' June said, heating the oil on the pan.

Tess stopped what she was doing momentarily. 'Who is?'

'Who do you think?'

'Really? I suppose there's no accounting for taste, is there?'

'Mrs Kelly is a rich and somewhat glamourous woman. What's she doing with someone like Malcolm Levy?'

'It's *because* she's rich and glamourous.' Tess nodded knowingly. 'It's called slumming it, June. Look it up. Some people find it quite exciting.'

'If you say so.'

Small talk rambled its way out of June in an attempt to distract them both.

'How do you know?'

'I saw them. *And* I cleaned the room.'

'I see.' Tess checked that the oil was sufficiently hot before dunking the basket of sausages in. 'Aaaand cook.' She smiled. She put the kettle on to boil, while June spread the potato slices evenly on the pan.

'Did you tell Liz?'

'Why would I do that?'

Tess nodded. 'So, none of them know that you know?'

June turned her mouth downward and shook her head. Tess

didn't need to know about Malcolm and what he did or didn't know. 'I wouldn't think so.'

Tess nodded again. 'Well, you make sure you keep it that way, you hear me? The last thing you need is the likes of them thinking about you at all.'

June nodded, flipping the potato slices one by one. But someone *was* thinking about her, weren't they?

'I will.'

THIRTEEN

MIA

The gravel crunched outside as Mammy's car pulled up. She'd been away for a few days, and this was the first time that Mia had ever felt relieved to hear her come home. This time, more than ever, she'd been wondering what it might be like to go there with her someday. She often saw the brochure for the Cedarwood Manor Hotel. She picked it up every time she cleaned Mammy's room, and to Mia it looked a little daunting. But the wording used in the brochure made it sound like paradise. In fact, that was one of the words they used. *Paradise*. Others were *opulent* and *haven* and *calming*, and she could imagine why Mammy loved it so much. She had very few calming days in her own house. For weeks now, Mia had been extra good at keeping her mouth shut, paying special attention to all her jobs and nodding and smiling in response to everything. Just like Daddy. But Mammy hardly noticed at all. She certainly gave no hint that she might have been more pleased than usual. Then one evening, she just packed her big brown bag, with the gold *L*s and *V*s all over it, and off she went without saying a word.

She used to like it when Mammy went away. Things were

always more peaceful and quieter during those few days. But something was different now. It only started a few months ago. On the day of her tenth birthday as it happened. The day that Mammy went on one of her trips. Not that Mia's birthday was ever anything special. It wasn't like anyone baked a cake and sang to her or anything. Mammy said that people like Mia didn't have the same kind of birthdays that other kids have, because sugar makes them worse. She knew that and she was fine with it. But that day, Daddy had asked Mammy not to go and they had a bit of a fight about it. Mia could hear their mumbled voices upstairs, but she couldn't make out what they were saying. Then Mammy left anyway, with her brown-and-gold case, and Daddy just kind of moped around the house for the rest of the day.

As it got close to teatime and she started preparing the disgusting fish for the pan, she turned and saw Daddy standing in the doorway watching her. If anything, he looked mildly confused by what he saw.

Instinctively, Mia checked the clock. She wasn't late with their meal yet. Still, she reminded herself that Daddy didn't really get mad. Not like Mammy and Kevin did. But sometimes Mammy and Kevin got mad on his behalf.

'Don't look so worried, Mia.'

Mia exhaled and carried on with the fish, trying not to let her face twist up in disgust.

'Today is your birthday, isn't it? How old are you now?'

'Ten,' Mia replied, still concentrating on the food.

'Ten, eh?' His voice trailed off then when he said, 'Has it been that long?'

It wasn't the kind of question that needed an answer, so she carried on with cracking an egg into a bowl and whipping it a little with a fork. It was ready then to dip the fish in. She'd already put breadcrumbs into another bowl, but she'd get some butter melted on the pan before she started all the dipping.

'Why don't you leave that? I don't feel like fish tonight.'

Mia stopped and turned to face him. 'But it's Friday. It's always fish on Fridays.' She started to feel hot and prickly. She didn't have anything else ready to cook. Friday was fish day, and it was ten minutes until teatime.

'What would you say to cheeseburger and chips?'

'A cheeseburger?' Her unease paused on its way from her stomach to her face. Mia had seen Kevin devouring cheeseburgers many times. They came in little Styrofoam boxes with deliciously scented grease stains and leftover lettuce in them. Aside from the leftover lettuce bits, she'd never had a cheeseburger herself because Mammy hated fast food. She frowned. Something about this felt like a test. Was Mammy waiting outside the door, ready to pounce if she said yes? Would she be punished over her willingness to waste the fresh fish?

Daddy laughed quietly. 'Mia, why do you always look so worried?' He nodded his head towards the hall. 'Come on.'

She did as she was told and followed him. He led her to the good sitting room with the white carpet and Mammy's armchair, beside the overstuffed couch. There, sitting on the coffee table, were two green Styrofoam boxes and a carton of chips wrapped in paper. They were unmistakable. The smell hit her as soon as she walked in there and it told her that it was actual fast food. Also on the table were two cans of Coke. Mammy would have an absolute fit if she saw this. Burgers *and* Coke in the good sitting room. *Mia* in the good sitting room, *eating* burgers and *drinking* Coke! Still, she couldn't help it. She allowed herself a small smile.

'Happy birthday, Mia.'

This was all new to Mia. Bubbles started popping in her stomach and up through her chest. But it felt different from the fizzing and popping that usually went on in there. Like when something bad was about to happen. So, this must be what it felt like when something *good* was about to happen. Her face broke into a big smile then. She wrapped her skinny arms around his thick waist and pressed her face against him. She did it without thinking and the way his body stiffened said that it was unexpected for him, too.

'Can I have some?' she forced herself to ask, letting go of him.

He smiled down at her. 'Let's eat, shall we?'

Mia nodded, still smiling, and hurried towards the table.

And that was the start of it. Every time Mammy went away after Mia turned ten, Daddy started being so much nicer to her. He still just smiled and nodded most of the time when Mammy was home. Only now he'd give her a little wink sometimes when Mammy wasn't looking. Usually just after she'd got angry with her. To Mia it felt like she had something that belonged to *her*. Something special that she could hold on tight to, and something to look forward to when Mammy went away. All things she'd never had before.

The next time, after the cheeseburger night, was a few weeks later. That time they had what Daddy called a midnight feast. A full tray of chocolates, crisps, jellies and fizzy drinks. Enough to make Mia physically sick. But she still ate as much as she could, knowing that she might never see the likes of it again. That night, he put on a movie. It was called *The Goonies* and the pair of them sat together on the couch, Mia at one end, Daddy at the other, and they laughed together at a chubby little boy called Chunk.

Now Mammy was arriving home from her third trip since Mia's tenth birthday. When she was leaving this time, Mia couldn't wait for her to go. She wanted to be left at home to be spoiled by Daddy.

He'd brought what he called *real* fish and chips home with him. They came wrapped in paper and the vinegar made Mia's eyes water when she unwrapped hers. Even though she hated fish, the smell made her want to not only devour the fish, but the paper as well. They'd been lodged in her chest since she ate them. Not because they weren't delicious. She was sure they probably were. But while they were eating them, Daddy pulled Mia onto his lap. She'd never sat on anyone's lap before, and she was sure that she was probably too big. But she didn't mind any of this. Not the fish and not the lap. She figured this is what it must feel like to be a normal girl with an actual dad. Not very comfortable. But normal.

He picked another movie to watch. It was called *The NeverEnding Story,* about a big flying doggy-dragon-type fella. Just as it started, he shook his head and kind of scowled to himself. Then he shoved her off his lap. He was acting weird, like he wanted to have a movie night with her, but like maybe she smelled or something. She was sure she didn't. She was careful about staying clean because it was one of the house rules.

'Are you alright, Daddy?' Mia asked, landing roughly on the cushion beside him.

'You shouldn't be calling me that,' he mumbled, rubbing his beard and glancing uncomfortably at her. Then he looked away again as if the sight of her face hurt him somehow.

Mia frowned. 'Why? That's wh...'

'We just... I mean, did you ever hear about boyfriends and girlfriends, Mia?'

Mia frowned and nodded. Of course she'd heard of them. She read the newspapers. 'Boyfriends are the fellas who kill their girlfriends,' she said, licking salt off her fingers, despite the strangeness of all this. 'Sometimes they kill themselves as well, but not always.'

Daddy frowned and shook his head, still looking at the telly. 'Sometimes. That's true. But they don't always kill each other. They do other things as well.'

'Like what?'

'Well, she and I... I mean... you're probably not even...' He sighed deeply and rubbed his face roughly with both hands. 'Look, just watch the movie and enough with the bloody questions, alright?'

He seemed cross all of a sudden and the fizzing and popping started in Mia's belly again. The older, more familiar kind. She didn't know why exactly, or what she was afraid might happen. But the fizz always warned her when something bad was coming. And it was always right.

'Did you have a girlfriend, Daddy?' she asked. 'Did she die?'

He stopped breathing for a few seconds, then jumped to his feet. 'Get to bed,' he shouted, and stabbed his finger in the direction of the door. 'Get to bed, and keep your mouth shut! You hear me? Don't ever ask about this again.'

Mia jumped to her feet, too, knocking her food onto the floor. She stood there, frozen. There was fish and batter scattered on the white carpet. If Mammy came home to a stained carpet, she'd kill her. 'But the fish...?'

'Bed!' he roared.

He'd never done that before, so Mia ran from the room. She grabbed her key from the pantry and took the stairs two at a time down from the kitchen. She jumped into bed with all her clothes still on and she lay there staring at the ceiling for countless minutes. She was so confused. Why did he get so mad? What did she do?

Eventually she scuttled under the blankets and pulled them up to her chin. But when she closed her eyes, all she could see were the faces of boyfriends and girlfriends she'd seen in various papers. There were loads of them. Headlines and photographs stuck to her brain like glue. They always had. There was the boyfriend with no hair who choked a girlfriend to death. The brown-haired one who stabbed a girlfriend. The curly-haired fella who beat a girlfriend with a golf club, and the one who shot a girlfriend and all her children. And himself. Though he might have been a husband. Why was Daddy talking about boyfriends and girlfriends? Did he have one that he was planning to kill or something? Or was it Mammy? Was he planning on killing Mammy?!

She opened her eyes again and turned on her side. She kept hundreds of coloured marbles in a clear plastic container on her bedside locker. They were there for nights like this one, when she needed to keep her eyes open. She got bad feelings sometimes. Like something was happening that she didn't understand. Something that would lead to trouble. On nights like that it was best if she didn't sleep, because if she did, a bad version of the dream always followed. She fixed her gaze on those marbles and tucked her arms under the blankets to ward off the cold. Then, beginning with the marble in the bottom left corner, she started counting.

FOURTEEN

JUNE

'Have you heard?' Heather asked, as she dragged two chairs over to the emergency exit door. She had an unlit cigarette dangling from her lips, just waiting for a spark.

June carried both plates expertly in one hand and two full cups in the other. 'Heard what?'

They exchanged a chair for a lunch, and both sat down with their meal resting on their lap. It was dry and bright today, so they were more outside the door than in. Heather lit her cigarette and gasped down a few lungfuls. Then she got going on her story.

'Well, according to the concierge...' She changed both her voice and her accent when she said *concierge*, just like she did when she said *Cedarwood Lounge*. 'Liz has been dodging calls from Isabelle Levy all week.'

'Really?' June took a small bite of her toastie. She liked to savour it. 'How would he know that?'

'Apparently, when she kept failing to reach Liz, she called him.'

'To say what?'

Heather shrugged. 'That Liz needs to stop avoiding her. Or

something to that effect. She doesn't contact this hotel from one end of the year to the next.' Heather turned and pointed her yellowing finger at June. 'The fact that she's so desperate to get in touch all of a sudden... something's going on. Mark my words.'

June nodded and took another bite, squinting towards the woods. She couldn't help agreeing with that. Liz was avoiding Mrs Kelly and now her boss, too. This was all very much out of the ordinary. 'How long have you worked here, Heather?'

Heather took another drag and blew out a grey cloud. June didn't get the appeal of smoking. From where she was sitting, it was disgusting, and quite frankly, it was destroying the flavour of her lunch.

'A bloody lifetime, is how long I've worked here. But if you were to press me for a number, I'd say around ten years.'

'Wow.' June nodded. 'And do you ever remember Liz behaving like this?'

Heather shook her head and stubbed her butt out on the sole of her shoe. 'No, actually. But then, she's nothing like she was back when I started. Physically, I mean. If I had a photo to show you now, you'd never think she was the same person. She had a bit of an innocent look about her back then. She'd already started having bits done, but nothing like now.'

They both sat and quietly ate their lunch for a few minutes between Heather's cigarettes.

Heather shook her head. 'You'd hardly recognise the girl she was back then. But this avoidance thing is new, too. Normally she's in her element when someone gives her a problem to solve.

'Don't get me wrong, she deserves her place here,' Heather continued. 'She worked her way up and she still works hard. She's good at her job, is what I'm saying. But she'd want to get rid of that yob, Malcolm, and sort out whatever is going on with the boss. Because Isabelle does not like to be fobbed off.' She lit another cigarette and took a drag.

'Then again, what do I know? No one acts normal around here.'

Normal. The only word in the English dictionary without a meaning. June looked down at what was left of her sandwich and nodded. She supposed Heather was right in a way. Could any of them honestly say that they were normal?

After lunch and after she'd finished the last two bedrooms on her floor, June went back down to the lobby area. She parked her trolley and brought a bucket of supplies for a walk around. The lobby didn't need any more of her attention, but she was keen to find out where Liz was. With a buffing cloth in her hand, she worked her way along the reception desk.

'Hi, Lauren.' She half smiled at the receptionist, who was tapping keys on her keyboard.

'Hi,' she replied curtly, without looking up.

'Is Liz in her office?'

'Who wants to know?'

June stopped what she was doing and looked pointedly at the girl who'd only been among them a wet week. '*I* want to know.'

Lauren glanced up and perhaps it was the look on June's face, but she cleared her throat and said, 'Sorry. I mean, no. She isn't. I'm fielding calls for her all day. That old woman in the Caymans keeps ringing.'

'Where is she?'

Lauren shrugged. 'She doesn't tell me that. As far as I know, she hasn't left the building or anything. But she's not in her office.'

June nodded. 'It's a good time to clean it, then.' She walked away and Lauren went back to tap-tapping on her keyboard.

June and Liz didn't have the type of relationship where they would drop in on each other for no reason, even though they'd worked together for six years, and Liz did vent to June some-times. But June was never silly enough to mistake that for friendship. The venting came down to June's station in life. It told people that their secrets were safe. After all, who would the weird hotel maid have to tell? But if June were to start asking questions, it would end all that. Whatever June wanted to know, she'd have to find out for herself.

She walked around Liz's desk, tracing the buffing cloth along the surface. Liz kept very little on top of her desk. Just a notepad, pen and her date book. There was also a Waterford Crystal ashtray and her laptop. June started with the notepad. She picked it up, tilted it and brought it close to her face. She studied it to see if there were any indentations on the clean page. Had Liz been writing any notes recently? There were none that she could see so she replaced it exactly as it was. The laptop's screen was black, but when she swiped her finger over the mouse pad, it came to life. Liz's home screen was, of course, an aerial photograph of the Manor. Across it was the password request.

June knew Liz's password. She'd been cleaning the office when Liz was here with an IT technician last year after the system was hacked. She needed to reset her password and she mumbled it as she typed it in.

Ladyofthemanor with a capital *L*. Even if she hadn't been there that day, Liz referred to herself as the lady of the manor so many times that June could easily have guessed it. She typed it in, and the screen came to life. Like Liz's actual desktop, her digital one was just as tidy. There were only a handful of icons. June clicked on the little envelope, opening Liz's email. She expected to be met with another password request, but instead it opened right into her inbox. Liz was already logged in. The most recent email was from Isabelle Levy. It arrived at nine seventeen this morning, meaning that Liz had probably seen it but had chosen to ignore it. June could not. She clicked it open.

Liz,

I understand why you're avoiding my calls, but I do not appreciate it. Quite frankly, I expected more from you. However, your avoidance doesn't change anything. The fact of the matter is, Erica Kelly is offering a very fair price for the Manor, and while it hadn't really occurred to me to sell, Frank is of the opinion that we should. With your refusal to engage in this conversation, I'm beginning to think that perhaps he is right.

If by the end of this week, you haven't found your big girl pants, then you will have lost your opportunity to convince me that my husband is wrong.

Yours in utter disappointment

Isabelle

June quickly marked the email *unread,* closed the app and locked the screen. She gathered up her bucket and left the office. Erica Kelly was trying to buy the Cedarwood Manor. That explained Liz's behaviour and why she was avoiding Erica Kelly. If this sale went through, then it would be an uncomfortable adjustment for all of them. But for Liz Sheehy, it might as well be the end of the world.

By the time June got back to the lobby area, Liz was at the reception desk dealing with a middle-aged couple. They were on their first visit to the Cedarwood Manor.

'Of course.' Liz smiled. A picture of patience and professionalism. 'I'm very sorry that that happened to you.'

The man was rubbing his wife's back in a soothing manor. But whatever the problem was, she didn't look like she needed his TLC. She stood right on the edge of Liz's personal space and was glaring at her, waiting for some kind of satisfaction.

June thought she looked like someone who just enjoyed a good old argument. But what did she know? Either way, she pretended not to notice any of them. She started polishing the brass plate on the wall, the one that let everyone know about the restaurant's Michelin Star. From there, she could hear their exchange.

'While there are so many perks to our stunning location, I can see how certain elements might come as a shock to guests who aren't used to it,' Liz consoled the pair.

June thought she knew what they might be complaining about. And she was pleased to see Liz handling it with the professionalism that she was known for. The couple were down from Dublin City on their holidays. That in itself was probably the crux of the problem.

'But you don't understand.' The woman was bordering on hysteria. 'That so-called woodland trail is a death trap. We're lucky to be alive!'

Liz nodded stoically. 'What exactly did the owl do?'

'What did he do?!' The woman threw her hands up. 'First of all, this was no ordinary owl. This thing was huge! I mean, two or three times the size of the ones you see on telly! And it came swooping' – she slashed her hand through the air – 'down out of the trees and it came right for us.'

'I'm sure he didn't mean you any harm, Mrs Delaney. He was just...'

'Don't you tell me that thing didn't mean any harm! It attacked me, knocking me to the ground! You didn't see it...'

'Chrissie, my love, why don't we...' the husband tried, but Chrissie batted him away.

'She didn't see it, Gerald! And there was no way out of there other than to traipse back the two miles we'd already traipsed! In fear for our lives the whole way!' She was pointing her finger at Liz now and her voice had risen significantly. 'You'd think a place like this, with your five stars and all your bells and whistles, would think of something as basic as an emergency bloody exit!'

'You're absolutely right, Mrs Delaney.' Liz nodded. 'I can only apologise to you both. And as a small token of that apology, I'm going to ring the chef and have him rustle up a nice charcuterie board and perhaps a glass of merlot to help you relax.'

Gerald rubbed his wife's back a little more forcefully now. His way of telling her they'd won.

'Yes, well...' Chrissie said, in a calmer but slightly petulant tone. 'I'm not one to normally complain, Miss Sheehy. I just thought you should be aware of what's going on out there.'

'And thank you for that, Mrs Delaney. I do appreciate it.' Liz extended her arm towards the Cedarwood Lounge and the pair walked away, passing June as they went for their free food and drink.

Liz waved her hand at Simon, the barman, and mouthed the word *merlot,* as the pair went and found a seat, happy to have had their concerns vindicated.

As soon as she turned and walked away from them, Liz's face crumpled. She'd been holding it up and together for the sake of her job, but June could see how much work the façade took. And now she knew why. She returned her attention to the brass before Liz caught her looking. Once she was finished and Liz had settled back into her office, June went and knocked on her door, bucket in hand as always.

There was a gentle clearing of the throat before Liz called, 'Come in.'

June stepped in and went straight to the wood furniture. 'Hi. Sorry to disturb you. I'll be quick.'

Liz was sitting at her desk, appearing so much older than the woman who just placated two awkward guests. June said no more and got to work quietly.

'Have you heard? Our woodland trail needs an emergency exit.'

'Really?'

Liz cleared the sarcasm out of her throat. 'Did you remember to leave some liquorice in room 202? Mr Lovell is on his way. He should be here shortly.'

Tess's *little Henry* was the VIP guest with a penchant for tea dances and a kind of liquorice that liked to play hard to get.

'I did.' June smiled. 'I added some Milky Bars to his fridge as well. On his last visit I must have found ten wrappers in his various bins. Mr Lovell has a sweet tooth.'

'Well spotted, June, and well done. Thank you.' She sighed a weary sigh. 'Sometimes I think you're the only one who gets it.' She huffed out a humourless laugh then. 'The quietest person within these walls, who knows exactly what sets us apart from everyone else.'

'Well, I'm not sure it's the Milky Bars that set us apart.' June gave a small smile but continued working. 'They are nice, though.'

Liz looked up at her. 'Was that a joke, June?'

June shrugged.

'I don't know if I've ever heard you joke.'

'I suppose what I mean is, the Manor isn't just any old hotel, is it?'

Liz sat back in her high-backed, leather bouncy chair. 'You're not wrong there, June.'

'And not just anyone could run it the way you do. Could they?'

Liz blinked slowly and her lips tightened into a straight line. 'Try telling other people that,' she mumbled.

'I'm sorry?'

Liz shook her head and then looked at June quizzically. 'Didn't you do in here already today?'

'I did. But I'm ahead of myself today, so I thought I'd give down here another quick run-through,' June responded, feeling sweat tickle the nape of her neck.

'Thank you, June.'

June packed up her stuff. 'Is there anything else you need, Liz?'

She shook her head. 'Go on home. You've done enough for today.'

June nodded. Before she left, she emptied the wastepaper basket beside Liz's desk. 'See you tomorrow.'

'See you tomorrow.'

When she returned her trolley to the basement, June took the small bin liner out of her main bin: the contents of Liz's wastepaper basket. There wasn't much in there. Just some tissues, some clear plastic wrappers and a balled-up piece of paper. June unrolled it and held the crumpled scrap behind her trolley so no one could see. Her hand felt clammy and began to tremble as she made sense of what was etched on the paper. It was a doodle. Or rather, a collage of doodles. There were some squiggly lines all overlapping to create a frame of sorts. It swirled and twirled its way all around the elaborately curly word, *BITCH*.

FIFTEEN

JUNE

'I'm home,' June called when she stepped through her front door.

Facing her was Tess's closed bedroom door. To the right was the closed door to the family room. That's what Tess insisted on calling the three rooms in one. Which was ironic seeing as they hadn't a single family member between them. On the left was June's closed bedroom door and the bathroom. Their closed-door rule went some way towards maintaining what little heat they had. Which, at the moment, was zero. They were all out of credit.

June's greeting was met with silence. Not that she expected an immediate response from Tess, but she always made some little sound. The flat was so small that even while Tess was sleeping in her room, June could still hear her breathing. So, the strangeness of that silence now stopped June in her tracks. Her senses heightened as she listened for any sign that she wasn't alone in the flat. As she stood there, she began to feel a heaviness in the air. Like it hadn't been disturbed in some time.

'Tess?'

No response. June went to the family room first, but it

looked exactly how it had that morning. Everything down to the single cereal bowl, washed and now dry, on the draining board was exactly as she'd left it.

'Tess?' she called a little louder, turning towards Tess's room. She stopped outside her door and stood quietly for a minute, listening. There was no sound coming from inside. Tess only left the house once a week, on Tuesday morning at nine am. She did that purely out of necessity because, like June, Tess didn't have a bank account for her pension to be sent to. If she did, then she'd probably never go outside. But this was Thursday evening, not Tuesday morning. Tess was here.

She's dead. This was the first thought that came to June's mind as she stood in the silence of their little home.

'Tess?' she said, more quietly now, and knocked on the door. Her heart beat a little louder in her chest and her stomach bunched up on itself. She closed her eyes, took a deep breath and opened the door.

The room was empty. But there was a big old, leatherbound book resting on her bed. June had never seen it before, although she and Tess never ventured into each other's rooms. 'Tess?' she called out again, but her eyes were on the book.

There was no response and still no sound in the flat. June hovered in the doorway for a second. This was Tess's private space and she didn't want to snoop. But she couldn't resist picking up the book and opening it. It was an old photo album. Each black page had two photographs taped to it. Some were black and white, others were faded old colours, cracked and yellowing. The first picture was a group of girls of all ages. Each of them had on a slightly different flowery dress and knee-high socks. The same group of children were in the next one, with presumably their parents. June looked closely at the faces, to see if she could recognise Tess. She didn't. But they were very young, and Tess was very old. June conceded that it might be hard to recognise the woman at the opposite ends of her life.

Each page had pictures of the same kids and the same parents, not all together, but in twos and threes. It was a family photo album. Presumably, Tess's family.

But on the last page was a picture of a different group of girls. They were in much shabbier old dresses, outdoors and standing over a crop of vegetables. Each of them was holding a gardening tool of some sort. Behind them stood four nuns and nearly all of them were smiling for the camera. June searched the faces of the girls in the shabby dresses. One of them must be Tess. Why else would she have kept it? The scene itself, in the large garden with a big imposing building in the background, meant that this was taken at the mother and baby home. But none of the girls, with their forced smiles, looked familiar in any way. June was just about to close the book, when her eyes found the nun on the far left of the photo. She stood dead straight, with her hands clasped in front of her and her head held high. She wasn't smiling, but her grin was the first familiar thing she'd seen in the whole photo album. It was hard to say for sure. But that grin...

A dog barked somewhere near the front door and June slammed the book shut. She dropped it back on Tess's bed and hurried from the room, closing the door behind her. She stood there in the hall for several minutes, breathing and thinking. It couldn't have been her. Tess was a lot of things, but a nun was not one of them. She hated the Catholic church. She'd said so many times. They held her prisoner and took away her child. June shook her head. It couldn't have been.

She turned to go back into the family room. 'Jesus!' She exhaled and every muscle in her body loosened. She clutched her chest and closed her eyes again. 'Tess? What are you doing?'

Tess was standing in the middle of the room, facing the door. Facing June. Her back was ramrod straight and her hands clasped together in front. Her hair was a mess, like she'd just woken up from a restless sleep. But her features were totally blank as though she hadn't *actually* woken up at all. She was just staring, trancelike, straight at June. Like something from a creepy old movie.

'Tess!' June said, a little more forcefully now. 'Where have you been?'

Finally, Tess blinked and came back to life. 'June.' Her face broke into a smile, as if she'd just realised she was there. 'Oh, I was sitting out the back, taking a bit of air.'

Tess went a bit funny sometimes. But usually there'd be warning signs before it happened, like she might be extra quiet for a few days before. Or she might spend a couple of days in bed. That kind of thing. But this had come out of nowhere and June wasn't expecting it. She wondered now if it had something to do with that photo book.

'You okay, Tess?'

'Me?' She unclenched her hands and turned towards the kitchen. 'Of course I'm okay. Why wouldn't I be? Fancy some rice and beans? Or will we have pasta and beans?'

'Eh...'

'Actually, I don't think we have much in the way of pasta. So, rice and baked beans it is. Yum.' She looked over her shoulder and smiled her wrinkly smile. If she noticed June coming out of her room, then she said nothing about it.

'Sounds lovely,' June muttered, doing her best to play along.

Thursday was bottom of the barrel day as far as dinner went.

June went and stood beside Tess, and they cooked together like they always did. But she couldn't stop thinking about that photo. The way Tess had been standing just now, just like that grinning nun in the picture. She glanced at her out of the corner of her eye from time to time, trying to see her as she would have been all those years ago. Trying to picture her in both a habit and a shabby old dress.

'Did you have a bad day, Tess?' June asked, as they sat down at their small table.

'Is there such a thing as a good one?'

Sitting there with her shoulder-length white hair and her sagging skin, it was hard to imagine that Tess had ever been a young woman. But of course she was. She'd told her often enough about having her youth taken away before she had any time to enjoy it.

'Were you thinking about her?'

'Thinking about who?' Her smile slipped, but only slightly.

'You know who.'

'What would be the point of that?'

'Him, then?'

'Who?'

June rolled her eyes. 'Seán Buckley.'

A cloud fell across Tess's face and her melting smile was replaced with a straight line. 'For a time, perhaps.'

'Tell me about him,' June said. She lowered her eyes and started to eat.

She'd heard this story many times. The more she talked about it, the madder Tess got. It wasn't that June wanted to make her angry. But getting it off her chest was what brought her back to herself. Some might call the telling of her story therapy. But tonight, it was June who needed to hear it. She needed to hear the emotion in her voice when she told it. The kind of emotion that couldn't be faked. She needed to know that the nun in that picture wasn't Tess.

Tess huffed. 'Why should I tell anyone about *him*? He doesn't deserve the airtime.'

June said nothing. She just slowly ate her rice and beans.

'That horrible fecker promised me the sun, moon and stars.' She twisted her paper napkin into a tight ball. 'And what did he give me? Five minutes, up against the wall of the picture house.'

June nodded but didn't look at her. Tess preferred to tell her story to the air around her. She didn't want or need audience participation, so June never gave it. But if the story stayed the same as it always did, despite the album and despite Tess seeing June coming from her room, then questions would have to follow.

'Seventeen years of age. Sure, what sense did I have?' Tess paused to breathe a little and she took a small forkful of food. She chewed it quicker than she usually would and gave a small, snide laugh. 'Yeah. But where was he when my belly started growing, huh? Fecking Houdini he was then – nowhere to be found.'

June got up quietly and went to fill two glasses of water. Tess hardly noticed that she'd moved, but June's impatience was growing.

'Where was he when my fecker of a father dragged me by the elbow to the doorstep of those nuns? Where was Seán bloody Buckley then, huh?' She looked at June finally. 'Did you ever see those nuns, June?'

June shook her head and sat back down, placing a glass of water in front of each of them. She'd never seen a real nun in her life. 'Only in films. And photographs.' She looked pointedly at Tess.

Tess nodded and looked into the middle distance again. She should have been wondering *which* photographs June had seen. Or maybe she just wasn't worried about it. Maybe it wasn't her at all. June was second-guessing herself and she wished she'd taken the time to look properly at the photo.

'Well, fact can be so much worse than fiction or snapshots.' She frowned deeply then. 'They had themselves up on pedestals, fully convinced that they were on some kind of mission from God. That they were *right* to punish girls who only needed help. Girls who just wanted to be loved. And to love their children.' There was a long pause then and Tess put down the fork that she'd been holding. 'Sideways, she came out. Did I tell you that?'

June glanced up. Tess's voice was fading into sadness now. She needed anger, not sadness. Anger brought Tess back. Sadness added days onto her strangeness. And June wanted answers, not the silence of her depression.

'Did you ever think about looking any of them up?' she asked, bringing the focus back to the villains of the story.

'Who, Buckley? On the line, you mean?' Tess snapped back, just a fraction.

'Or those nuns.'

'Why would I want to do that?'

'To let them know what they did to you?'

'Why?'

June shrugged. 'So you can stop staring at walls?' That's what Tess did when she went a bit funny. She sat for days, staring at the wall.

Tess's smile came back. 'I like our walls.'

June looked around at the grubby, off-white walls that so often closed in around her. Black mould crept around the four corners. She looked back to Tess. She was still smiling, just a little.

'Anyway, I wasn't thinking about him, and I wasn't looking at the walls. I wasn't thinking about the wife he probably has now either. Or the proper children they probably raised together. I wasn't thinking about any of that. Not today.'

'Do you think about her a lot?' she asked, despite knowing it was entirely the wrong question to ask. But she'd always had a curiosity about Tess's daughter. She found herself wondering now if she even existed.

'Ah.' Tess gave a small nod. 'You mean the tiny little baby who was loved with all her mother's heart? Is that who you mean? The little girl who was pulled from her mother's body and carried out the door by the holiest of the women. Never to be seen again. Is that who you're talking about?'

June stared at Tess and Tess stared back, both curious to see each other's response. Tess had been left there: bleeding, crying, scared and alone. Her baby was taken away before she'd even had a chance to hold her. Or so the story went. Neither of them said anything for a minute. But then Tess broke the silence.

'But no, I wasn't thinking about her just then. I was thinking we might get chicken *burgers* tomorrow instead of goujons. It's payday. What do you think?'

June frowned. Sometimes it was hard to tell if she was joking or being serious. 'Really?'

'Mmm.' Tess nodded, her wrinkly smile fully back in place. She took a small forkful of rice. 'So, how was everything at the Manor today?'

'I saw the photo book.'

'Hmm?'

'The one on your bed.'

'Oh! That silly old thing.'

'Was that your family?'

'Once upon a time, I suppose it was.'

'And the picture at the back?'

She stopped chewing then and swallowed. She frowned and tilted her head with a curious expression.

'The one with all those girls in shabby old dresses and the four nuns.'

Tess looked confused now and shook her head. 'I'm not sure which photo that is. I never kept anything from that time. As you can imagine, I didn't have many fond memories of that place, June.'

They ate in silence for a few minutes, but the atmosphere in the room had become heavy. The temperature had dipped as well.

'I'm sorry I let us run out of heat,' June found herself saying.

She knew Tess well enough to know when she was lying. She was lying now about that picture. But June needed to think about her next question, before accusing her outright.

'You didn't *let* us do anything, June. We simply ran out.' Tess nodded, still chewing and smiling, despite the awkwardness surrounding them.

'I'll top us up tomorrow when I'm paid.'

'A tenner will do. Don't go mad. If we go easy on it, that'll see us through till Tuesday.'

June nodded. She often wondered how Tess was able to keep smiling. Especially when she was having a day like this one. A whole day stuck in a dark past is most unpleasant. June knew that only too well. But to finish the day on the spot like she was now, caught out in a lie... how was she still smiling?

'Tess?'

Tess blinked slowly and lowered her fork. She dabbed her mouth with a paper napkin and then placed her hands in her lap. Each movement was slow and deliberate. She looked June square in the eye, as if knowing what was coming. 'Yes, June.'

'One of the nuns in that picture looked very much like you.'

Tess looked down at her plate again. She frowned. Then raised her eyebrows and looked around as if thinking, her lips moving in silent conversation with herself. 'You know that Malcolm Levy fella?' she said, finally.

June frowned.

'He reminds me of Seán Buckley.'

A mental image of Tess, up against the wall of a picture house with Malcolm Levy, came to June's mind. She couldn't help it.

'Not to look at.' Tess rolled her eyes.

June just stared at her, incredulous. It was as if she hadn't heard any of what June had said.

'I mean, the way he is. The kind of chap who always gets what he wants. And *only* what he wants.'

'Did you hear what I said?'

Tess shook her head and waved away the question.

'I'm stuffed,' she said, shoving her plate towards June. She'd eaten less than half.

June looked at the plate and shoved it back towards Tess. 'So am I. Tess, did you hear what I said? That nun in the picture...'

Tess got up from the table. 'He'd a fine arse all the same.'

'Tess!' June couldn't hide her annoyance anymore.

'Buckley, I mean.' She headed for the door. 'That other fella only has an arse for kicking. Goodnight, June.'

June had no choice but to sit and watch her go.

Left in the silence of that cold, damp room, a crushing weight pressed down upon June's chest. Tess was the only person that June had ever trusted in life. The closest thing to family she'd ever had. But a sudden crack had appeared in that picture now. Just like the cracks in the old snapshots in Tess's book.

SIXTEEN

JUNE

June's favourite time of day had always been first thing in the morning, before the other maids arrived at the Manor. Before the sleepy night concierge went home and the motor-mouthed one came on. Before there were guests milling around the halls and phones ringing. Before all the noise and chatter that might still have seemed quiet and peaceful to others, but only because they never got to experience the Manor like she did. Even its darker underbelly, every inch of which she knew, was special. The creak of the door leading to the locker room. The hum of the machines, always going, in the laundry room. The maze of corridors, only some of which were visible. Others were secret, running behind the walls and accessed via an old servant's staircase, built of stone. Most of the staff knew nothing about those, or the building's history, which was entirely their loss. Now the grumble of the pipes made the whole place sound like it was waking up and stretching. Like her, it was getting ready to face the day.

And that was just downstairs, in the belly of the beast. Upstairs had its own, separate personality. Warm, welcoming; always ready to impress. Upstairs gave everyone exactly what they wanted, whether they knew they wanted it or not. Upstairs, downstairs. Light and dark. Ying and yang. June had become enamoured with it all.

A piece was missing this morning, though. It took June a while to figure out what that piece was, and it was Liz. Again. With few exceptions, Liz was always first to arrive and last to leave. June felt her absence now because, at seven forty in the morning, Liz *should* be roaming the lower echelon, keeping tabs on everyone's arrival times. But she wasn't. Neither was the unmistakable scent of her perfume that lingered wherever she'd been. It was unusual for this to happen once. But twice in such a short space of time? That was unheard of. June wouldn't normally concern herself with Liz's problems. The woman seemed to have so many. But she worried that this particular problem would go on to affect them all. The Manor was June's safe place, but not anymore. Notes howling at her from her old life. That weird old photo of Tess. And now the Manor was on the verge of being ripped out from under her. It was as if the very ground beneath June's feet was turning to liquid and soon, the life she'd built for herself would cease to exist.

She still had time before she had to get ready, so she entered the stone staircase and moved quietly upwards until she came to the ground floor. She could exit through a concealed door into Malcolm's office, but instead she just peered through the peephole. He wasn't in there and the bank of monitors was blank. The cameras had been switched off. Nothing too unusual there. Malcolm often switched the cameras off, for a price. But he'd been absent from his post and now it seemed Liz was as well. June headed back down to basement level and out into the corridor. Today would not be a normal day.

By the time June shoved her trolley into the storeroom, she could hear the echo of the other maids' voices coming through the hall from the back door. She quickly checked her stock and took what she needed. A little more, just to be sure. She was rushing and didn't want that to be the reason why she'd have to come back later for something she'd forgotten.

'Well, aren't you the early bird?' Skinny Annie said, and not in a complimentary way.

'I sure am,' June replied, shoving her trolley past them and out into the hall again.

'Lick arse,' she heard the tall one mutter, as she dragged her heels around the locker room.

June tuned them out and headed for the elevator, glad not to have to see them again for several hours at least.

'June?' Lauren hissed, as June stepped out into the lobby.

She pulled her fully loaded trolley backwards out of the lift and glanced over her shoulder at Lauren, who was frantically beckoning to her. June parked up. She unhooked her bucket and brought it with her to the reception desk.

'Where's Liz?' Lauren hissed again, even though there was no one else around.

June shrugged and started polishing the shiny surface. 'Did you try her office?'

'Of course I tried her office. I tried her office, her mobile, the bar, the staff room, the laundry room, the kitchen and the restaurant. No one's seen her.'

'Maybe she's taking a well-earned day off,' June said, above her own mounting curiosity.

Lauren's face said that she no more believed that than June did.

'Anyway, it's eight in the morning. What could be so urgent?'

'209 will be on top of me any minute, demanding to see her. That's what's so urgent.'

'What's the problem?' Despite her maid's uniform, less experienced staff always defaulted to June on the rare occasion when Liz was unavailable to help them. Probably because she'd been working there for longer than most of them put together.

'They said there was a racket in the room next door during the night.'

'Room 208? That's vacant. What kind of a racket?'

'Some loud bangs in the early hours of the morning.'

'And did you send Malcolm up?'

'Well, I wasn't here when they called during the night, June. I've just come on and that old biddy who does nights didn't mention anything about it before she shuffled out the door. So they caught me completely off guard. They nearly ate me without salt on the phone! You'd swear *I* was the one banging around and waking them up.' She exhaled dramatically.

'Did you apologise for their inconvenience?'

'Of course I did. Even though they're bloody bluffing. They're just trying to get something for free.'

June frowned. 'Is that the owl couple?'

'The ones looking for an emergency exit from the garden. Yes. The sooner they go back to the city, the better.'

'Tomorrow, I think.'

'Yeah, well, in the meantime they're demanding to see Liz. And if she's not here by the time they get down, then it'll be me who gets it in the neck. It's always bloody me!'

'Well, if they get here before she does, please don't tell them you think they're bluffing.'

Lauren rolled her eyes. 'Do I look thick or something? But you said it yourself! The room beside them is vacant. There's no one in there. And secondly, it's the Cedarwood bloody Manor! People don't exactly come here to get sloshed and trash the place, do they?'

Clearly Lauren had never seen the things they did to the beautiful pieces of furniture all around her. June started cleaning her way away from Lauren.

'Well, what am I supposed to tell them?'

'Tell them that you've reported their concerns to Miss Sheehy, and she is currently investigating the matter. She'll make a point of speaking with them soon and then tell them to enjoy their breakfast.'

'Oh. Okay.' She nodded, pleased. 'Good idea.'

'I'm full of those,' June mumbled. But she was already wondering about room 208. She'd done a vacation clean on that yesterday and its next expected occupancy wasn't until later that week. So, what, or who, was banging around in there during the night?

She thought about the blank monitors earlier that morning and mentally ran through the Manor's current staff. From the kitchen porters, to the manager's office, and everyone in between. Whoever it was would have had to pay Malcolm at lot for the use of a vacant room and June wanted to know why. She hung her bucket back on her trolley and pulled the lot back into the lift. When the door pinged open on the second floor, she pulled out the trolley, parked it against the wall and stood, listening for a while. The halls were quiet. She took her bucket and walked slowly towards room 208. She stood outside for a minute with her ear to the door. She couldn't hear anything.

Suddenly the door to room 207 swung open. June took a dusting cloth from her bucket and started working on the wall-light fittings.

A relatively young couple stepped out, not looking very happy.

'Good morning,' June said, throwing them a small smile.

'Not really,' said the man. He was in his mid-thirties and everything about him screamed tech success.

'Maybe you can give them a wake-up call.' His equally glamourous partner jabbed her manicured finger towards the next room.

June looked at the door, confused. 'Oh, these guests haven't checked in yet.' She stopped cleaning and gave them her attention, which they were instructed to do if they were being spoken to. 'This room is vacant.'

'Well, vacant or not, someone was having a right old party in there last night.'

June pulled her eyebrows together. 'Really? Oh... that's very strange. Maybe it was the Lady of the Manor.' She forced a half smile.

'The who?' the woman asked.

'The Lady of the Manor. Legend has it, she had her husband murdered. Right on this floor, as it happens. That was more than two hundred years ago, but apparently, she never left.' June took a small step closer and lowered her voice. 'There's been a few sightings of her over the years. But always around the anniversary of her death, there'd be some strange noises, alright.'

'What, really?' The woman perked up.

'Oh, here we go.' The man rolled his eyes.

'Oh, yeah! This place has a very dark past. People have seen and heard all sorts of things.' June made herself sound as excited as possible. 'I've heard a few strange things myself over the years. And always on this floor.'

'Oh my God!' The woman slapped her husband on the chest. 'That room is empty, Shane!' Her eyes were wide with excitement. 'Do you think it was her?' She turned to June then. 'Do *you*?'

June raised her eyebrows and shrugged.

'Oh, Christ.' The man shook his head. 'Can we please just go get some breakfast?'

The woman nodded and looked much more enthusiastic than she had when she stepped out of their room.

'Enjoy your breakfast.' June gave a small wave, glad that they were leaving. Her own paranoia was heightening. She wanted to know what was going on in that room. She wanted to know what was going on everywhere.

They both ignored her and walked away. She was already forgotten. But the Lady of the Manor was not.

June kept her eyes on them until they stepped into the lift. When the doors slid shut, she used her key card to open the door, and she stepped into the supposedly vacant room 208.

The smell was the first thing to hit her. Vomit. She'd know it anywhere. She'd smelled it in this exact room many times during Mrs Kelly's darker moments.

'Hello?' she said, stepping a little further into the entrance hall, but holding the door open. She leaned forward and peered into the room.

Of all the things she expected to see in there, a dishevelled Liz sitting with her back against the headboard, still in yesterday's suit, was not one of them. It was crumpled and stained, and she looked a million times worse than she had the last time she'd been seen in it.

'Liz?' June's fingers fell away from the door and it slammed shut.

SEVENTEEN

JUNE

'Liz?' June said again, more cautiously this time.

Liz looked at her with bloodshot eyes. She held a bottle of Erica Kelly's expensive red wine limply between her hands. The bottle was empty. So were the other two that had smashed against the wall. The famous racket.

'Are you okay?' June kept her voice low as she looked around the room for further damage. It was a mess, but nothing else seemed to be broken. Aside from maybe Liz.

'I'm fucking marvellous, June.'

June lowered her bucket and went to the Nespresso machine. 'I gave Mrs Kelly these limited-edition Nespresso pods,' she said, slotting one in. 'Intensity ten.' She put a cup under the spout and set the machine going.

'Fuck *Mrs* Kelly and fuck her limited-edition fucking pods.' She was still drunk.

'Too right. Let's drink them.' June injected a smile into her voice, but her back was to Liz. She pulled another cup over and had the second pod ready to go for when Liz's cup was full.

June didn't drink coffee. She hated everything about it, including the smell. But she filled a second cup anyway, sensing that Liz wanted to take back as much as she possibly could from the woman. And she'd probably need the second cup. She put a drop of milk and two sugars into the first one and handed it to Liz, taking the wine bottle from her.

Liz didn't respond, but she took the cup.

'Dharkan, I think it's called,' June added.

'I know what it's called, June. Who do you think ordered it?'

'Of course. I suppose we have a few more weeks before we have to think about her coffee requirements again.'

'Oh, we'll see her well before that.'

June paused. 'Will we?'

'Ah, yeah! She can't get enough of us here at the Manor.'

'Right.'

'He thinks she's his golden ticket.' She snorted out something like a laugh.

June glanced at her. She knew about Malcolm and Mrs Kelly.

'He's an idiot!'

June agreed wholeheartedly. But she kept her response to herself and continued with the task of pouring a second Dharkan in silence.

'They both want what I have.' Liz muttered, swinging her legs off the bed. She wasn't really speaking to June now. She was thinking out loud, so June said nothing. Liz sat for a minute with her back to June. 'He wants my job. *She* wants my whole life.'

June went and put milk and sugar in the second cup of coffee. The first had already been abandoned on the bedside table. Suddenly the whole thing seemed clear in June's mind as well. Malcolm would never choose an older woman to have an affair with. He was too shallow to cope with any signs of maturity. But Erica Kelly wanted to buy the Manor and Malcolm was the black sheep of the family who owned it. Did he think she was his way into the top spot, where he felt he so richly deserved to be? Liz's spot. Could he really be that stupid?

Liz got up off the bed, staggered slightly and used the windowpane to right herself. June noted the handprint she left behind on the glass and the paranoia on her boss's face.

'Do you know, she actually wants to *buy* the Manor?' She was incredulous now. 'Buy it!' She stormed her way around the bed. 'Well, I hope she's ready for a fight. Because I'm *not* that easy to get rid of.'

June just stood there with her eyes wide, still holding the full cup. She didn't have to feign surprise. She *was* surprised that Liz had let her in on the fact that Mrs Kelly was trying to take the Manor from her.

'She's has been having affairs here since the eighties, did you know that?' Liz's smile was a snide one now, and for the first time, June could see her hatred for the woman.

'So I believe,' June replied. She'd heard the stories and she believed about half of them. 'But why would she want to own this hotel? The Manor has always been a haven for her. Or at least, that's what she told me once. So why would she want her haven to become a job?'

Liz rolled her eyes and turned to face June. 'That woman wouldn't know a *job* if it slapped her in the face. She just wants what I have.'

June put down the cup and started picking up the larger shards of broken glass from the floor, just to be busy again. Liz had many insecurities, but paranoia hadn't been one of them until now. June didn't believe for a minute that Liz meant that much to Mrs Kelly. She was right that she wanted the hotel. June had seen proof of that. But her reasons couldn't be as simple as wanting to upset Liz, surely.

Liz was pacing the room now and finally she headed for the bathroom and stood in front of the mirror. From where she stood, near the door, June saw her flinch. The light in there could be quite unforgiving.

'Maybe she wants the hotel, so that she can leave home?' June said, quietly.

'Don't be ridiculous! She lives in a fucking mansion surrounded by horses and servants, June! Why would she want to leave that?' Liz leaned closer to the mirror and touched her fingers to her face. She looked disappointed in herself suddenly as she turned away from the mirror again and came back out to the room. She pulled her bag out from under the bed and brought it with her, back to the bathroom.

June didn't respond. She'd overheard Mrs Kelly on the phone to her solicitor. Plus, she'd gleaned enough of the woman's secrets over the years to know that her home life was not one of opulence and bliss. She had reasons far bigger than Liz Sheehy for wanting out of there, but June kept those reasons to herself. They were no one else's business really. She glanced again at the three empty wine bottles, two of which were shattered to a million pieces and *all* of which were supposed to be reserved for Mrs Kelly.

Liz was unravelling. She was storming through cotton wool pads trying to clean yesterday's make-up off her face. Today's was all lined up and ready to be applied, but it wouldn't mask her fury. Or the irrational thoughts written all over her face. Erica Kelly did want to buy the Manor. That much was true. But she didn't need Malcolm to do that. He was merely a plaything for her and contrary to Liz's belief, Mrs Kelly wasn't thinking about *her* at all. She just had her eye on the prize. But Malcolm. He knew exactly what he was doing. *He* was the one betraying Liz and it was at *him* that Liz should direct her fury. But she wouldn't. She'd save it all up for the other woman. A woman who she stood no chance of winning against.

Eventually Liz came out, looking impressively fresh, considering how she was thirty minutes earlier. 'Can I have that other coffee?' she asked.

June went and got it for her. 'Are you feeling okay?' she asked gently.

Liz nodded. 'I'm sorry about the mess, June.'

'Don't worry about it. It's why I'm here, after all.'

Liz paused before taking a sip. 'You know, I think you might love this place as much as I do.'

June frowned at the sudden turnaround. The bitterness that flew like daggers off her tongue just moments ago seemed to have vanished. Rubbed away by a cotton wool pad perhaps.

'I'm... not sure if *love* is the word I'd use.' She forced a half smile to go with her response. June had a much more complicated relationship with the Manor than that. 'But I suppose I'm exactly where I should be when I'm here.'

'Me too.' Liz stood in front of the long mirror then. 'And whatever *friends* Erica Kelly thinks she has in Malcolm's family...' She was speaking to her reflection now and her sentence trailed off.

'I'm sure this will all turn out to be nothing more than one of Mrs Kelly's whims.'

'You sound awfully sure of that, June.'

June shrugged and shook her head. 'Well, this place wouldn't be *quite* this place without you in it, Liz. I'm sure about that much and I'd imagine Mrs Kelly knows that, too.'

'Yes, well – I just need to remind Malcolm that I'm the one who keeps him in the good graces of his grandparents. And I can change that any time I like.' She smiled to herself then turned and walked to the wardrobe. She slid open the door and hanging inside was a fresh suit shrouded in plastic. She ran a hand over it, took it down from its rail and then headed for the bathroom again. 'I'm not going anywhere, June. I can promise you that. You can leave this room until last and then give it a full turnover.' She pulled the plastic off her suit. 'That'll be all, June.'

June nodded and picked up her bucket. She let herself out, closing the door behind her.

EIGHTEEN

JUNE

The next time June saw Liz was closer to lunch time. She was smiling and chatting with some guests in the restaurant, looking just like she always did. The Lady of the Manor. All traces of her destructive behaviour from the night before were gone. Having worked through the bedrooms early, including the 208 shambles, June carried on past the restaurant and went to tend to the lobby table. Her favourite child.

'June?' Lauren called. She was lowering the phone back into its cradle. 'Can you please go to the bar? And bring a dustpan. There's some broken glass on the floor.'

'Sure. On my way.' June nodded. More broken glass on a floor that didn't deserve it. She swapped out the items in her bucket and brought the tall dustpan and brush set to the Cedarwood Lounge.

She stopped short just as she went inside. Malcolm Levy was sitting at the bar drinking coffee. Malcolm was rarely seen around the hotel during the day. But this was something he used to do in the early days of his relationship with Liz. He used to perch at the bar throughout her shift. Not to keep her company while she worked or anything, but to let her know that he was always there. Always watching. June's stomach tightened as that heaviness came to rest upon her again. The atmosphere in a room always felt like a physical thing to June. Or maybe it was a person's aura or something. Whatever it was, she always got a keen sense of it as soon as she came within range.

Malcolm turned and offered a lazy grin. 'Scrub that up, will you, maid?' he said, pointing to a shattered crystal water glass beside his high stool.

'No problem, Mr Levy.'

He was trying to embarrass her. He always did and he always failed. If June allowed herself to be embarrassed, then she'd feel that way constantly. But always oblivious to his failures, Malcolm continued to try.

'I'm surprised to see you here on your day off, Mr Levy,' she said, as she got going with her dustpan and brush.

'Someone has to keep an eye on my family jewel, don't they?'

June nodded in agreement, while she swept up the glass. 'I'm sure Miss Sheehy appreciates a second pair of eyes.'

Malcolm's eyes narrowed while he tried to work out if she was brave or stupid. June might have been able to sense danger, but she also drew it on her sometimes. A side effect of having nothing much worth losing.

'I don't know how she does it, to be honest,' she continued, resting the full dustpan against the bar while she retrieved her spray bottle and cloth. 'Superwoman,' she said more quietly, with a deliberate hint of awe in her tone.

Malcolm's foot shot out and kicked the dustpan, sending fragments of glass in all directions. June stopped what she was doing and stood up tall. She looked around as if wondering where the sudden mess had come from.

'I think I'd better get the hoover out for this, after all.' She picked up the dustpan and her bucket and turned to leave. 'Don't worry. I won't disturb you with the noise for long, Mr

Levy.' She smiled, wondering if it would push him over the edge. The look on his face told her that it just might.

But June's smile vanished as she left the Cedarwood Lounge and walked briskly through the lobby. Why couldn't she keep her mouth shut? *He* was the only one who ever really threatened her. If he was sending those notes, then he *would* follow through on them. And what if he got his hands on this place? He'd fire her from here as quickly as Erica Kelly would fire Liz. She was losing the Manor. She was losing Tess. She was losing everything. When she got to her trolley, she reached into the bottom shelf and removed the little black velvet pouch she always kept there. She brought it, along with the dustpan and her cleaning bucket, to the guests' bathroom. All she had to do was keep her mouth shut. But it seemed she'd lost that lifelong skill, right when she needed it the most.

'Hello? Anyone here?' she called when she went inside. 'Housekeeping.'

There was no answer.

She walked along the length of the stunning bathroom, with its imported tile floor and antique sink units. The relaxing scent of ylang-ylang in the air did nothing for June just then. She still felt the overwhelming need to inflict some damage upon herself. She hunched so she could see under the hand-crafted cubicle doors. No feet. She was alone.

She returned to the sink area and lifted a large shard of glass from her dustpan. She squeezed some soap into her hands and made a lather, which she used to wash the glass, taking care not to cut herself. Not on the hand, at least. She rinsed the glass thoroughly and took it with her into the furthest cubicle from the door. She dropped the lid on the toilet seat, lowered her trousers and sat down. She opened the drawstring pouch and rested it on her bare lap. Then, bringing the glass shard to an old scar, she opened it quickly and without mercy. She bared her teeth and squeezed her eyes shut. She directed a silent scream up to the heavens while her hands worked on autopilot. They retrieved gauze from her pouch and stemmed the flow of blood before it reached her clothes or the tiled floor. One hand controlled the bleed, while the other sprayed wound adhesive. June doubled over on herself. She cried fiercely but silently as the elation of her pain both filled her up and hollowed her out, at the same time.

The adhesive worked fast. June continued to clean the blood off her skin while she gathered herself back together again. It took a few minutes to get her breathing under control. And the tears. Her self-loathing was at an all-time high, as it always was right after. She was weak. Too weak to fight the urge to do this. She was no better than any other addict when they heard the call of their chosen substance. Or rather, the substance that had chosen them. Some did it so that they could stop feeling. Others, like June, did it so they could start.

But the effects never lasted long enough, in either case. This morning alone she should have been assailed with worry, embarrassment, fear, caution, among so many other emotions. But only with the help of a sharp object could she feel any of those things. Then all together at the same time, the wave came in. And just as quickly, it flowed back out again.

NINETEEN

MIA

Mammy had just arrived home from the Cedarwood Manor and as soon as she walked through the door, Mia could tell she was in a very bad mood. For one thing, she nearly took the front door off its hinges when she slammed it. She dropped her bags with a loud thud in the hall, but then there was silence for a while. Mia didn't dare look out the kitchen door, but she could tell that, for some reason, Mammy was just standing out there, not moving. Could she see evidence of the mess that Mia and Daddy had made in the living room? Mia was intensely worried all of a sudden and found herself frozen to the spot in the kitchen. When Mammy finally did come through the kitchen door, Mia jumped with fright.

'Hi, Mammy,' she almost shouted, trying to busy herself.

Mammy's lip curled. 'Coffee.'

Mia nodded quickly and got to work. While she prepared the coffee, her gut warned her against asking dumb questions now. But those instincts, as strong and as trustworthy as they'd always been, were drowned out by the noise inside Mia's head. So many questions were hurtling around in there that she worried her brain might explode if she didn't let them out.

Questions about Daddy. About boyfriends and girlfriends, about... everything. She had *so* many questions that desperately needed answers.

'Mammy, can I ask you something?' The words tumbled out as she poured the coffee.

'Ah. Questions. My favourite.'

Mia still had her back to Mammy while she put milk and sugar in the drink, but the tone of her answer set her instincts off again. They screamed at her now to stop talking.

Mammy sat down and waited in silence for her coffee. Mia placed it carefully in front of her, but then Mammy looked into the cup and made a face like it was filled with horse dung. She did that sometimes when she came home from the Cedarwood Manor. It made Mia wonder how much better everything must be there.

'Can I ask you something?' she persisted, but her voice caught in her throat this time.

Mammy sighed. 'I thought you'd want to know someday. Sit down.'

Mia frowned, confused. Mammy was smiling. She was pointing to the chair beside her and suddenly Mia knew with complete certainty that this was a trap. A voice in her head screamed, *Don't sit down! Do NOT ask her!*

'You want to know about your mother, don't you?' Mammy continued, shoving the chair out for Mia to sit in. 'Your so-called *real* mother, I mean.'

Mia shook her head vigorously and felt like she might wet herself. She *did* ask about her real mother once and she'd sorely regretted it to this day.

'It's okay. It's natural you'd want to know.' Her unnerving smile was still there.

'I already know.' Mia's voice shook.

'Remind me, which bit do you know?'

The questions that felt so important earlier were gone now.

She closed her eyes and tried to put back into words the things they'd said about her real mother. Things she'd shoved as deep down inside her as they'd go.

'Eh, well... she didn't have any money. So she couldn't look after me.'

Mammy sniggered. 'Oh, Christ. Penniless women have children every day, Mia. What else do you know?'

'Well... Daddy said she had to move to America to get a job. He said she got married and had a real family over there and forgot all about me.'

Mammy nodded and made a sympathetic sound. But Mia knew it wasn't real sympathy. Just like her smile wasn't a real smile.

'Well, I suppose you were young when he told you that and it was an easy answer for him to give.' She took a sip of her coffee. 'You're older now, aren't you? Old enough to hear the truth, I mean?'

Mia nodded hesitantly.

'Mia, your mother was our housekeeper. She worked for me.'

Mia's forehead crumpled and her stomach closed in on itself. The noisy questions were back. Different ones now, pinging and bouncing around inside her head. But it didn't matter. Mia wasn't stupid enough to ask any of them.

'She was a very simple woman,' Mammy continued, examining her nails. 'And by that, I mean she was dumb, Mia. I'm sorry to have to tell you that. But the woman could hardly string a sentence together. She might have looked like a woman, but she had the intellect of a child.'

'So, why did she have to go to America if she already had a job here?' She tried to stop herself, but the question slid out.

Mammy gave a small laugh as she reached out and took Mia's hand. Mia frowned again. She was deeply confused. She knew her real mammy was dumb. She'd been told that many times. But she was *here*?

'I worry sometimes that you inherited your mother's... brains, Mia.'

Mia lowered her eyes. Her stomach was twisting painfully now, but she dared not move.

'I took the best care of your mother. I gave her a job when no one else would have considered it. I paid her fairly and fed her three meals a day, every day that she worked. I had the basement converted into a bedroom for her. I treated her like family, Mia.'

Mia's hand was shaking now. She could hear the words. She understood the words. And yet, they made no sense. Mammy clutched her hand a little tighter.

'But you see, Mia, your mother betrayed me.'

'Oh... okay.' She tried to pull her hand back and stand up. She desperately wanted to go back to work. To go anywhere, other than where she was. But Mammy wouldn't let her.

Mammy let go of her hand finally and sat back. Her fake smile vanished 'I came home one evening to find your mother on my good couch with my stupid husband, and boy, they were having a right old time in there. Do you understand what I'm telling you?'

Mia sat up straighter in her chair and felt a wave of panic come over her. It started at her ankles and worked its way up, warming her whole body as it went. She nodded yes. Then shook her head no. With *Daddy*?

'Never sign a prenup, Mia.' She mumbled, bringing her cup to her lips. But a laugh burst out of her before she could take a drink. 'Actually, I don't think you'll ever have to worry about that.'

'So, where did she go?' The question fought its way out.

'I sent your mother back to the hole she crawled out of with enough money to do the decent thing. But clearly, she went ahead and had you anyway.'

Mia's eyes flitted this way and that, while her brain tried to make sense of anything. 'But... how?' she tried again.

'Ah. Now, that's a whole other story. And I'm hungry.'

Mia didn't hear her. She just sat there, staring blankly back at her. Waiting.

'Didn't you hear me?'

She still didn't move.

'I said, I'm hungry.' Mammy slapped the table, and then, finally, Mia jumped up and stumbled towards the fridge.

TWENTY

MIA

Mia's hands worked of their own accord, preparing Mammy's 'go-to' meal. The same one she always made when Mammy was hungry, but not willing to wait: buttery scrambled eggs with fresh chives and white pepper. Never black. Served on three slices of sourdough bread. But her brain had shut down and her body was threatening to do the same. Her stomach was churning, her hands were shaking and her whole head pricked with pins and needles.

Her real mother was here. Probably standing in the exact spot where Mia was standing now. Her hands stopped what they were doing, and she looked down at the floor. She was right here. Did she touch this pan? Her eyes went to where her hand rested on its handle. Had she ever used the black pepper by mistake, like Mia once had?

She could feel Mammy's eyes on her back, so she got to work again. The tension in the room seemed to hum and everything felt wrong. She wanted to ask a hundred different things, mostly about her real mother. But what about all the other questions that were lined up in her head since before Mammy came home? She had wanted to know if she could go with her to the

Cedarwood Manor next time. She wanted to know about boyfriends and girlfriends and the weird way Daddy had acted last night. She stopped what she was doing again, as a thought occurred to her. Is that what he was trying to say? That he and Mia's real mother were boyfriend and girlfriend? Was he her *real* father?

Did he *kill* Mia's mother?!

'What's wrong with you, girl?' Mammy snapped.

Mia was frozen to the spot, but Mammy's voice spurred her into action again. Her belly told her that she'd get in serious trouble if she asked about any of this, so she decided to keep her mouth shut. But all the questions swimming around inside her head were getting jumbled up. They became so tangled that all she could think to say was: 'Did you have a nice break away?'

'I did, Mia.'

Mammy had that false happy tone in her voice, the way she sometimes sounded when she knew Mia had done something wrong. An explosion was coming, she was sure of it.

She put the plate on the table in front of Mammy and moved hesitantly away. She desperately wanted to hear more. But she knew better than to ask.

'You look like you have ants in your pants, Mia.'

'Sorry.'

Erica gave her a bemused smile while she ate, which only added to Mia's confusion. Then, with her mouth full, she used her fork to point at the opposite chair, where Mia had sat earlier. She settled back into it quickly. She dared not breathe in case Mammy changed her mind.

'You want to know how *I* came to rescue you from that stupid woman. Is that it?'

Mia couldn't respond.

'It's simple really, Mia. I didn't see why we should be pumping money into that woman's hand for the rest of our lives, when *she* was the one who betrayed *me*. What did *I* get out of that arrangement, hmm? What was in that for *me*? I mean, I was hardly going to hire another housekeeper for my husband to cast his greasy eyes on, was I?'

Mia shook her head, no. She didn't know what else to do.

'So, I went to see her, and ugh, you should have seen where she lived. You were small then. Probably *too* small to be out playing with a bunch of teenagers on bikes. One of them had you on their crossbar, flying around that filthy estate. Honestly, I would never have hired her if I'd seen where she lived.' Her mouth turned down in disgust. 'I don't know how you weren't killed. I shudder to think what would have happened if I left you there to be raised by that idiot.'

Mia froze. This story felt familiar somehow and she found herself thinking about the dream she had from time to time. In her dream, she was the one cycling the bike. Or someone else was, with her on the crossbar. But she wasn't a baby in the dream. Or at least, she didn't think she was. But she'd never thought about it. All she knew was what it felt like. The fear. The exhilaration. The wind in her hair. The freedom.

Was that real? Did that really happen, just like Mammy was saying?

'Did you talk to her?' The question just popped out.

'Of course I talked to her."

Her mouth turned down again. 'She didn't care about you, Mia.' Erica pointed to the coffee maker again and Mia stood up on shaky legs to make another cup.

'I told her I was done sending her money.' She paused then. A long pause and Mia held her breath throughout. 'Do you want to know what she said?'

She didn't. As desperate as she was to find out the rest of this story, she worried that it would be more painful than anything else. But Mammy didn't wait for an answer.

'She said that if I didn't keep giving her money, she'd throw you in the river. She had no use for you, she said.' She exhaled loudly. 'The only reason she kept you in the first place was for the money, Mia. But she didn't take any kind of care of you at all. She just spent it all on herself.'

'Okay,' was all Mia could think to say, as her knees began to buckle. Her mother was going to throw her in the river.

'Really? Is that all you have to say?'

'Sorry,' she whispered, desperately needing the toilet all of a sudden. Everything inside her was looking for a way out.

'She said she hated you. Did you know that? What a terrible thing for a mother to say.' Another pause, but shorter this time. 'It's like she just wanted to get it all off her chest while I was on her doorstep or something. She said all kinds of terrible things, like she couldn't stand to look at you and how you ruined her life. She just went on and on. So, you know what I did, Mia?'

Every ounce of Mia's energy was absorbed into clenching everything shut. Her suspicions had been confirmed. She was a bad stain on the world. One that no one liked to look at, but that no one could remove. Some people were meant to be born and some people weren't and Mia Kelly, or whatever her name was, was *not*. A cramp shot through her guts, and she desperately wanted to let it all out. And then to flush herself away with it.

'I need the toilet.' The words barely came out and Mammy didn't hear them.

'I offered to take you home.' She threw her hands up. 'And she said *fine*, and closed the door in my face. She didn't even kiss you goodbye. Not so much as a wave.'

Tears ran off the end of Mia's nose like a small stream and splashed onto the floor. She couldn't hold it. 'I need to go.'

'She just gave you away.' She shoved her plate away and stood up then. 'I'll have that piece of lamb for dinner. You'll want to get it in the oven now.'

She walked out the door as if she hadn't just shattered someone's world, while Mia lost control of her body, all over the kitchen floor.

TWENTY-ONE

JUNE

'June, I need to talk to you about something.' Tess was standing right inside the front door when June arrived home. She looked like she'd been there for some time.

Tess still wasn't right, and neither was June. Clearly both of their minds had been restless that day.

'Have you been standing there all day, Tess?'

'No. But you are ten minutes later than you usually are.'

June looked at her watch. Tess was right. She was late. She'd cut a little too deeply in her haste that day and the wound kept opening. She had to pause her work to clean herself up twice more during her shift. It had been years since she'd cut at work. She had more self-control than that, usually. But today she did it because she *had to*. The compulsion to rip into her flesh was so strong in that moment, right after leaving Malcolm Levy in the bar, that she couldn't ignore it. It's what she imagined a heroin addict felt like when they needed a fix. She couldn't have stopped herself no matter how much she wanted to. But Tess didn't need to know any of that.

June took off her jacket and hung it on the back of the door. Their evening would not go well. June knew that. But she needed to gather herself, so she went with Tess over to the kitchen. Even now, with all this turmoil between them, they fell naturally into their daily routine. Today was fish fingers and spaghetti hoops day. Tess insisted they have fish fingers once a week, even though she knew that June didn't like fish. She said they needed their omega three. What she didn't know was that June had been buying chicken fingers for some time. She'd kept an old fish finger box and simply swapped them out. Either Tess never tasted the difference, or she never said it if she did.

June glanced at Tess and at her arthritic fingers, which were fighting with the ring pull, and June stopped herself from taking it from her. She didn't feel much like helping Tess tonight.

Before long, June was scooping two chicken fingers onto each plate, and after sixty seconds in the microwave, Tess followed with spaghetti hoops. June carried the plates to the table while Tess filled two glasses of water from the tap.

'So?'

They sat down opposite each other, and Tess scooped a few hoops onto her fork. 'Hmm?'

'Why were you standing inside the door, waiting for me to come home?' June looked pointedly at her. 'Is there something you want to tell me?'

'Oh, that.' She put down her fork again and sighed heavily. 'We both missed out on an awful lot in life, didn't we, June?' she said, much more quietly now. 'Both of our childhoods were snatched away.'

'Were they, though?'

'You know, I thought that place was like a hospital or something. Somewhere where the sisters minded girls until their babies were born.' She laughed then and it sounded genuine. 'Can you believe what they called themselves? Mercy and Good Shepherd and all kinds of lovely notions attached to the evil, conniving little...' She closed her eyes and took a deep breath, then exhaled with a smile. 'Listen to me. Going on as if I'm a saint myself.'

'Is this the real-life version of the story that you're about to tell me, Tess? Because that's the only one I want to hear tonight.' June's voice was lower now and dripped with menace. She was done with the lies. One more and there would be no going back for them.

Tess nodded, resignedly. 'I suppose we can't leave all the secrets buried forever. Can we?'

'I wasn't aware you and I had any secrets. Not from each other at least.'

Tess pushed her plate away, having barely touched her food.

'I lied to you, June.'

June nodded. The truth at last.

'I told you that I was dropped off at the home by my father after getting pregnant. And that the nuns beat me and berated me for the full seven months. I told you how my child was coming out sideways and that they gave me nothing for the pain. Remember?'

'I remember.'

'Then my baby finally made it out into the world and that evil bitch in the black habit took her from me and carried her out the door. You remember that?'

Colour was draining from Tess's face now and she looked unwell.

'That was me, June.'

'Which one?'

Tess shook her head and twisted her hands in her lap. 'Not the bleeding girl who'd given birth to a sideways baby.'

June, unaware that she'd been rocking in her seat, stopped suddenly.

'The evil bitch who carried the child away. The evil bitch who beat and kicked and berated that girl, and so many others just like her. Day in and day out. *I* was that evil bitch, June. Me.'

'The grinning nun in the back of that photograph. *Sister Tess*.'

She shook her head. 'Tess died that day. About twenty minutes after I took her baby away from her, she bled out on the floor, all alone. She endured me for the last seven months of her life and I've been begging for forgiveness ever since.'

June scraped her chair back from the table and hurried from the room.

She ignored Tess, or whoever she was, calling after her as she ran into her bedroom and slammed the door.

'No, no, no, no, no!' she cried, dropping to her knees. Her whole life had been a lie. She fumbled around in her drawer, looking for her washbag. She found it and tipped its contents out onto the mat. Her fingers pulled clumsily at the tissue protecting her blade. As soon as she had a grip on it, she drew it sharply across her wrist and immediately followed with the other one.

June Calloway inhaled a deep, sharp breath and waited for the darkness to come.

TWENTY-TWO

JUNE

The harsh overhead lights burned June's eyes when she finally opened them. She groaned and squeezed them shut again, turning her head away. But there was no escape. She was lying on her back and when she tried to move, she found that it required far more effort than usual. She felt like death and her head was filled with a thick, heavy fog. She peeled one eye open and then the other. When they found their focus, she was looking at a blue armchair. The kind with wooden armrests and wipeable upholstery. Without moving her head again, she glanced down at her hands. Both her wrists were tightly bandaged and there was a cannula sticking out of the back of one hand. It was held in place by a plaster and some tape. There was also a clamp on her index finger, which was attached to a monitor above her.

June's breathing quickened and a sort of panic took over. Her legs flailed as she tried to sit up, while at the same time, reaching across to pull out the cannula. She grimaced at the sting of it. Next, she yanked the clamp off her finger, which set off an alarm on the monitor. This alerted staff to the fact that she'd come back from wherever it was that she'd been. The curtain surrounding her narrow trolley was quickly pulled back.

'There you are.' A nurse stepped in. She smiled at June, while simultaneously checking the monitor and clocking the missing cannula and finger clamp. She was an older nurse. The no-nonsense sort. Or at least that would have been Tess's deduction.

Tess.

'Where am I? Where's Tess?' Her voice sounded like an echo in a deep cave. Her thoughts were lost somewhere in there, too.

'We've been waiting for you to wake up, so you can tell us who we can call for you.' She was still smiling, but her full attention was on June. June didn't like it. 'Who's Tess, love? Is she your friend? I'm Niamh, by the way.'

June tried to sit up again, but Niamh pushed her gently back.

'I want to go home.'

'Okay. That's no problem, June. But look, they're some nasty injuries you have there. I'm just going to get the doctor to have a quick look at you, yeah? Then we'll see about getting you on your way.'

We'll see about getting you on your way. This sounded to June like she didn't have a choice in whether or not she stayed. Her chest tightened and she pressed her knuckles against it. But it didn't help. She couldn't breathe.

'Listen to me, love, you're alright,' Nurse Niamh said reassuringly, putting one hand on June's shoulder, while the other slipped the clamp back on her finger. She glanced up at the monitor and then brought her attention back to June.

'Okay, I need you to breathe for me, June. Just breathe.' She placed her two hands on June's shoulders now and put her face right in front of June's, so that she had no choice but to look at her. Then the nurse put one hand on her own chest and the other covered June's hand, on hers. 'Breathe with me now. In.' She took a visibly deep breath in. 'And out.' She blew out a long breath.

June tried to do the same, but she couldn't get any air to go in.

'That's good, June. Now again, in.' She breathed in and June almost envied her the ability to do so. 'And out. Good. Now keep going.' She used a finger to tilt June's head so she was looking up at her. She smiled and continued with the exaggerated breathing. In and out. In and out. 'With me, June. That's it. Good girl, you've got it.'

It was working. Her own breathing was slowing down, but there were little black dots floating in front of her eyes.

'You're okay, June.'

June's eyes darted all around her, but they wouldn't focus on anything. Only the black dots that moved with her. Everywhere she looked they were there. 'Where am I?' she cried out. 'Where am I?'

'You're in the Cork University Hospital, love. You're alright. Do you hear me? You're alright. You're safe.'

She looked again at her bandaged wrists. Black dots swam all over the otherwise bright, white fabric. She'd cut them. She'd cut her wrists. Tess.

'I need to go. I should be at work!'

'And you can, June. But just wait for the doctor to see you. She's on the way now, yeah?' Niamh sat down on the narrow edge of June's trolley and leaned back to look around the curtain. 'Ah! Here she is now.'

'June? I'm Dr Linda Egan. Good to see you awake.' She picked the chart off the end of June's bed. Niamh stood up and with her back to June, she spoke quietly to the doctor. The doctor listened carefully and then nodded.

'Right, June. I'm going to leave you in Dr Linda's capable hands. But I'll see you again in a little while, okay? I'll be just over there.' She pointed towards the nurses' station, which was inside the ward. There were five other beds in there, each separated by a blue pleated curtain.

'How are you feeling, June?' the doctor asked, taking a seat alongside June's bed.

'Fine.'

She nodded, with her head down. She was studying June's chart and June worried about what it might say.

'Can you tell me what happened?'

June shook her head.

Dr Linda lowered the chart onto her lap and crossed her hands on top of it. She made eye contact with June for the first time. June didn't like it. She didn't like anything about this.

'The paramedics found you in a residence on Wellington Road,' Dr Linda said in a low, semi-sympathetic voice. 'The front door was open, and you had a note pinned to your chest. But there was no one else in that flat, or in the flat upstairs. Do you remember any of that?'

'What did the note say?' She felt a glimmer of hope.

'It said, *My name is June. I didn't mean to do this.*' She looked up at June again. 'Is that true?'

June shrugged.

'Because deep, clean cuts to both wrists would be considered a very unlikely accident.'

June shrugged again. 'It was an accident.'

'You don't seem so sure.'

'I am sure.'

'June... is that your name?'

'Yes.' June was measuring her words, letting as few as possible slip out.

'What's your surname, June?'

'Calloway.'

She wrote it down, making June feel a deep sense of unease. Why was she writing it down? What did this woman want from her? Her breathing quickened again, and she gripped the blanket under her.

Dr Linda looked pointedly at her, then up at the monitor. She leaned forward a little. 'Okay, June. Try to relax. Deep breaths.'

She couldn't. The doctor stood up and put the clipboard down on June's legs. She reached up to examine the clear bag that was hanging over her bed. Whatever had been dripping into June, through the cannula in her hand, was gone. The bag was empty. Whatever it was, was already coursing through June's body, but she didn't care. She needed to get out of there and she was going the wrong way about it.

Calm down, she told herself. *You're drawing too much attention. You're going to ruin everything.* She closed her eyes and focused on her breathing.

'Do you know who pinned that note to your chest, June?' Dr Linda again. 'Did you write it?'

With her eyes still closed, she imagined the woman's pen was hovering over the page again. She shook her head.

'Who lives there with you?'

'No one. I live by myself.'

Dr Linda nodded and made another note. June could hear the pen scratching at the paper.

'You told the nurse that you needed to get to work. Where do you work?'

June opened her eyes and continued with her slow, deep breaths. 'At home. I meant I must get home.'

'So you don't work?'

June shook her head. 'I do. I'm a cleaner. I take cleaning jobs wherever I can get them.'

'Okay. And you live alone?'

'Why are you asking me all these questions?'

'I'm not trying to be nosy, June. I'm not trying to trip you up either. There are no right or wrong answers here. But as you can imagine, given your injuries, the old ones as well as the new, we're quite worried about you. We'd like to make sure you'll be safe if we were to let you go home now.'

'*If* you'll let me go home?'

'Is there someone I can call? Anyone at all?'

June shook her head. 'I'm pretty sure you can't keep me here against my will.'

'That's not what we want to do at all. But I would like to know more about what led you here.'

'I'm tired. Can I rest please?'

'Sure. I can come back later. But, June, I want you to know that this is a safe space. If there's something going on in your life that you need help with, that help is available. Can you think about that?'

June nodded and turned on her side, facing away from Dr Linda. She squeezed her eyes shut to try and prevent the tears from rolling down her cheeks. She needed to get out of here. There were already too many questions, which would only lead to more questions. The kind that led to suits and uniforms knocking on their door. But she couldn't make a scene by demanding to leave. To do so... Even the very fact that she was here at all could open a can of worms that would bring her whole life, what was left of it, crashing down around her.

TWENTY-THREE

TESS

Tess stood in her flat facing the locked door. Her hands fidgeted with her clothes while she stared at it, hoping that whoever was knocking might go away. The trouble was, she'd had the wireless on when they started. It was always up loud because her hearing wasn't what it used to be. But then she made the mistake of turning it off, so whoever was out there, knew she was home. They knocked again. The third time, so they weren't going away. She took a breath, smoothed down her hair and her clothes and opened the door.

'Oh, hello.' She smiled the most endearing old-woman-smile she could muster.

'Hello.' The woman smiled back.

Someone had let her in through the main door. Or maybe the lock was broken again. Either way, here she was. She was a well-rounded woman with a long floaty green skirt. She wore low-heeled boots, a black overcoat and a purple floral scarf. The scarf was pretty, but really, there was no dressing her up. Her hair was a shambles and she seemed old before her time. But the battered leather bag hanging off her shoulder, bulging with files, told Tess to keep her guard up.

'Hi there! My name is Elsie Jennings.' She held out her hand and Tess shook it hesitantly. With her other hand she offered Tess a card. Tess didn't have her glasses on, but she recognised the HSE logo on top.

'Oh, you're a doctor?' Tess smiled. 'Well done, you!'

'Oh gosh, no.' The woman chuckled. 'I'm a social worker.'

'Oh. Well, that's lovely, too.'

'Most days, not so much, I'm afraid.' She smiled half-heartedly. 'Do you live here, Mrs, eh...'

Now it was Tess's turn to chuckle. 'Oh dear, I'm not Mrs anything. Just call me Teresa.'

'Okay, Teresa. Is this your flat?'

'Oh, well, I don't own it or anything. But I do live here. So yes, I suppose it is.'

'And do you live here alone?'

Tess made a show of looking concerned now. 'I'm sorry, but did the Gardaí send you here?'

'Why would you think the Gardaí sent me?'

'On account of what happened yesterday?'

'Oh. Can you tell me what happened?'

She dithered for a few seconds, which she could tell was endearing her to the woman. This *Elsie* character.

'Well, I went out to do a bit of shopping. Nothing much now, mind you. I just needed a half pound of sausages for my tea. So I popped up to the Centra at the top of the hill. They have the nice ones. You know, the Clonakilty ones? Anyway, I'm not as quick on that hill as I used to be, so I was probably gone a while.' She smiled again. Then she wagged her finger as if she'd just thought of something else. 'And actually, I went to the post office as well. I had to get a stamp because, you see, a friend of mine sent me a mass bouquet last week. I hadn't been feeling well. A touch of the flu is all it was, but I was miserable all the same. You know yourself the way you'd be, Elsie.

Anyway, they sent the mass bouquet, just to let me know they were thinking about me. Wasn't that nice?' She paused for another little smile. 'So, I needed to get a stamp so I could send a thank-you card. I only just made it before the post office closed for the day! Then I was on my way home when I met Martin. He's the man who makes deliveries to the Centra. I don't know why, but he always wants to stop for a chat. We talked about the weather and about the price of bread nowadays. You know. All that kind of thing.'

She could see the woman was fading. She didn't look like someone who suffered fools. But what kind of social worker would she be if she cut off the flow of a dithering old woman who perhaps was lonely?

'And did something happen, Teresa?' she gently pressed.

'Oh.' Tess giggled. 'Yes, I'm sorry. I always get sidetracked and give too much information. Isn't that what they say?'

The woman forced an understanding smile.

'So, yes. I came home to find the front door open.' Tess pointed over the woman's shoulder at the main entrance. 'And the door to my flat was also open. Now as far as I could see, nothing had been taken or anything like that. But the lady who lives upstairs wanted to call the Gardaí. She was out as well, you see. Actually, she's always out. Anyway, I said I didn't think there was a need because, honestly, I could have gone out and left it that way myself. It wouldn't be the first time. And as I said, there was nothing taken.' Then she put a finger to her chin. Thinking. 'But there was some blood on the floor. I'm sure that wasn't mine.' She looked at her hands, like maybe she'd forgotten that she cut herself.

'Teresa, do you know someone by the name of June?'

'June?' Again, she brought her finger to her chin and looked off to the side, brows furrowed. 'I know a Jill? She works in the post office, I think.'

'But no June?'

'Not that I can think of.'

'Teresa, someone called an ambulance to this flat yesterday. When they got here, they found a woman with severe injuries inside. She had a note pinned to her. Do you know anything about that?'

Tess produced a shocked expression. The best one she had. 'Oh my, no!' Then she shook her head sadly. 'But you know, I've seen some young people around here who seem to have problems with,' she whispered, 'drugs.' She shook her head. 'It's terribly sad really. Sometimes they just can't see a way out.'

'So you don't know anything about this woman? Who she might be or why she was in your flat?'

She shook her head. 'Gosh, no. Like I said, I went out to the shop and the post office and to chat to Martin about the weather and whatnot. And when I came home, the place was open. I didn't think there was any reason to call anyone. I had no idea there'd been so much of a fuss around my little flat.'

'Okay,' the woman said.

'Maybe I left the place open, and that poor girl just saw somewhere warm and quiet where she could end it all. Did she die?' she asked, trying to sound as nonchalant as she could. But her heart was racing in her chest.

'No. She didn't die.'

'Oh, that's good. So how come you're here so quickly then? All this only happened yesterday, wasn't it?'

The woman smiled an exasperated smile. 'Honestly, Teresa, I don't know. I was meeting with another client near here, when I got a call from a friend of mine over at CUH. She's a nurse there and she's a bit worried about this June lady. I said that as I was passing the door, I'd call in.' She hiked her bag up onto her shoulder then and turned to go. 'I came, I saw, I conquered,' she joked. 'And none of us are any wiser, as usual. You take care, Teresa. And be sure to lock those doors.'

'I will. It was lovely to meet you, Elsie.'

Elsie waved over her shoulder and ambled out the door. Tess shoved her own door closed and breathed as her well-practiced smile fell away.

TWENTY-FOUR

JUNE

Millie was the name of the student nurse who came and introduced herself to June earlier in the evening. Considering they'd just met, June felt like she knew everything there was to know about the girl. In the first few minutes alone, she told June that she was about to turn twenty-one and planned to go to Australia as soon as she finished her training. She was on a psych placement right now, but really, she wanted to work in paediatrics because she just *loooooved* kids. Also, she was exhausted. She said that four times in twenty minutes.

June pretended to sleep for most of the day, so that she could avoid speaking to anyone. It also gave her time to think. She *should* be at work now. In the six years she'd been at the Manor, she hadn't so much as missed one day. Where did Liz think she was? What was happening there in her absence? All of her energy should be put into getting back there and she resented Tess even more for getting in the way of that. Why would she have lied to her all these years? Why would she make up that story about Seán Buckley and the baby? She told it in so much detail and the story never changed. She thought back to the night they met, completely by accident. June was in crises, as she so often was back then. Tess helped her. She got her a job. Her first and only job, at the Cedarwood Manor Hotel. But why?

The answer surely lay with Tess and her baby. June had heard so much about them, it was as if she knew them. Whoever they were, they had to mean something to... June realised that she didn't even know her name. This woman who was the closest thing to family she had. The real Tess, whoever she was, was dead. That only left the nun and the baby. June's eyes shot open. Sister Whatever-her-name-was just happened to be there at the exact moment when June needed her most. And she'd acted like a mother to her ever since. June started to shake. Was *she* the sideways baby? The one ripped from her mother and...

Her fists clutched the sheet under her as the low beeping quickened overhead. She squeezed her eyes shut and begged Nurse Niamh to appear, but only in her mind. *Breathe in. Breathe out.* A chair squeaked on the other side of her half-drawn curtain, indicating that the nurse had heard the quickening pace, too. *Breathe in. Breathe out.* June forced her face and shoulders to relax, but her mind raced on. She heard the curtain move slightly on its rail. She kept her eyes shut. *Breathe in. Breathe out.* She could sense the nurse standing over her before she felt her fingers brushing against her skin when she adjusted the finger clamp. *Breathe in. Breathe out.* She sensed her watching for a moment as the beeping slowed to a more normal rhythm. Then finally, she moved away again.

June opened her eyes. That didn't make sense. June *knew* who her mother was, so it couldn't have been her. But that baby was *someone*. She was sure of that now. What did any of it have to do with June, however?

Most of the patients were asleep by then and at least one was still pretending to be. But she would not stay in that hospital bed another minute. She needed to go home. She needed to find Tess and make her tell the truth. No quirky side stories. No humorous cover-ups. June needed to know who she'd shared more than a decade of her life with.

She reached down beside her bed to where the green plastic bag was. It contained the soiled, bloody clothes she was wearing when they brought her in. She'd unknotted the bag and opened it wide, earlier in the day. That meant she could keep the noise to a minimum now. She slipped out the black leggings without rustling the plastic and wriggled into them. She was still in bed, concealed behind her pleated blue curtain, which was only pulled halfway. She suspected the nurses didn't put a lot of trust in their patients on this ward. Slowly and silently, she pulled out the black jumper. She could smell the blood on it, but she imagined it wouldn't be easily spotted. Not at first glance, and not in the dark at least. She folded the jumper and flattened it as much as she could. Then she tucked it into the waistband of her leggings. With the hospital gown pulled back down, it was perfectly well hidden.

The sound of a nurse's shoes squeaking against the floor had faded into the distance. June got up quietly. The nurse's station was in the ward and the toilet was right beside it, next to the open door.

'You okay, June?' Millie whispered, so as not to wake the other patients.

June nodded and smiled. She pointed to the toilet.

Millie returned a tired smile and nodded back. Then she lowered her head again and pretended to read whatever piece of paper was in front of her.

June opened the door to the toilet wide, intentionally letting the light flood out into the darkened ward. Then she closed it again and slipped out into the corridor. Rather than running, she walked. The same slow, fed-up, mournful sort of a walk that she'd seen several other patients doing that day. The *I need to stretch my legs* walk. She passed another nurses' station where several nurses and care assistants were gathered. They didn't even look up at her.

It seemed everyone was too tired or too busy or too over-worked to take any notice of her as she shuffled mournfully past them. Or maybe they just weren't too worried. After all, where would she be going in a hospital gown? How far did she think she'd get?

Still, she continued to look like she wasn't going anywhere in a hurry. She ambled out through the double doors and down another long corridor, which was empty aside from a row of parked trollies, waiting to be occupied. She looked behind her and in front. There was no one around. She took off the gown without stopping and pulled her jumper on over her head. She dragged the long sleeves down over her bandaged wrists, then rolled up the gown and shoved it down behind some seats. She kept going forward, with no idea *where* she was going, or how to get out of this hospital. She only increased her speed to that of a normal, non-psychiatric person, despite feeling an urgent need to run. She helped herself to a face mask outside the lifts and put it on. When the doors slid open, she stepped aside to let two porters out. They were wheeling a trolley with a very fed-up looking man on it. The man gave her a weak smile, but the two porters looked more quizzically at her.

'It is really only three?' June grumbled with a roll of her eyes. 'This night is dragging.' She stepped into the lift. 'I don't think I ever needed nicotine more.'

'Tell me about it,' the porter at the back end of the trolley agreed. 'Good thinking with the jumper. It's cold out there.'

'Don't forget, smoking kills,' the other one said with half a smile. But she'd smelled the smoke off him as soon as he stepped out of the lift.

June pressed G as a safe bet. Exits were usually on the ground floor. She gave the lads a small wave as the doors slid shut.

As the elevator rumbled downwards, her whole body tensed. Her shoulders were hunched, her stomach clenched, and her fists were clutching the bloodstained sleeves of her jumper. She was thankful for the fact that she favoured black clothing. Blood wasn't very visible against black, even under harsh hospital lighting. Not unless someone was looking closely.

Soon she arrived at another set of double doors. To the right was a switch on the wall, beneath a sign saying *press to exit*. She did. But it wasn't a real exit. It was just an exit from the hospital proper, into the hospital's accident and emergency department. Here, things went from calm to bedlam. There were people on trollies everywhere. Staff squeezed themselves up and down the narrow paths between them, trying to avoid being physically caught by patients desperate for care. And probably sleep. People were calling out, singing, some were even fighting. Bells and alarms beeped, buzzed and rang out. It was chaos.

June felt her shoulders relax slightly as a drunk old man rolled off his trolley and onto the floor. Staff went running to help him, as another man started shouting, 'Is that what we have to do to get a bit of attention around here? Do we all have to hit the fucking deck?'

'Give it a rest, Dennis,' a nurse called back to him.

'I wish I bloody could, Josephine.'

'It's Sarah,' she retorted. She was pulling a hoist over to her colleagues who were kneeling beside the fallen man. 'It was Sarah last Saturday night and the Friday night before. And it'll still be Sarah when you come back to see us again next weekend.' There was humour in her tone, despite what she was dealing with.

'Yeah, whatever, Karen.'

No one noticed June as she slipped past the main reception and out into the cool evening air.

TWENTY-FIVE

JUNE

The walk from Cork University Hospital to Wellington Road took well over an hour and the sunrise had yet to make an appearance. June was drained by the time she got there. She had no idea how much blood she'd lost or how much they'd replaced. But she felt depleted in every way imaginable.

Still, June always carried on regardless of physical weakness. She never had any other choice. But this morning she was fuelled by rage. When she reached her doorstep, she rang the bell for their flat. She had nothing with her. No phone, no money, no key. She rang again and again until finally she could hear someone shuffling towards the door. But the sound stopped right inside.

'It's me.' She tried to keep her voice steady. She needed her to open the door. She did.

'June.' A dishevelled old Tess greeted her with tears in her eyes.

It seemed for a minute like she might hug June, but the moment passed quickly. Which was just as well. June didn't have the energy to push her off. She walked in and stopped just inside the door, suddenly not wanting to go any further. She was repulsed by the woman. June turned and looked back out the door, but she didn't think she could physically make it if she tried to go anywhere else. And where else *could* she go?

'June.' Her voice was low and quivery. 'Please come inside. I'm sorry. I'll tell you everything you need to know. Get your strength back and then you need never see me again, if that's what you wish.'

Never see her again? Tess knew June's secrets. All of them. How could she simply never see her again?

'Who was she?' June asked, her voice as low as she felt.

Tess frowned. 'Come inside.' She tried to put her arm around June's shoulder and lead her to the family room. But June shrugged her off and walked there ahead of her.

June's body was exhausted, but her brain was alive and pouncing from one thought to another.

'Sit down. Let me make you some tea. Would you like some beans and bread?'

'I'd like you to tell me the truth. Who was she?'

Tess nodded and her whole face quivered. But still she went about making their early breakfast, which would comprise of the baked beans that had been scheduled for that evening's dinner. 'Okay. Just let me do this first, so I can straighten things out and...'

'Come up with more lies?'

'No. No more lies, June.'

Food preparation had always been the catalyst for free-flowing conversation within their home. Which is why June didn't try to stop her now. Tess took the last tin of beans down from the cupboard and immediately began struggling with the ring pull. June forced herself up from the table. She went over to her and took the tin. She pulled the tab, peeled back the lid and shoved both back at her.

'Would you like to change into something a little less smelly, love?'

June couldn't smell it anymore, but she knew it was there. She'd got the strong stench of blood when she first put the jumper on, so she turned and left the room. She, too, needed a minute to straighten out her thoughts. And to calm them. Her legs were threatening to go from under her. She felt so weak and tired. But she needed the truth more than she needed rest and she no longer trusted Tess to give her that.

She closed the door to the family room as she left. But rather than going straight to her own room, she let herself into Tess's first. She stood just inside the door. It was neat and tidy as always, but there was no sign of the photo book. She opened the little wardrobe, but there was nothing much in there. Only the few items of clothing that Tess owned, hanging neatly on the rail. Beneath, her spare black shoes and slippers sat side by side. June closed the wardrobe door quietly, her eyes drifting to the top of the wardrobe. There were some folded blankets up there with a spare pillow resting on top. June reached up and pulled the blankets down and dropped them onto the bed. There was a rectangular box shoved into the fold of one. It was the same size and shape as the photo book and the same colour brown. June pulled away the lid and dropped the box onto the bed.

She covered her mouth and looked away for a minute. Then she took a deep breath and tipped the box, emptying its contents onto the bed. Pictures of Erica Kelly scattered everywhere. Newspaper cuttings mostly, showing her at various horse events. In several she was all dressed up, holding the reins of a horse in one hand and a trophy in the other. In others, a younger Erica Kelly in riding gear, in various stages of showing off on horseback. She was even *smiling* in some. But there was one photo that jumped out of the pile. Erica, with her equally unhappy looking husband and two children. A big, brutish looking boy and a haunted red-haired waif of a girl. Her whole body turned cold.

She pulled the rest of the blankets apart, but there was nothing else there. Her nostrils flared and her brain began to burn. But she forced herself to be still. To take a moment. She closed her eyes and once again she conjured up the image of Nurse Niamh, telling her to *breathe* as she squeezed her fist around Erica Kelly's family photograph.

She replaced the lid and brought it with her to her own room. There she sat on the edge of her bed and struggled out of her clothes. She put on fresh black leggings and a hoodie. She picked up the box and brought it with her to the family room. When she got there, Tess was sitting at the table with her hands in her lap. There were two plates of food cooling in front of her.

June placed the box on the table between them. Tess froze momentarily as she looked at it but recovered herself quickly and picked up her knife and fork.

'I should never have let you believe you were the only one who'd done terrible things in life, June. I should never have done that. I was just afraid that if you knew the truth' – she put down her utensils again and blew out a shaky breath, ignoring the box somehow – 'you'd hate me as much as the rest of the world does.'

June didn't say yes or no or anything at all.

'Back in my day...'

June slammed her hands down on the table and Tess jumped. 'What is this?' She placed a hand on the box.

Tess responded by pounding her own fist on the table. She looked defiantly back at June. 'Okay! But I need to explain, God damn it.'

'You have one minute, Tess.' June looked her up and down. 'Or whatever your name is. One minute.'

Tess's face was a mix of all known emotions. She looked around her and then nodded. 'Like I was saying, back in my day, everyone felt they should have either a nun or a priest in the family. Call it an honour thing, I don't know.' She waved away the idea. 'But in our family, it was me.'

'What is this?' June muttered, hand on the box again.

Tess glanced impatiently at it and then at June. But still she continued. 'I didn't want to be there, June. No more than those girls did.'

June flipped her untouched plate of food and most of her beans flew into the storyteller's lap. 'What did you do with the baby?'

Tess didn't flinch. 'Which one?' she asked quietly.

June took a second to answer. That was a trick question. One designed to lead to another story. 'You're running out of time,' she said after a while. 'Tell me who she was. And tell me what this is!' She slapped the box with both hands, denting the lid.

Tess said nothing.

June felt even more drained than she had before. 'What's your name? Can you even tell me that much?'

'Again, I could ask, which one? I was born Margaret Higgins, but the name later given to me was Sister Bridget.'

'And Tess?'

Tess looked to the ceiling, exhaled and shook her head. 'Tess was the girl who changed everything. I grew up with Tess. She lived three doors down from me and we used to play together outside on the street after school. She was the cleanest living girl I knew. Believe it or not, she was the one who actually wanted to enter the convent. That was all she talked about growing up. So you can imagine my surprise when she turned up on our doorstep with her father clutching her by the elbow. I'll never forget her. The tears running down her face and the look of sheer horror on her face. The way her father just released his grip on her and walked away, without so much as a backwards glance. I was so shocked to see her there. But when she saw me, there was a glimmer of hope in her eyes. I saw it as clear as day. I was a friendly face, or so she thought. But Sister Clemence saw it, too. She was our Mother Superior, and she had an evil streak that the Devil himself would envy. She instructed me to give Tess her first penance. Which was to say, she handed me shearing scissors and made me scalp the girl. Just in case it wasn't already clear that I was no longer her friend.' She shook her head and finally brought her eyes up to meet June's. 'And that was how it went. I continued to do as I was told by the Mother Superior. But I took no pleasure in it.'

'That was big of you.'

'I believed in what we were doing. I'd been conditioned to believe it. I believed that those girls had offended God and deserved to be punished. But if I'm very honest, a part of me did want to be the one who punished them. For having the choices I never had and for being stupid enough to squander them. But Tess's arrival there made me question everything. I continued to do as I was told by the Mother. I had no choice in that. But I wasn't so convinced that we were right anymore. I was so sure that Tess did not belong there.'

She took a moment for some deep, shaky breaths.

'Who. Was. She?'

Then, with a loud exhale, Tess slowly lifted her head to continue. 'The baby, you mean? Well, she's the reason we're both here, isn't she?' She glanced at the box.

June lowered her head onto the table. She was right. Somehow, knowing that she'd got one thing right in her life, brought some strength back into her. She raised her head again and looked the woman in the eye, all traces of emotion gone.

'I kept a close eye on her,' Tess continued quickly, putting her own hand on the box, finally. She'd sensed the shift in June. It was by no means a subtle one. 'Tess, I mean. She quickly made friends with another one of the girls, which wasn't surprising. Tess was like that.' She half smiled at a distant memory. 'Everyone liked her. She could strike up a conversation with just about anyone. Lorraine was the other girl's name. And while we discouraged those friendships, I overhead them talking one night. Tess broke down and cried in Lorraine's arms. She said that it was her father's friend who'd put her there. She'd begged him to leave her alone. Begged him to stop, but he didn't. The baby she was carrying was his, but the sin was hers. Of course, we heard so many similar stories. But we believed them all to be lies, you see. Excuses. The bitterness I felt towards these women was fierce, June. But I knew Tess. I knew she wasn't one who flaunted anything or tempted anyone. I knew that this couldn't possibly be her fault. It was the first time I considered the possibility that the wrong people were being punished. And yet, I did as I was told, and I continued to punish her for it anyway.'

'She died, yes?'

Tess nodded. 'That much was true. In fact, everything I told you about what happened to Tess in that home, was all true. She gave birth to a beautiful baby girl, without any of the medical attention that she so desperately needed. The pain the poor girl must have been in would have been immense. I was handed the child and instructed to take her to the couple who were waiting in the building. By the time I came back, she was gone. Her beautiful face a mask of pain for all eternity.'

'But taking her life wasn't enough? You had to take her name, too?'

She blanched at last. 'A part of me died that day, too, June,' she said defensively. 'I left there not long after that. In the middle of the night, I just packed my bag and I went. I couldn't go back home. Margaret would be disowned by her family, and as for Sister Bridget? Well, I grew to hate that woman as much as the girls who had the misfortune of crossing paths with her. I took Tess's name so that I'd never forget the part I played in her life. And in her death.'

'All the lies...'

Tess looked up hopefully. 'I told you the truth about every-one, June. I just... I suppose I just swapped around a few of the names is all.' She sighed then. 'Seán Buckley was my sister's boyfriend by the way. Luckily for her, he went on to marry her after that thing behind the picture house.'

June frowned, then she laughed out loud 'Oh! What about the book? What kind of an elaboration was that?'

Tess had been reading *The Count of Monte Cristo* to June for years. She still did from time to time. Nights like this, when June was at a low ebb, would be exactly the kind of night when the Count would come out. Before all these confessions started, that is. Tess told her that her best friend from the Mother and Baby Home, Lorraine, had given her the book and she treasured it above all else. Lorraine had inscribed it to her on the day her own father came and took her home.

Tess nodded, lowering her head again. 'After handing her baby over, I found myself sitting on Tess's bed. They had no possessions in that place, you understand. But she had the blouse she came in wearing. It had yellow flowers embroidered on the collars and I knew that it was her mother's handiwork. She was gifted with a needle, that woman. I was admiring that and thinking about her family, when I felt something hard under me. I lifted the mattress, and I found the book. The inscription was to Tess, from Lorraine. That book was the first thing I packed. And I left there that night.'

They sat in silence for some time, both staring at the table, the box and the mess of soggy bread and scattered beans.

June squeezed her eyes shut and took a deep breath in. 'Who was the baby?' she muttered first. Then she lifted the box and slammed it down on the table. 'Say it!' she screamed. Spit flew from her lips, and she hardly noticed the look of shock on Tess's face.

'If I told you that part first, it wouldn't really have made sense,' she stammered.

June brought her hands to her face and rubbed it roughly. A sharp pain shot out through both of her wrists.

Tess's eyes were drawn to the bandages.

June looked at the bandages, too, then lowered her hands and drew her eyes back to Tess. 'Don't worry. There won't be a repeat performance.'

And she meant it. Strangely, she felt no urge to cut or to inflict any sort of pain upon herself. If anything, she could feel herself hardening. A coldness came over her thoughts as they ran back over everything she thought she knew. Every*one* she thought she knew. A steel barrier came down in her mind and she felt herself moving further away from all of it. From all of *them*.

'What do you want from all this, June?'

'What do I want?' June laughed, incredulous. 'What do I want! I want a life that's *mine*! Is that too much to ask for, *Sister* Bridget? I want to live!' she shouted, and again, she lifted the box and slammed it down. 'Now answer my fucking question! Say the words!'

'For a girl who wants to live, you sure do dance with death a lot.'

'Answer the question,' June growled.

'I've carried Tess with me every day of my life since then, June. I felt I owed it to her to keep tabs on her baby somehow.'

June stared unblinking at Tess, her thoughts cooling even more.

'I know Tess had a name picked out for her child before she was born. But of course, the family gave her their own name.'

'And what name did they give her?' she asked, sounding devoid of all emotion suddenly. She needed her to say the words.

'Well, the name her mother picked was... well, it was June. June Calloway.'

June's eyes went wide, and she had to fight the urge to pounce across the table.

'But that wasn't the name she ended up with,' she said quickly. 'She went to a well-to-do couple called Frederick and Mary Ellis. They called their new daughter Erica and they spoiled her rotten.' She placed her hand on the dented lid of the box again. 'She went on to marry a veterinarian, changed her surname to Kelly and, well, I believe you may know the rest.'

TWENTY-SIX

JUNE

Seven fifty the following morning, June loaded up her trolley.

'June?' Liz sounded both surprised and relieved to see her.

'I'm sorry, Liz. I wasn't feeling myself yesterday.'

Liz glanced at the bandages poking out from the sleeves of June's blouse. She'd pulled them down as much as she could, but they didn't quite cover them fully. Liz stared at them for a minute, then looked up again.

'That's okay. It's good to have you back.'

'Everything okay?'

Liz took a while to answer. 'No. I feel like I owe you an apology.'

June stopped rooting in the stock cupboard and gave Liz as much of her attention as she could. 'Why would you owe me an apology? I'm the one who didn't turn up to work yesterday.'

'Yes. But clearly you had a good reason. In fact, you probably shouldn't have turned up today either. You look absolutely frightening. No offence. I mean...'

'So, why are you apologising?'

'I...' She raised her eyes to the ceiling. 'I thought that maybe you were off somewhere with Malcolm.'

June frowned. 'Why would I be anywhere with Malcolm?'

'Erica Kelly is trying to buy the Cedarwood Manor. You know that.'

June nodded but went back to loading up. 'And what's that got to do with me?'

Liz just stood there like a schoolgirl, wringing her hands, waiting for someone to tell her what to do. Or at least, that's how she looked to June. She pulled the door of the storeroom closed.

'I don't know why she wants the place. But I think it has a lot to do with the fact that she wants me gone. And, of course, she's rich and bloody bored.'

Liz was still labouring under the assumption that Erica Kelly factored her into her decision-making process, but June didn't say anything. She just nodded again.

'You don't seem surprised to hear that.'

'Which part? I'm not surprised that she wants to buy this place because you already told me that. Mrs Kelly likes to have nice things. What could be nicer than the Manor? Plus, she insults you every chance she gets, so you're probably right.' June was done placating her. It was time instead to add some fuel to Liz's fire.

Liz flinched.

'And don't forget, she also took your boyfriend from you. It seems to me that she wants what you have. Like you said. And so does Malcolm.'

And that one was a kick in the gut.

'June.' Liz brought her hand to her chest and looked away. She frowned then and turned back to June. 'That was a very cold thing to say.'

June nodded. She was right. It was. 'I'm sorry, Liz. But it's what you're thinking, too, isn't it? That they're colluding against you? And you thought maybe I was in on it as well?'

Liz stared at her for a minute and her eyes started to water.

Then she nodded and looked away. 'Yes. I suppose it just sounds a bit more... harsh coming out of someone else's mouth.'

'And that's why you thought I was off somewhere with Malcolm?'

She shook her head brusquely. 'If you're as tuned in as I think you are, then you can understand why I might be feeling a little paranoid, June.'

'I do. But you needn't feel paranoid when it comes to me, Liz.'

Liz's face softened slightly. 'I think I know that. Sometimes it can be hard to see the wood for the trees.'

'I understand. Well...' She returned her full attention to her work. 'I'm sure it'll all work itself out.'

'I hope you're right. What about you? Would you continue to work here if she were your boss?'

June shrugged. 'Sure, where else would I go?'

The door swung open, and the two noisy maids ambled in. They were momentarily caught off guard by their boss and another maid huddled together in there. They made no secret of the fact that they thought June was weird, but judging by their faces, she looked a million times weirder today. They soon recovered themselves, however, and dragged their trollies in. June backed away, pulling her one out with her.

'You're late, ladies,' Liz admonished.

'It's bang on eight,' said the more annoying of the two.

'It is. Which means you should already be cleaning something by now.'

'And so should I.' June passed them all, Liz included, on her way out.

'June?' Liz called, and followed her, out of earshot of the other two. 'Are you sure you're okay?' She nodded towards June's wrists again.

'Of course.' June forced a smile as she turned her wrists inward and carried on ahead, towards the lift.

·   ·   ·

By lunchtime that day, Malcolm was back in the bar drinking coffee and grinning at the staff around him. As June worked the lobby, she could see that Liz's paranoia had notched up significantly. It was a visible thing now. She was standing near the reception desk, craning her neck to look through to the bar. Then she'd look over at June. If she noticed anyone looking at *her*, she'd pretend to be reading something behind the desk. The atmosphere between Liz and Malcolm oozed deviance now, and judging by the way Lauren was watching Liz, other people had started noticing it, too. It was a timely distraction, as far as June was concerned. But she wanted no part of it, so she carefully put down her container of oil soap and walked over to Liz.

'Liz?' she spoke softly. 'Would you like me to remove my bandages?'

Liz blanched. 'What? Why would I want you to do that?'

'So you can stop looking at me like that – like maybe I was somewhere other than where I said I was yesterday. I can show you exactly what I was doing if it'll put your mind at ease.'

She tried again to frown and actually managed to get a small crease on her forehead that time. Her Botox was wearing off, which was unusual for Liz. 'June, you seem... different today. And you really don't look well. Your face is practically grey in colour.'

'I feel different. I really do. But then I did try to kill myself yesterday.'

'I know. I... I'm sorry, June.'

June nodded. 'But I feel much better now. Wherever Malcolm was, it wasn't with me.'

TWENTY-SEVEN

MIA

As far back as she could remember, Mia had always been able to sense it when something bad was coming. She had that feeling now, as she sat on the step outside the back door, peeling potatoes. She had her head down, focused on the task at hand, when some movement caught her eye. She glanced up to see not one, not two, but four little robins huddled together on the grass.

She slowly put the peeler and the potato back in the bucket and stood up. She tiptoed down the steps towards them.

'Don't be afraid,' she whispered. 'I won't hurt you.'

When she got just close enough that they could see each other properly, one of them looked up. He let out a little tweet and they all flew away.

'Don't go,' she said quietly, as she watched them take off into the cloudy sky. Mia loved robins and had never seen four of them together before. She continued to look upwards, as her brief moment of happiness flew away with them.

She was about to go back to her step when she spotted something on the ground where they'd been. Something they were huddled around. She went closer for a look. Nuts. Two little nuts and some crumby stuff.

'I'm sorry, birdies,' she said softly.

There wasn't a lot of food around for small birds like robins at this time of year. But these four managed to forage some and she'd scared them off before they had a chance to eat it.

'Stupid Mia,' she muttered. She picked up the nuts and put them in the pocket of her dress. Then she went back to her step, picked up the peeler and the half-peeled potato, and went about finishing the job.

'I'm not having it in my house.'

Mia closed her eyes and slowed her peeling. Mammy was at it again. Her heels click-clacked on the tiled floor, right on the other side of the back door. She could only assume that Daddy was in there, too. Mia was glad she'd pulled the door shut when she came outside. She sat with her back to it.

'Do you hear me? I won't stand for it. Not this time.'

'Do you know how ridiculous you sound?'

Mia stopped what she was doing and looked up in surprise. His voice was low and flat, but he answered her! He never answered her.

'I'll walk, Evan.' Her voice was lower again. More threatening. 'And while you might think life would be just fine if I weren't here, I meant what I said. I'll take all your dirty laundry with me, and I'll air it for the world to see. I'll fucking ruin you, you bastard. Do you hear me? I'll ruin you.'

'*My* dirty laundry. Is that right, Erica? Tell me again, who was the one who brought *her* back here, hmm? It sure as hell wasn't me. Now if you had wanted the child, I'd say something. But you haven't a maternal bone in your shrivelling body, my darling. So, when we talk about dirty laundry, whose do you think reeks more? Mine, or yours?'

'You...'

'I'm done here, Erica. If you want to go, then by all means, fuck right off and take her with you. This house without the blight of women would suit me just fine.'

Mia sat there with the peeler hovering above the potato, listening. Her eyes were wide, and she dared not breathe in case they heard her. Mammy was threatening to leave. Would she really take Mia with her? Something told her that she wouldn't. She did not like spending time in Mia's company, so she couldn't imagine her wanting to be with her all the time. No. She'd go and leave Mia here with Daddy and Kevin, and the whole lot was making her insides turn watery.

There was more click-clacking and then it all went quiet. One of them had just walked out. Maybe both of them had. She started peeling again, but the action was more automated this time. She was too distracted by what she'd heard. There was so much talk about dirty laundry. And the way they said it, made Mia think they weren't talking about socks and underwear. She couldn't help thinking it all had to do with her and her real mother. But Mia had been in Mammy's house all her life. Why would she suddenly not stand for it now? Mia wasn't very clever, she knew that. She probably had the whole thing all wrong. But still, she wondered about it anyway.

If her real mother used to be their housekeeper, and Mammy found her with Daddy in the good room, that must mean that Daddy was Mia's *real* daddy. She'd read enough to think this could be right. Is that what they meant when they talked about laundry and secrets? She rubbed her head with one hand, wishing that people would just use proper words when they spoke.

None of it made sense. Mia was adopted. She'd always known that because Mammy had been telling her all her life. Her real mother didn't want her, and she had no father. She knew that. *Real* fathers do not adopt their *real* daughters. Do they? No. Mammy brought her home just as the other woman was about to throw her in the bin. No one else wanted her. That's what she'd always been told.

She tried to stop herself from thinking round in circles. The only thing she knew for sure was that no one *actually* wanted her. Everything else was just confusing.

'What are you doing?' Kevin's voice behind her made her jump. He came out the back door and stepped over her, down the steps.

'Peeling potatoes.' She stiffened. She forced herself to focus on the mundane task so that he wouldn't be able to see inside her head. She never knew where she was with Kevin. He could completely ignore her at times, just like Daddy ignored Mammy. But other times he was the cruellest person in the world. Even worse than Mammy when she was in her most terrible mood.

'You're doing it like an idiot.' He started mimicking her actions, but with his tongue sticking out and his eyes crossed.

She didn't respond and continued to peel the only way she knew how.

'You know what they're fighting about, don't you?'

Mia kept her head down.

He stepped in close to her. 'You.'

Her stomach tightened and her face flushed red.

Kevin laughed, like he was genuinely amused. 'You look so dumb right now.' He sighed loudly, then explained it like she was simple. Which she supposed she was.

'He was screwing your tinker of a mother and now' – he laughed again – 'now she actually thinks he's screwing you as well! How fucked up is that? I mean, he's a piece of work and all. But even *I* know he's not that way inclined.'

Mia's heart was thumping in her chest now. She didn't really know what he was saying, but she knew it was something bad. Something that would get her in big trouble.

'H... he's not!' she stammered, thinking back to the movies

and the sweets and the seconds spent sitting on his lap. Was that what Mammy was so upset about?

'Doesn't matter, though, does it? It's all coming to a head, either way. You're starting to look a bit *too* like her, if you know what I mean, and it's clouding everyone's judgement.'

Mia tore the peeler through the potato, her hands starting to shake as she made them work faster. The peeler slipped and skinned her finger, and a stream of blood ran towards the bucket. She dropped the potato and stuck her finger in her mouth to stop it.

'Hang on.' Kevin looked thoughtfully at her. 'You wouldn't be that stupid, surely... would you?'

She looked up at him, her finger still in her mouth. She wanted to run away so she didn't have to listen to him. But to try would be useless. He'd just follow her. He always did.

'You don't think that maybe, one day, all this will be yours, do you?' He waved his hands over the house, and the trees, and the paddock behind him.

Mia never thought about that. She never thought about anything other than getting from one job to the next. Besides, how could this place be anyone else's but theirs?

He pointed down the yard then. 'She'll have you buried under those stables before she lets that happen and he won't do a thing to stop her. He probably has kids all over the county, but he doesn't give a shit about any of them. Me, and certainly you, included. You don't get it, do you?' He stopped pointing and let his arms hang down by his sides. 'They hate us. Both of them, not just her.'

This surprised her. *Us?* They hate *us?*

'*She* hates me because I'm his son and heir and I came about the same way as you did. Pretty much. Thankfully, I'm not hers. But she keeps me around because I help her to keep you down where you belong. *He* also hates me because I'm his son and heir. Could you imagine if he knew I was gay, on top of all the other reasons he has to hate me?' He laughed then, but there was no humour in it. 'You can imagine how bad that would look for a man like him?'

Mia desperately wanted to ask what other reasons Daddy had to hate him and whether they were the same reasons why *she* hated him. But she kept her mouth shut.

He was looking at the closed door behind her now and his voice dripped with sarcasm. Finally, he glanced back down at her. 'I remember your mother.'

'Do you?' Mia asked, a hint of desperation in her voice.

'She was thick. Like you, but much better looking. Mammy kicked her out as soon as Kate got too fat for her dress.' He paused and stared at her for a while then. 'You know, I was with her that day when she went and got you.'

Mia just stared back at him, afraid to speak. She desperately wanted to hear what he had to say. But she worried that if he knew that, he'd stop talking just to spite her.

'Kate?' Mia froze. She'd read that name before, but not in any of her newspapers. It was in a letter she found when she was cleaning Mammy's room nearly two years ago. She knew that because she wasn't long after turning eight and the letter was sitting right there on Mammy's bed. It was in a white envelope with really scratchy writing on it. Mia didn't know why she took that page out of the envelope, but she did. And she remembered the words as clearly as she remembered everything else she read.

Dear Erica,

I thought I might come for a visit next Monday. I want to see her and I don't think you should be able to stop me. I know you said she doesn't want to...

Mia only got to read the first two lines, because Mammy

called her from downstairs. Quick as a flash, she had to fold it along its three creases and shove it back in its envelope. That's when she saw the name, Kate, at the very end.

'Yeah, Kate.' He grinned, waving his hand in front of her face. 'What, didn't you even know her name?'

Mia lowered her head. Kate. Kate. Kate. The name went round and round inside her head and she desperately wanted to go back in time and read the rest of that letter. Was Mia who she wanted to come and visit that Monday? Why didn't she ever come?

'I'm not sure what else she said to her, to be honest,' Kevin continued, and Mia did her best to tune in to what he was saying. 'I was too busy watching the lads on the bikes. But all I know is that the woman was on her knees, crying and calling out your name, as Mammy carried you away and put you in the car.'

'Why?' Mia's face started burning now as a fury rose up through her. 'Why did Mammy want me so badly?'

He laughed again. 'She didn't *want* you. She *hates* you. I told you that. But she hated your mother more. If Mammy doesn't like someone, she'll take everything they have away from them, just to see them suffer. It's the only thing that makes her happy.'

'Did my... did Kate ever write letters to Mammy?' Mia lowered her hand and let her finger bleed into the potatoes.

'Letters?' He laughed. 'Never mind the bloody letters. She thinks he has his eye on you now!' He sucked air in through his teeth. 'That's history repeating itself in her twisted little mind, isn't it? And he's happy for her to think that, so you're done for, girl.' He chuckled and made it seem like he was about to walk away, but he stopped and turned back. 'Trouble is, if she kicks you out, what's to stop you running to the cops about them?'

Mia shook her head. Why would she do that? *How* would she do that? Mia Kelly knew nothing outside of this house.

Aside from all the dangers that Mammy had warned her about. All the things she was shown in the newspapers, that they'd been keeping her safe from. That's why she never went anywhere. People wouldn't understand her. She was not right in the head and would be taken somewhere and dumped by the first person she met. *This* was her safe life. That's what she'd always been told. Just like she'd been told that her mother didn't want her. The same mother who fell to her knees and cried when she was taken away. The same one who wrote at least one letter, asking to come and visit.

It was as if the whole world just fell away. The potatoes, the trees around her, the horses down in the paddock. The door behind her and the steps underneath her. They all vanished. Only two things mattered now. One was a woman called Kate and the other was a letter begging for her back.

TWENTY-EIGHT

JUNE

'Oh, thank Christ.' Heather visibly slumped when she saw June standing in the laundry room, just outside the door to the hotel's junk room, an almost hidden entrance that had been painted shut some years ago. Today it was Heather holding the toasties and two cups of tea.

June gave her a small smile and went to pull the chairs out the door. 'Did you miss me or something?'

She handed June a plate and a cup and they both sat down. 'I bloody well did, as it happens. You're the only normal person I have to talk to around here. Plus, you make a much better toasted sandwich than I do.'

'Heather, if I'm the most normal person you have to talk to, then you're worse off than I am.'

Heather glanced at June's wrists and looked away again, out towards the woods. 'Are you alright? You look half dead.'

'Maybe I am. But the other half is better than ever.'

Heather blew out a long stream of smoke and shook her head. 'What did you go and do that for, June?'

June looked at her sandwich. All the extra cheese Heather

had put in oozed out each side of it. She took a small bite and chewed. This was far better than the frugal ones she made.

'June?' Heather turned to look at her. 'Why did you do that?'

June shrugged and kept eating. 'You're wrong about the toasties. This is far better than mine.'

'Forget the toasties. What does' – Heather gave an over-exaggerated shrug – 'mean?'

'It means, I don't know. Just one of those things, on one of those days, I suppose.'

Heather guffawed. 'One of those things?' She glared at June. 'One of those days!'

June lowered her sandwich and turned to face her. 'What would you like me to say, Heather?'

Heather looked away towards the woods again. 'Nothing, girl. You're right. You don't owe me any explanation. But can I just say that I'm glad you fucked it up?'

'Thank you.' June took another small bite and picked up her cooling tea.

'Well, herself is on some kind of mission. She's stalking the halls. And I mean, she's bloody everywhere.'

'Who, Liz?'

'Who else? And Malcolm is back.'

'I know. He's up in the bar.'

Heather rolled her eyes.

June sipped her tea, thinking. Then she glanced at Heather. 'She's going to do something. I can feel it.'

'Who? Liz?'

June nodded.

'Like what? What can *she* do? I heard that Malcolm's grand-parents are retiring.' She bobbed her head from side to side. 'I mean, even more than they already are. They'd be handing this place over, like. But what I heard is, they're only leaving half of it to Malcolm.' She leaned in and lowered her voice. 'Apparently, they're selling the other half to Erica fucking Kelly of all people! Could you imagine if that was true!'

'It is true,' June muttered.

'Seriously?' Heather looked at her with eyes like saucers. 'That's the stuff of bloody nightmares, June! I'll tell you what, the day that woman becomes my boss, is the day I down tools in this sweatbox. And as for him! I'll be gone like the clappers.'

June picked up the last of her toastie.

'Would you work for them?'

June shrugged. 'I don't know where else I'd go.' She put the last corner in her mouth. 'But I'm not sure it'll come to that.'

'What makes you so sure?'

'Liz,' June said, matter of fact.

'What's she going to do about it?'

'The Manor is her life, Heather. What would you do if your boyfriend and his bit on the side were trying to take everything away from you?'

Heather huffed. 'I'd fucking kill the pair of them. That's what I'd do.'

June nodded. 'Well, I don't know about killing them. But she won't sit back and take it, that's for sure.'

'Well, I hope you're right. Let's hope that Liz has finally decided she's taken enough.'

'Can I use the machines later? I don't have it in me to go to the public laundry.' June stood up and wiped the crumbs off herself.

'Of course you can.'

'Oh, and, eh...' She lowered her voice to little more than a whisper. 'Do you by any chance have anything that might help me sleep?'

It was common knowledge that Heather had more pills than the local pharmacy and was willing to hand them out like Smarties for a price.

She looked suspiciously at June.

'I'm not sleeping, Heather.'

'I can see that, June. But you've never asked me for anything before.'

'I've never slit my wrists before either.'

Heather's face softened. 'I'm sorry, love. Of course I can help you. But, eh...'

'I won't take them all at once.' June gave the woman the reassuring grin that she needed. 'I mean it when I say the urge has passed. I just need to sleep. That's all.'

Heather exhaled and nodded, returning a small smile. She rubbed June's arm then. 'I get it. Look, I'm knocking off at four and you know yourself, Liz will be here until about five. But I'll leave some powder and softener on top of the machine and... a few of my pharmaceutical friends. Help yourself, love.'

'Thanks. And, Heather?'

'Hmm?'

'You make a really cheesy toastie.'

Heather smiled and June went back to work.

For the first time in as long as she could remember, June's mind was as clear as a bell. Even her self-loathing seemed to have vanished into thin air. She hadn't felt so much as a tingle in her thighs since leaving the hospital. Her beloved blade had lost its appeal. Everything had. Everything, but the Manor. This was where she needed to be. And this was where she planned to stay, for as long as she was needed.

That afternoon she got changed out of her uniform and clocked out at four. Same as every other day. She said goodbye to Liz who always came to the basement at three forty-five to make sure no one tried to leave early. Then June left through the staff entrance. But she didn't go home. Her conversation with Tess had made it impossible for her to go back there that night. Instead, she walked around the outside of the building and towards the woods. She found a spot to sit at the base of a tree with line of sight to the hotel carpark. She opened her bag and took out two packets of individually wrapped biscuits. They were plain shortbread, which would have been nicer dipped in tea. But they would be her dinner for that evening, so she took her time to appreciate them as much as she could. The hour passed quickly as she sat there thinking. Running through all of what Tess had told her in the days before.

All this time Tess had spoken about Erica Kelly, the same way she had about all the other guests at the Manor. Like she knew them all personally. June thought it was just one of Tess's quirks. That because she didn't leave the flat, she was somehow living vicariously through June. Tess allowed her to think that.

But she did know Erica Kelly. She'd been watching her since she was a baby. Keeping tabs on her, her whole life. June didn't usually think too much about coincidences. But this was a big one all the same. Tess injected herself into June's life. She became her family, when neither of them appeared to have one. And June worked in the very hotel where Erica Kelly passed as much of her time as possible. What exactly did Tess hope to achieve in all this?

It was Liz's distant laugh that snapped her out of her own thoughts. She was leaving, arm in arm with Malcolm. Of course she was. She was laughing, but her body language was off. June nodded to herself. Liz was clever enough to know the whole *keep your friends close and your enemies closer* theory and that seemed to be what she was doing.

June waited until Malcolm finished trying to eat Liz's face and he'd closed her driver's side car door for her. He waved her off as she drove away. Then he walked back in through the main entrance to begin his shift. Whatever that entailed for Malcolm, June didn't know. But she suspected it wouldn't be too taxing for him. When they were both out of sight, she got up, wiped the seat of her pants and went back in the staff door. She moved quickly and quietly through the hotel basement to the locker room.

From another locker, not the one she'd used that day, June pulled out a black holdall and brought it with her to the laundry room. Like everywhere else in the basement at this time, the laundry room was deserted. As promised, Heather had left a cup full of powder, some fabric softener and a little bundle of crumpled tin foil on top of the machine. June took them down and opened up the foil. There were eight pills in there. They were all white in colour, but four were round and four were oval shaped. June had no intention of actually taking them. She didn't trust pills because she'd seen what they could do to people.

She opened the washing drum and opened her bag. Into the machine she put three pairs of black leggings, two black hoodies and three T-shirts, along with one large towel and a set of almost matching bed sheets. Everything she owned. She put in the powder and softener and set the machine going. Then she sat down on one of the plastic lunch chairs, facing the hidden door to the hidden junk room. A small smile played on her lips. No one noticed that the door was no longer sealed shut. Not even those who worked alongside it every day. But June had been getting that room ready for a while now and she was pleased with how it was going. As she sat there, looking at the door and waiting for her laundry, she let her mind drift once more to the woman she thought she knew better than anyone else.

A part of her knew that she should feel sad or angry, or something, to have lost her. But a door had closed in June's mind. On the other side of that door was funny, quirky, strange little Tess. Whom she could never see again.

TWENTY-NINE

MIA

It was roast lamb for dinner today and Mia usually felt a little anxious when she had to make it. Daddy was so particular about lamb. But anxiety wasn't what she was feeling tonight. She hadn't thought much about the food at all, in fact. Not the blood in the potatoes, or the amount of herbs she'd thrown on the meat. Instead, Mia was filled with an unfamiliar rage as she worked in the kitchen that night. Her brain was making so much noise that it was hard to hear, and she had to mutter, just to let some of that noise out. Feelings like these had never afflicted her before and she didn't know what to do with them.

She'd always believed them when they said she was thick. Dumb. Everything else they told her she was. Even now, in her rage, she knew she must be all of those things, surely. But according to Kevin, her real mother still wanted her. They'd kept Mia from her all her life, just because they could.

As the lamb baked and Mia stewed, she heard Mammy come thumping down the stairs. The front door opened and slammed shut. Another minute and her car started up. Mia went to the good room and watched out the window as she screeched down the driveway. For the first time in her life, she felt pure hatred for that woman.

She stayed there for a while before returning to the kitchen and when she did, she looked at the pot of potatoes, ready to be mashed. She glanced in the oven at the tray of roasting vegetables. They were done. She stood there staring at the food, her young mind making a list of all the things she now believed to be true in life.

1. Things she read in the newspapers. Newspapers always told the truth. Most of the stories she read were about bad things happening to people. But sometimes there were good things, too.
2. Good things happening must mean that good people made them happen. Didn't it?
3. *He* had put a baby in Mia's real mother's belly. *Mia.*
4. That meant that *he* was her real daddy. Kevin had said as much and Mammy had, too, just with different words.
5. But real daddies don't let bad things happen to their children. So, he wasn't a *real* daddy.
6. *He* had allergies and would die if a nut went anywhere near him.
7. *She* took her away from her mother.

Right on the stroke of five, he came into the kitchen. Mia sliced up the lamb that crumbled away because it was too hot to carve it properly. She heaped food onto his plate and put it in front of him, along with a cold glass of milk. She opened the butter dish and put that on the table as well. He sat down and started eating, without saying a word.

'Is Mammy...'

'She's gone.'

'Oh.'

'You shouldn't expect her home for a few days.'

'Oh.'

'Try not to sound so dumb, girl.'

She stared at him for a few seconds and nodded. Then she started tidying the cooking area on autopilot. When she turned to put the milk back in the fridge, he was looking at her, chewing a mouthful.

'This is a good piece of lamb.'

She nodded.

'She's cross with me, Mia.' He smiled then, his voice softening again. He shoved another forkful into his mouth. 'Do you want to know why?'

She didn't. She really didn't. But she had to respond, so she shrugged one shoulder.

'She's a fierce jealous woman, is my Erica.' He put down his fork and wiped his mouth with his napkin. 'She was jealous of our last girl and now she's jealous of you.' He sat back in his chair and looked at her, smiling.

Mia turned and busied herself cleaning the countertops. 'What happened to the last girl?' she found herself asking, her voice flat and void of emotion.

He shrugged. 'I've no idea.'

Mia's throat tightened and the whoosh-whoosh sound of her blood pumping past her ears got louder and louder. 'Was she my mother?'

'She used to be a right stunner in her day. Erica, that is.' He ignored her question. 'But now she sees someone younger and prettier and, how can I say, more appealing than herself, and she flies into a blind rage. Half the time it'll make no sense to anyone but her, but that's just the way she is.'

Mia stayed quiet, but her heart was thumping louder in her chest and heat rose up through her. Her hatred for him, for *them*, became all consuming. But Mia had been raised to be a meticulous thinker. One wrong detail could land her in the height of trouble. She was conditioned to think out her every move and never to speak or act on a whim.

'Can you hear me, Mia?'

She nodded and kept wiping, not daring to let him see her turmoil.

'Will I pick out a nice film for us to watch tonight? While Mammy's away...' He smiled brightly.

'I think she wasn't happy the last time,' she said, thinking ahead through the evening, step by step by step.

He nodded. 'You're right. And if I know my wife, she won't let this go. So, we're going to have one more movie night, just to stoke her flames.' He chuckled.

'I need to get Kevin his dinner.'

'Don't you worry about Kevin.'

Mia kept her back to him and continued to clean the already clean counters. Her mind was handing her ideas that she couldn't fathom putting into practice. But then there was the rage. That was screaming at her that she had no choice. No one in this house would ever tell her the truth about her life. She knew that suddenly. But she had to know. Somehow, she had to find out if life outside this house was possible for her. Perhaps a life with a real mother, who'd written letters begging to have Mia back.

'I'll go find us something nice to watch. Bring my éclair into the good room – and Mia?'

She half turned to look at him, holding onto the counter for fear she might fall down. Or maybe charge at him with her head down.

'Bring one for yourself as well. Mammy won't be wanting hers.' He smiled the same smile he always gave her. The one that made her think he was the only friend she had in the world.

She nodded to him and forced herself to smile. 'I'll finish here and bring them through.' The words caught in her dry throat and made her sound old and croaky.

Mia breathed heavily for a few seconds, then she reached into the pocket of her dress. Her fingers rolled the two nuts around. The thought had entered her head as soon as she saw them lying on the grass. *They'd kill Daddy if they got near him.* She knew she should have binned them and then disinfected her hands thoroughly. She certainly shouldn't have picked them up and brought them into the house. She'd been unsettled ever since the last movie night and while the thought of doing something about it hadn't actually occurred to her, she thought now that maybe her mind was a few steps ahead. Or maybe she had an angel, whispering in her ear. Bringing those nuts to her, today of all days, and telling her to keep them. And now here they were, rolling around between her fingers.

She pulled the nuts out of her pocket and held them in the palm of her hand. They were so small. So innocent looking.

'Mia?' he called again.

'I'm coming,' she called back.

She'd go to jail for it. She knew she would. But what was jail anyway, only being stuck in one place, unable to leave. It would be home, minus the liars who'd stolen her life.

She placed the nuts gently on the counter and held them in place with her finger. She took a spoon from the top drawer, and using the back of it, she pressed down on them, trying not to make a loud noise as she crushed them into powder. Her breathing quickened as she pulled the éclairs out of the fridge and put them on two plates. One blue, one brown. She ran to the door, opened it a crack and peeped out. She could hear him at the whiskey tray in the good room. He was getting himself a drink. She hurried back to the counter and opened one éclair. She swept the nut powder into the palm of her hand and sprinkled it onto the cream. Then she used the spoon to mix it just enough that the cream didn't get messy. She closed it up again.

'Mia!'

She took some deep breaths, picked up the plates and went

to him. Her heart was crawling up her throat, but her hands were steady. Steadier than they'd ever been.

'There you are.' He patted the couch beside him. He'd turned it so that it faced the telly. That would be the first thing Mammy noticed when she came home.

Mia sat on the very edge of the cushion and handed him a plate. The brown one. *His* one. He smiled and sat back with the plate on his lap. He pointed the remote and pressed play, then kind of wiggled himself to get comfy. As the music started and a giant bear with a big silly smile bounced onto the screen, Mia already knew that this movie was a kid's one. Not that she planned on watching it. The knot in her stomach began to loosen.

He glanced at her and smiled, then he ruffled her hair, looking like he was really enjoying himself. He picked up his éclair with a chuckle of delight. Mia took the tiniest bite of hers, because she knew she should. But she dared not look at him. Instead, she stared at the TV, without actually seeing it. He took a bite. She held her breath and waited. He looked at her again and smiled, a dollop of cream at each corner of his mouth. She took another tiny bite and kept looking straight ahead. It wasn't working. The story about the nuts was another lie.

He took another bite. An enormous one this time, taking half the éclair into his mouth. He chewed it up and then stuck the rest in. She watched him now as he chewed and swallowed and wiped at his mouth with his thumb and finger. He licked the last of the cream off, wiped his hand on his trousers and picked up his whiskey glass.

'Are you eating yours?' He nodded to her barely touched pastry.

She shook her head and held her plate towards him. Her brain was on fire now. The movie was playing on: *The Bear in the Big Blue House*. She might have loved this a few weeks ago, back when she was still thick. But tonight, it just seemed ridiculous. Beside her, Daddy was alive and grinning, and it seemed he would live the rest of his life doing whatever he wanted to do. While she...

She let go of the plate before he had a grip on it, and it dropped on the carpet.

'Damn it, Mia!' he shouted. 'Can you ever come into this room without fucking the place up?'

'I'm sorry.' She dropped to the floor, picked up the pastry and put it back on the plate.

He sighed. 'Look, don't worry about it. Mammy can clean it up when she gets back.' He smiled then. 'Come back up here now and let's watch this. Let's just have a nice evening.'

He sat back again, but his smile slipped from his face. He coughed a little and pulled on the collar of his shirt. Then he coughed some more and sat up dead straight, pulling at his collar with more urgency.

Mia stayed kneeling on the floor, watching him. His face grew redder and redder, and his eyes bulged. He couldn't breathe. Butterflies in her stomach felt more like birds as they fluttered and punched their way up through her chest. She stood up, her watery legs solidifying under her. He was pointing to the dresser near the whiskey table. Mia looked to see what he was pointing at. He was wheezing and pointing, looking terrified and like he wanted to kill her, all at the same time. That look of terror on his face ignited something in her. Something that hadn't been there before. She found herself smiling. But a proper smile. One she didn't need to control or manufacture. It happened all on its own and he saw it, too.

He dropped off the couch and onto the floor. He tried to crawl towards the dresser, reaching out with his hand, desperate, *desperate* for whatever was over there, just out of reach. He collapsed onto his belly before he could get close.

Mia turned and walked over to see what he was going for. She opened the drawer. Inside, resting on top of some papers, was some sort of medical thing. A yellow tube with an orange top on it. She picked it up and looked at him. His eyes looked desperately at it, and he tried to reach a hand out to her. He gasped and slumped flat onto the floor. She could hear wheezing for another minute before the room fell silent.

Mia stood there staring at him. He was dead. She'd killed him. And she didn't feel anything about it.

THIRTY

MIA

Mia left the stupid movie playing and walked out of the sitting room. She stood in the hall looking around, thinking about where she should go and what she should do. His keys were in the bowl on the hall table, along with the clicker for opening and closing the big gates at the end of the very long driveway. She picked them up and put them in her pocket. She looked back out towards the kitchen first, and then up the stairs. Kevin was here somewhere. She knew she should probably leave right now, while there was no one trying to stop her. But where would she go? Which direction would she take when she got to the gate? No. Mia could not leave this house until she'd found something to direct her. Something that would tell her how to get to her mother.

She turned and walked back to the kitchen. There she took a moment to look around, before reaching for the knife block on the counter. She slid out a boning knife and held it up to look at it. She smiled again. She'd never felt so free in her entire life. All the anxiety, all the fear, all the uncertainty seemed to have left her and now all she felt was strong. They'd used her as a weapon and now that's what she was. For the first time in her life, *she* was in charge.

She slipped the knife into the same pocket where the nuts had been, and she went quietly upstairs. Mammy and Daddy had their own separate bedrooms. She went to Mammy's first. She stood there looking around, trying to think where Mammy might keep all the things she didn't want Mia to see. Well, that could be anywhere because Mia was only allowed in here to change the beds, clean the bathroom, hoover the floor, and dust the surfaces. She was never allowed to open the wardrobe or the chest of drawers. She'd been specifically warned that the wardrobe was out of bounds. She glanced at it. Surely it should be the first place she looked.

She blinked when she heard a sound coming from the room next door. Kevin's room. She didn't move, but different scenarios played out in her mind, which was much quieter now. She could actually hear her thoughts. One was that he might come in here unexpectedly, while she was searching the wardrobe. He'd overpower her and she'd lose. The other was what might happen if he didn't come in. If she found what she needed and left. In that scenario, *she'd* send him after Mia. And they'd make sure he found her.

She turned and walked quietly into the hall and along to Kevin's room. She placed her ear against his closed door and listened. After a while, she heard a single, rough snore. She stayed there a while longer, waiting for the heavy rhythmic breathing. As soon as she heard it, she opened the door as quietly as she could, and crept inside. She hadn't decided what to do yet, so for a while, she just stood beside his bed looking at him. His mouth was wide open and he was drooling. A slob, living like a king. She was never allowed in his room either, only to collect his laundry, so now she took a moment to look around. She compared it to her windowless room in the basement. He had the same plush carpet that ran throughout upstairs. He had sage green wallpaper. Shelves filled with books and video games and all sorts of stuff that belonged to him. She looked down at him again. The ugly, hairy beast. She hated him. She slipped the knife from her pocket and placed the tip of it near his stomach. But the knife looked awfully small beside his swollen belly. She didn't think it would work.

Michael Jackson's daughter, Paris, called suicide hotline before slitting her wrists.

Another bold headline flashed in her mind. People who wanted to kill themselves, cut their wrists. They did that when they wanted to actually die.

His hands rested limply on his stomach. She grabbed one of them and quickly pulled the sharp blade across his wrist. The pitch of his scream was startling, and his arms and legs flailed. She just managed to grab the other hand and repeat the action before he could comprehend what was happening. That was when she saw his father in him for the first time. *Their* father. That look on his face. The bulging eyes, the disbelief. He grabbed at himself, his fingers slipping and sliding as dark blood came out of him in spurts. The knife had cut him bone deep and soon he was almost drowning in his own blood.

Mia took a few steps backwards and away from the blood. She watched him flail and weaken and fall off the bed and onto the floor. She watched the life draining from his eyes and she wondered how happy this would make Mammy. She hated them as much as she hated anyone else. She'd be glad to see this. But it would be some days before she would. No doubt, Mammy was at the Cedarwood Manor Hotel. Maybe she was thinking up ways to do this very thing herself. Maybe, for the first time in her life, she would *love* Mia for doing it for her.

Mia stood there for a while after he stopped moving. The thick grey carpet was almost black now and she looked around in awe at the amount of blood that had come out of him. And so quickly. If only she could have been strong enough to do this before now. But of course, she didn't know she had a reason to before now. She dropped the knife beside him and left the room, pulling the door closed as she went. When she released the door handle, she saw the bloody handprint she'd left behind on it. She frowned and used the sleeve of her dress to clean it. When she was done, she pulled the sleeve back up and looked at her hands. His blood was already drying into them, so she went straight to the bathroom to wash it off. She didn't like having his blood on her. It might seep in through her skin and taint her somehow. She scrubbed them five times with soap and once she was satisfied that they were clean, she found herself cleaning the bathroom sink out of habit. She stopped as soon as she realised what she was doing and smiled a little. There was so much freedom in that. Being able to stop. She dried her hands and went back to Mammy's room.

She didn't waste any more time looking around. She went straight to the wardrobe and changed her clothes. Hers had blood on them. She put on a warm Aran jumper and some black stretchy pants belonging to Mammy. She had to pull the pants up as far as her chest and roll the waist several times. Then she started rummaging. Shoeboxes, handbags, drawers, cupboards; everything had papers in them, but nothing that Mia could make sense of. She didn't care enough to try either. She was looking for the white envelope with the scratchy writing on it. Then she found it. Or rather, one very like it. The same scratchy writing, but on a different envelope. *Lots* of different envelopes. When she pulled all the hangers right to the end, she found a biscuit tin on a shelf, tucked right in the back. In it was a whole bundle of handwritten letters. She picked one up at random.

Dear Missus Kelly,

I don't know if you've been getting my letters, because I didn't never get nothing back from you. I have my own room in a shared house now and it can fit me and my little girl in it. It's just that, I think I made a mistake. I know you have more money than me and you can give her loads more than me. But I was thinking, I didn't have a lot when I was growing up. And the more I think about that, the more I think, it doesn't really matter. I was still a happy enough girl most of the time. I think if I just love her enough, then she can be happy too. With me, I mean. Can you please let me have her back? I did come the other day, but your gate is locked and I think the code has changed since I was there. I couldn't get inside and I don't think you were at home.

I miss my little girl, Missus Kelly. Please? Give her back.

Yours,

Kate

Mia checked the date at the top. Seven years ago. She flicked through all the envelopes, checking the dates. Some were as old as eight years, while the most recent one was less than six months ago. She dropped the one in her hand and opened the most recent one next. That's the one that would tell her where her mother was right now.

'I'm coming, Mammy,' she muttered, pulling the single page out of the envelope. The writing this time was very different to the last letter she'd read. Mia picked the other one up again and held them side by side to compare. It was kind of the same, but even more scratchy. This time the writing was slanting off the page. It was a mess.

Erica

You promised you'd tell her about me and how much I love her.
If you told her all that, then why would she say she never wants
to see me again? Why would she be so cruel and say all the things
you used to say to me when I worked in your house. I might be
stupid. My baby might think I'm a stupid mother and I bet that's
what you've been telling her. But I still know how I feel. I gave
her to you coz you promised you'd mind her better than me.
That's the only reason, but you never told her that. I know you
didn't. You knew the guards would never believe me because of
the drugs and you was right. I am stupid. Have you been telling
my baby that she's stupid, too? You heartless bitch.

I shouldn't never have gave her to you. Without her, there's no
point in anything. I can't go on anymore without my baby. Tell
her I love her. Tell her I always loved her. Tell her I'll be her
angel now and I'll always mind her. Tell my baby goodbye.
Please. Do that one last thing with honesty in your heart, Missus
Kelly.

Kate

Mia squeezed the paper to her chest and screamed, as every feeling that had abandoned her tonight returned with a vengeance. She scooped up the bundle of letters. Holding them close, she cried more fiercely than she ever had in her life.

She stayed there, crumpled on the floor until she was spent. Each letter she pulled from the pile was meek and begging, asking how Mia was, asking if she could see her, asking if she'd been missing her. Some were unbelievable responses to things she could only imagine Mammy saying. *What do you mean she doesn't want to see me ever again? Don't break my heart, Missus Kelly.* And, *But why would she want me to stop writing?* One letter even asked Mammy to stop sending money. She didn't want the money. She wanted her daughter. Her *baby*. That's what she called her in every letter. Mia spent her life thinking no one wanted her. But here was a woman who was desperate to be with her. So desperate that she killed herself thinking it might somehow bring them together. Mia stopped crying and read the words again. *I'll be her angel now and I'll always mind her.*

'It was you,' she whispered. Her mother had brought those nuts to her. She hugged the letter to her chest. 'Thank you, Mammy.' She smiled. 'Thank you.'

THIRTY-ONE

JUNE

It was not yet seven in the morning when June let herself out of the groundskeeper's shed. He didn't start work until nine, but June would be long gone before he, or anyone else, turned up. He'd find no evidence that she was ever there. But after a night spent on a concrete floor beside a ride-on lawn mower, she desperately needed a shower. She figured she had at least fifteen, maybe twenty minutes before Liz turned up and the night staff were getting ready to leave.

She locked up the building, which looked more like a quaint cabin than a gardener's shed. With her black holdall on her shoulder and a hotel blanket rolled up under her arm, she walked around the back of the hotel and in through the staff entrance. She moved quickly towards the laundry room. It was still dark and sleepy. Heather hadn't arrived yet.

The so-called *hidden door* wasn't really hidden at all. It just blended in with the wall, just like the doors to the secret staircase and the passages behind the walls. Up until recently, this door hadn't been opened in years. It led to the junk room. That was where all the broken stuff went to be forgotten. There was a dismantled washing machine, several broken chairs, an old bed, some mattresses and a huge number of odds and ends. It was essentially a dumping ground, but it hadn't been used since three maintenance managers ago. A few hundred years before that, back when the Cedarwood Manor was a private home, it used to be the kitchen. It would have been a perfect place for June to spend a few nights now. But she wouldn't. The last thing she wanted to do was draw attention to this room. Not now.

There was a huge open fireplace in there, which once would have heated the whole place. Now it was full of black bags and other junk. There was a big old aga against the wall beside it, which, June figured out some time ago, still worked. She'd been filling it with long burning woodchips and lighting it on and off over the past few months. She lit it again while Heather was making lunch yesterday. She did this for several reasons. Firstly, to see if it worked. And secondly, to see whether or not anyone would notice. It did. And they didn't. Most of the staff didn't even know about this room and those who did, had more or less forgotten it was there. The extra door in the laundry room was just one more thing that had become invisible over the years. But June had the key. She let herself in and went over to the aga. A small bundle of supplies that she'd gathered sat on an old table beside it. She added a plastic-wrapped package to it. Now everything she'd need was there. She opened the hatch and dropped in another bag of wood chips. She stoked the flames and found herself smiling as they warmed her face. But she wouldn't allow herself the time to get comfortable. If she was seen coming out of this room, then it would cease to be invisible. And that would ruin everything.

She left as quietly as she'd entered and locked the door behind her. Then she went to the locker room. When she got there, she walked all around the bank of lockers, to make sure she was alone. She was. She shoved the blanket into an empty locker and locked it. Then she found another one, at the other side of the room, for her holdall. On a rail against one wall, their uniforms, laundered, starched and pressed, hung in bags with their names on them. As they did every morning. June took hers along to the shower room, as well as her own towel and toiletries. Under normal circumstances, she'd never shower at work. There were too many opportunities for someone to walk in on her, accidentally or otherwise. The last thing she needed was for her mess of a body to become fodder for hotel gossip. So, she washed as quickly as she could, and she was out of the shower again and drying off in less than five minutes. It was only when she was packing her bar of soap, wrapped in a face-cloth, back into her wash bag, that she noticed yet another piece of paper which had been deposited in there. This time it was wrapped around her deodorant stick.

She slapped the bag down on the sink and yanked the note out. She wasn't afraid of it this time. She was done being afraid. She opened it up and read it there and then.

I know what you're doing.
I'm watching you.
Killer.

June blinked slowly as she scrunched the note into a tight ball. She put it in the pocket of her waistcoat and walked calmly out of the shower room.

Freshly washed and folded into her new uniform, she made her way to the staff canteen. June popped two slices of white bread in the toaster and switched on the kettle. Her neck ached a bit from her night on the floor, but otherwise this felt like a bit of a treat. Toast for breakfast. She and Tess always had corn-flakes. Or sometimes Weetabix. Not the real cornflakes or

Weetabix obviously, but the affordable versions of them. Bread was usually kept in the freezer and used only for their weekend toasted sandwiches. June couldn't remember the last time she'd eaten a lunch that didn't consist of toasted bread and melted cheese.

While she waited for her breakfast, she sat down at the scratched old table and took a moment to enjoy the silence. The Manor made its own sounds, of course, letting her know that she wasn't alone. That it was there, ready to protect her when she needed it to. She listened and smiled and felt completely at peace. It was Friday morning. She had a busy weekend ahead, but for now she was happy just to live in the moment. And relish it.

'Oh.' Liz stopped suddenly as she came through the door. She looked a little disappointed and June knew that it was because she, too, liked to have the Manor to herself in the mornings. 'You're early.'

'Morning. Yeah, I woke up early. No point in lying there, so I came in.'

Liz went and switched on the kettle.

'It just boiled.'

'Oh, thanks.' She put two scoops of instant coffee into a mug, then turned to look at June. 'You want one?'

June's toast popped and she stood up. 'That's okay. I'll look after myself.' It would have felt too weird to have her boss serving her coffee. 'Have we a lot of check-ins today?' June knew they did. Mr Lovell was checking in as well as Mr Morrisson. Two VIPs and another honeymoon couple. Those were the ones she knew for sure.

Liz didn't answer. She was rubbing her forehead roughly with one hand, while she poured boiling water onto her coffee granules with the other. She looked stressed.

'Are you okay?' June asked. She didn't mention having seen

her with Malcolm. Or knowing the game she was playing
with him.

'Guess who arrived here unannounced last night?'

June turned to look at her. Surely not.

'She checked in after eight pm. She only rang through to
Rita at six to say that she was coming. Not to *ask* if we had a
free room, but to *tell* her that she was coming, and that room
208 was to be ready for her.'

June pursed her lips. 'That's unexpected.'

Erica Kelly was back. She wanted to ask if she'd bumped
into Malcolm during his shift, but she could tell by Liz's face
that she was already asking herself that very thing. It seemed
everyone's plans were accelerating suddenly.

'Is it *really* unexpected, though?'

June took a bite of her toast and waited for her to continue.

'She's here to make a point. She wants me to know that she's
coming for me.'

'Maybe she's here to tell you the deal is done? That the time
is now.'

'Let her bloody well try,' Liz snarled into her cup.

'Well, then.' June put the last bite of toast in her mouth. She
chewed it slowly and swallowed, then stood up. 'Let's give her
nothing to say.'

'You still have ten minutes,' Liz said, looking at her watch.
'And a second slice of toast. Don't let her fluster you, June.'

June raised her eyebrows and smiled at the irony of that.
She patted her belly and gave half a smile. 'I'm full. Besides, I
like to load up before the others arrive.'

'Can't say I blame you there.'

'I don't think she'll win this time, Liz. Mrs Kelly, I mean.'

'What makes you so sure?'

June shrugged. 'From the little things you told me over the
years. Isabelle Levy took you on as a girl, didn't she?'

Liz stiffened and her face flushed red. Most of the personal details divulged by Liz over the years were given in moments of weakness. Or those moments when June was the invisible non-person who just happened to be in the room when her thoughts came spilling out.

'I mean, I was hardly a *girl*. I was eighteen. But yes, I suppose she did.'

June nodded. 'I've only met Mrs Levy a handful of times, but I could always see her affection for you. She thinks of you like a daughter. She won't do this to you.'

Liz sniffed and turned to face the kitchen sink. 'Yeah, well, time will tell.'

'Or... I suppose they *do* say money talks. But maybe Mrs Kelly will back down when she realises that you won't be pushed around,' June added, like an afterthought.

Liz half turned her head.

'You need to let her know that, Liz.' June's voice was low. 'You need to let her know that this is *your* home. She already has one.'

A short silence grew between them, before June exhaled and brought the smile back into her voice. 'Anyway, I'll go load up. Have a good day, Liz.'

Liz stood with her back to June and both palms flat on the countertop. Her shoulders were squared, and her head was down. She didn't respond.

June was loaded up and gone from the storeroom before the other two maids arrived. The day was off to a very good start and by the time she got to the lobby, Malcolm was finishing up his shift. He was usually long gone before she got there, but now he was talking to Rita, the night receptionist. She was also ready to go home after an eventful night, no doubt. Rita looked like someone's nanna, and as such, it was strange for Malcolm to pass the time of day with her. That's why June decided to stand facing them while she slowly cleaned the lobby table.

When he'd got whatever information he needed from her, Malcolm rapped his knuckles on the reception desk, indicating that he was done with Rita. Then he pulled his backpack onto one shoulder and walked towards the main entrance, passing June as if she wasn't there.

June left the table for now and went to start on the reception desk.

'Good morning, June.' Rita smiled, glancing at the clock. Lauren was five minutes late.

'Morning, Rita. Busy night?'

'You could say that. Mrs Kelly decided to just stroll in the door, as if we were some roadside B and B. She was already on her way when she called to book. Now, June' – she leaned forward, her elbows on the high desk – 'I know how good you are at your job. But it was the way she said, *have my room ready when I get there.*' She mimicked Mrs Kelly and June smiled. It sounded very strange coming from nanna Rita. 'I have to say, I felt a bit threatened. So, I grabbed a cleaning bucket myself and ran up to give the place a quick once-over.' She looked aghast. 'She has that kind of a way about her, doesn't she? I mean, she only has to say hello, and that's the bejesus scared right out of me. It's an awful way to be, isn't it?'

June raised her eyebrows and nodded, while she polished the wood around her.

'She says jump! And we all shout, how high? Ah! Here's Lauren now.' She smiled, looking towards the lifts. She turned to June again. 'Malcolm seemed a bit jumpy about her arrival.' She arched one eyebrow and grinned. 'The shine must have worn off.'

'Oh, yeah?' June offered. 'Did she say how long she plans to stay?'

'Monday. But who knows with her.' Rita stepped back from the desk as Lauren came around it.

'I must say, that whole thing caught me off guard. I mean, she's a woman of my own vintage. What's she doing with a fella like him?'

'What's he doing with a yoke like her?' Lauren joined the conversation. 'Oh, wait!' She smiled a sarcastic smile and waved her arms around at the Manor.

It seemed they were all done pretending.

' I'm pretty sure he dumped her,' Lauren said, coming to stand primly on the spot that Rita was vacating. 'Or at least, he's pretending he did.'

'What makes you say that?' Rita asked.

Lauren shrugged. 'I hear things. And what I hear is that he fancies that big leather, bouncy chair in Liz's office, more than he fancies either of those women. And one of them is his ticket into it. I hope he knows what he's getting into.'

'Right. Well, on that happy note, I'm off home.'

'I heard her son killed someone,' Lauren whispered.

Rita stopped and turned back to her. 'You shouldn't listen to rumours, Lauren.'

Lauren shrugged. 'I'm just saying what I heard.'

Rita lowered her bag and looked around. Then in little more than a whisper, she said, 'It wasn't her son. I believe her whole family was wiped out when she was young. They were all killed.' Then she dramatically mouthed the words *murder, suicide*.

Lauren looked at her. 'And you tell *me* not to listen to rumours.'

June said nothing as she continued with her polishing.

'Right. Now I really am going home. Have a good day, ladies.'

'You, too,' June replied to a departing Rita. She glanced at Lauren and continued polishing. Keeping her voice low and conspiratorial she leaned a little towards her. 'I don't know about you, but I can't see Liz letting Mrs Kelly push her out,' she said, to stir Lauren's cauldron. 'I think she's been making her feelings on that pretty clear, hasn't she?'

'Oh, she's like a demon about it! What's she gonna do, though? That's what I'd like to know.' Lauren took up her spot and smiled serenely, like the pleasant receptionist she pretended very well to be.

THIRTY-TWO

MIA

As well as the Aran jumper, which was down to her knees, and the rolled-up black pants, Mia also took a small bundle of cash that she found in the drawer of Mammy's bedside table. But it didn't occur to her to go through the rest of the house. If she had, then she might have found enough cash and jewellery to live off for several years. Instead, she left her bloody brown dress on Mammy's bedroom floor and went back downstairs. She glanced into the sitting room, to make sure Daddy was still where she'd left him. That he really was dead. He was. She glanced around one last time, then she opened the front door and set off. She half ran down the long, dark, tree-lined drive-way, towards the electric gates at the end. She used his remote to open them, just enough that she could walk out. Then she closed them again behind her, sealing them both inside. It was about another half mile to the main road and by the time she got there, her body felt so much weaker, and her legs were threatening to go from under her.

Mia didn't know much about adrenaline. She didn't know that its abandonment was what left her feeling so washed up just then. But even if she had, there was nothing she could do about it. She had to keep moving. But where would she go? Which direction should she take?

She stood at the turn off to their house and looked left, right and straight ahead. On either side of her was just a long, straight country road. It was tree-lined on the left, behind which was their property. On the right, there were miles and miles of open fields and some kind of mountain shooting up towards the night sky. It was pitch dark and there were no lights on the road, but her eyes had adjusted to the darkness. She could see as far as the half-moon shone. She glanced back in the direction she'd come from and thought briefly about going back until morning. Her life there had felt completely normal until the revelations about her real mother. Could she stay there for one more night with those two? They *were* dead, so it's not like they could hurt her. She could sleep in any room she wanted, except Kevin's. She could watch TV and eat anything she liked.

She shook her head and rolled the sleeves of Mammy's jumper up over her hands. She could smell her on it suddenly and she wanted to rip the jumper off. But it was too cold. She didn't know what to do. Should she go left, or right? How far would she need to walk before reaching... somewhere? She looked at the Cedarwood Manor brochure in her hand, but she couldn't make out the writing on it now. Which road would take her there? She cried then out of frustration and started walking. Left.

She'd only been going that way for a few minutes when a flood of light came from behind her. A car was coming. She stumbled to get out of its way, scared that they'd see her, while also scared that they wouldn't. She twisted her ankle on the verge and fell awkwardly into a gully.

The car passed by, then it slowed down and stopped just up ahead. A woman got out, leaving the car door open and the engine idling, and came running back.

'Dear God! Are you alright?' She came right up to Mia and crouched down to help her.

Mia looked up, her eyes wide. She nodded, not knowing what else to do. She knew she should be frightened now. What if this woman brought her back and found Daddy and Kevin? What if she brought her to the police? What if she kidnapped her? But Mia didn't feel frightened. She wasn't worried about any of those things. She'd already decided that jail would not be a problem. It would be just like her old life, only without all the liars. That's how she thought of it now. Her *old* life and that made her feel happy. Plus, if this woman kidnapped her, Mia now knew how to escape. So, no. She wasn't afraid. But she could see the concern on the woman's face and Mia knew exactly what she looked like. She was a skinny, freckle-faced ten-year-old girl. Maybe she was dumb as well. Or maybe they were more lies that they'd told her. Either way, the woman looked like she might be from one of the good news stories she'd read in the newspapers over the years.

'I'm frightened,' she said, in a soft voice that suited her physical appearance perfectly.

'Where's your mother? Or your father? What's a little girl like you doing somewhere like this, all alone?'

Mia made herself cry a little harder then. 'Please don't take me back there. Please?'

In the moonlight, Mia could see the woman's face change. Fear and maybe fury replaced the concern that had been there. Her mouth turned down and she looked all around her. Up and down the road.

'Okay.' She caught Mia by the arms and pulled her up.

But Mia couldn't put her foot under her. She'd twisted her ankle and now it sent pain shooting up through her leg when she tried to stand.

'Here.' The woman pulled Mia's arm around her shoulder. 'Come with me. I'll mind you.' She hunched to Mia's height and walked towards the car, with Mia hopping along, hanging off her shoulder.

Her car was an ancient, yellow banger with white smoke and strong fumes billowing out the exhaust as it sat abandoned in the road with its engine running. She opened the passenger side door and slotted Mia in. Inside the car was very clean, but it looked nothing like the inside of Mammy's car. It was very old-fashioned. The woman got in beside her, but instead of driving away, she turned in her seat to face Mia.

'Okay. Before I just drive away with you, I need to know that I'm not kidnapping a young girl.'

Mia twisted her fingers around each other, her breathing slow and steady. Her mind felt clearer than it ever had. She thought of all the headlines she'd read over the years, and she knew exactly what to say. The truth. Or at least, a version of it.

'My real mother is dead,' she said quietly, into her lap. 'I've been living with a family who... well' – she took a deep breath – 'they hurt me. The mother... she lets them do it. Please don't send me back.'

The woman turned in her seat again. She gripped the steering wheel with her two hands and stared straight ahead. Her knuckles were glowing white, and she looked like she was concentrating hard on her driving. But the car didn't move.

'I can take you to the police.'

Mia nodded, her lip quivering. 'Will they bring me back to them?'

She shook her head, but her face was deathly serious. 'They'll investigate it.'

'And what will they do with me?'

'They'll call social services.' She was still staring straight ahead.

'What does that mean?'

'You'll go in the system.' Her voice was lower now.

'What does that mean?' Mia asked again, looking at the woman.

'How old are you?'

'Ten.'

'Hard to place,' she half whispered, more to herself than to Mia.

'Are people kind in the system?' she asked, craning her head to see the woman's face. She was talking about the foster care system. Mia had read about it many times and none of them had been good news stories.

The woman didn't answer for a while, but eventually she shoved the gear stick forward and the car made a loud grinding noise. They bounced out onto the road and drove away.

'Why don't we think about all that tomorrow when we're a bit fresher?' she said after a while. 'You can stay with me tonight.'

Mia sat back in her seat and looked out her window at the passing treeline. Knowing what was beyond those trees, hidden from the rest of the world, she couldn't help letting a small smile play on her lips. Wait until Mammy found out what she'd done.

They drove in silence for ten minutes, with the woman checking her mirrors the whole time, like she expected to see someone coming up behind her. But before they could reach anywhere that might have been somewhere, she turned onto a small, tree-lined road that just kind of faded away after a while. Then they bumped and rocked their way upwards until they came to a single old house. There was nothing else for miles around, except the mountain that grew up behind it and the forest below. It looked like an old farmhouse, but there was no actual farm that Mia could see. Just a few chickens behind some wire at the side of the house. Mia couldn't help feeling a twinge of frustration. This was too close to *their* house. And just as isolated. Her new life was not here.

'Come inside,' the woman said. 'I'll take a look at that ankle.' She got out of the car and went around the bonnet. She opened Mia's door and as she helped her out, she threw Mia's arm over her shoulder again. The pair hobbled towards the old and crooked-looking front door.

Inside the house was drab and dark, but it was warm, and it smelled nice. Like something might have been baking before they got there. There was a big range in the kitchen, which was where the heat and the smell were coming from. They had one of those, but theirs was shiny and cream and modern. Hers was black and looked as old as the house itself. Mia liked this one better and she felt herself relaxing slightly. It was still very much on her mind that once again, she was in the middle of nowhere, tucked away from the rest of the world. But here was different. There were no fences or high walls. No locked gates. Regardless of everything, Mia needed to rest.

'Are you hungry?'

She thought of the éclair abandoned on the sitting room floor and her stomach turned. She shook her head.

The woman nodded and hunkered down. 'May I?' She pointed to the leg of Mia's pants.

'Okay,' she mumbled, a little unsure.

She gently rolled up the trousers and peeled off Mia's thick wool sock. Her cold fingers felt their way gently around her foot and ankle. 'Does this hurt?' She put a little bit more pressure on with the tips of her fingers.

Mia shook her head.

She leaned in and studied her ankle. 'I don't think it's too badly injured. Maybe just a sprain. I'll get some ice.' She stood up and went to the small chest freezer beside the under-counter fridge. She pulled out a packet of frozen vegetables and wrapped them in a tea towel.

'You must be tired. Come with me,' she said, pressing the veggie pack against the tea towel and kind of mushing it around.

Mia followed her to a bedroom on the ground floor. There was a sharp chill in the air, and it hit them when she opened the door.

'Sorry. I only put the heat on in the rooms I normally use. But I have some spare blankets.' She went to a press in the hall and brought a bundle of neatly folded grey blankets back into the room with her. She spread them out on the old, metal-framed bed that already had a sheet and a pillow on it. The room was bleak, but Mia didn't consider that. It had a window overlooking whatever mountain was out there. That was already more than she was used to.

'Hop in.' She pulled back the sheet and blankets.

Mia got in, with the Aran jumper and pants still on. It was cold enough that she'd need them.

The woman tucked her in tightly. Then she placed the ice pack snugly around Mia's ankle and pressed the blankets around that. 'Leave that on for about twenty minutes. You can kick it off then, okay?'

Mia nodded.

'Would you like it if I read you a story?'

No one had ever tucked Mia into bed before. No one had ever read her a bedtime story either. Or maybe they had. Perhaps her real mother used to read them to her when she was a baby. Before *she* came and took her away. Either way, Mia found herself nodding. She wanted the experience of it. To know what it was like to have someone read to her while she fell asleep. She felt a flutter of something in her stomach then, when she thought about all the new experiences she might get to have. Or maybe there was just one more experience waiting. But this one was new, and she would take it with both hands.

'Okay.' The woman smiled. 'Wait there.' She got up and left the room and Mia watched her go.

It was hard to put an age on her, but she looked ancient to Mia. Her shoulder length hair was grey down to her ears and then black the rest of the way. She was tall and skinny and wore old lady clothes, an ankle length black skirt and black jumper. She seemed kind of jumpy. But then she did just find a ten-year-old on the side of the road. Imagine if she knew what the ten-year-old had done! She came back a minute later carrying a book that looked as old as she did. It had a dark cover with gold writing.

'Have you ever read this before?' She held the book up. 'It's *The Count of Monte Cristo.*'

Mia shook her head.

The woman looked at the book and smiled. 'I love this book. It's about a fella who was sent to a horrible prison for no good reason. But after years and years, and against all the odds, he managed to escape.'

Mia felt herself smiling. This sounded perfect. Suddenly she wanted nothing more than to hear this story. 'It looks like a really old book,' she said.

'Oh, it is.' The woman looked at the cover of the book again, turning it over in her hands. 'This book was given to me by my best friend when we were girls. Lorraine was her name. She wrote a little note for me on the inside, and would you believe, I haven't seen her since.' She hugged the book to her chest. 'It's very special to me.'

Mia pulled her arms out from under the blankets and shoved up her sleeves. She was warming up now.

'What's that you've got there?' the woman asked, nodding towards the brochure that Mia had tucked up inside her sleeve. She slid it out gently and looked at it, turning it over in her hand. 'The Cedarwood Manor Hotel? Very fancy.' She half smiled. 'Thinking of checking in?'

Mia took the brochure back. 'Mammy is staying there. I'm going to go stay with her tomorrow.'

The woman's smile faded. 'Oh.' Then she lowered her head to think. When she looked up again, she said, 'Did you come from the Kellys' farm?'

Mia looked at her sharply. The pair locked eyes for a minute, neither of them speaking. Then the woman said, 'I know them, but...' She looked away.

'Are you going to take me back?'

She shook her head. 'There's something about *him* that I don't like.'

Mia nodded, the small smile returning. But the woman didn't see it.

'So, Mrs Kelly is at the Cedarwood Manor?'

Mia nodded.

'And you *want* to go stay there with her?'

She nodded again.

'Will she be happy to see you?'

Mia didn't say anything.

'I suppose what I mean is, is she good to you – Erica?'

Mia shook her head, no.

She frowned and gave an imperceptible nod. 'But you're going anyway?'

'Yes.'

'What's your name?'

'Mia.'

The woman stayed quiet for a while and Mia could tell she'd become more uncomfortable. 'My name is Tess.' She exhaled loudly. 'Okay, then. Stay here with me tonight. Let's read this fantastic story and then tomorrow, I'll take you up to Cork. I'll get you to Erica at the Cedarwood Manor.'

Mia smiled and turned on her side, getting comfortable. The woman stared at the inside cover of the book for a long minute. 'I'll get you to her,' she said quietly. Then she turned the page and started reading.

THIRTY-THREE

JUNE

June woke early, having not really slept at all. It was still dark outside, and she was cramped and aching from another night spent on the shed floor. She didn't want to risk the much warmer junk room, with its abandoned mattresses and aga. As appealing as they were, she couldn't draw attention to that room. She sat up and stretched out her neck and shoulders. She took a moment to look around, glad that she was almost done with this place. The shed, that is. She was sure she'd miss the Manor. Her body ached like that of a much older woman, as she shuffled backwards so that she could lean against the wall. She pulled her holdall onto her lap and opened it up. Rooting all the way to the bottom, her fingers soon found what she was looking for: the padded brown envelope containing her life savings. She pulled it out and held it there in her lap. Looking at it now in the pre-dawn light made her think about the other brown envelope she'd left at home, with Tess. Or rather, the contents of that envelope.

June had forced Tess to write a letter. She could never have imagined forcing that woman to do anything before now and it didn't sit well with her. But Tess gave her no choice. She'd been telling her lie after lie after lie, all her life. June angrily wiped a single tear from her cheek. Just thinking about their last conversation was making her lose control of her emotions. But Tess didn't deserve her tears. Or rather, *Sister Bridget* didn't.

Even as she sat there, confronted by June and a box of vile memories, the woman was still convinced that she was right. That June somehow didn't understand. But she was wrong about that. June understood it perfectly. Erica Kelly had always been Tess's priority, despite knowing what kind of woman she'd become. She'd simply been grooming June since the night they met. Trying to mould her into another person. Someone who might forget about the life Erica Kelly had stolen from *her*, and instead help Tess to atone for the life *she* stole from Erica Kelly. The lives of Sister Bridget and Erica Kelly intertwined in a vicious circle of lies and deceit, with June at the very centre. She understood that perfectly. But that would no longer be the case.

It was Tess who produced the pill bottle. Temazepam, according to the label. But it was June who provided a glass of water big enough to wash the whole lot down. Tess had cried then. Perhaps the pills were only meant as a threat. She probably thought June would try to stop her. But June was done playing games. Clearly Tess agreed that she had a penance to pay, or she never would have introduced the idea of killing herself. But first, the letter. Sister Bridget lost the right to slip away quietly, when she set foot in that home and stirred up the lives of everyone she met.

June shoved a blank page and a pen towards her and instructed her to write. As she did so, June read and memorised every word, which was the habit of her lifetime.

To whoever finds me,

I am Sister Bridget of the Good Shepherd Sisters and I've chosen you to be the recipient of my confession. I am here because of Erica Kelly, whose mother was once my peer. That is, until she became my charge at one of the world's most notorious Mother and Baby Homes. She did not deserve to be there. None of those girls did. They did not deserve the wrath that we brought down upon them. That I brought down upon them. I will atone for every act of cruelty I bestowed upon those girls, when I meet my maker. He knows. There are so many. But to you I confess this much. Erica Kelly's mother died in my care, and I have been watching over Erica ever since. Despite going to a good home and having never known anything about me, or the home, I watched her become a cruel and vindictive woman. No different from the ones her mother was subjected to. I just can't watch anymore. I'm sorry, Erica. Your whole miserable life was my fault. Everything was my fault.

I am leaving this world of my own accord. As I go, I beg for the forgiveness of all those whose lives have been affected by me, and those like me.

Goodbye

Sister Bridget

As soon as she started writing, the realisation hit June. It was *her*. Tess was the one leaving notes for June. On top of everything else she'd put her through, Tess was threatening her as well. Trying to make her lose her mind. Trying to stop her from taking back everything that her precious Erica Kelly had stolen from her.

June's tears dried up and her blood started to boil again. Just like it had when she sat across the table from Tess, watching her writing her confession. A part of her wished she could have denied her the right to confess. But she needed it as much as Tess did.

She calmly watched Tess lower her pen and pick up a pill. She glanced up at June as she placed it gently on her tongue and washed it down. She followed it with another. Then another and another. June watched as she slowly worked her way through the bottle. She watched the woman's tears roll off the end of her nose and onto their table. She'd listened to her apologies and her pleas for forgiveness, but June never responded. And she never looked away. When the bottle was empty and Tess fell to the floor on the way to her room, June did not help her up. But she did stay there by her side. She silently watched the rise and fall of Tess's chest. She waited until her body rattled with her final breath and that's how Margaret Higgins left this world. Sister Bridget went screaming after her, while a forever young Tess Calloway waited somewhere in the wings to have her name back.

June placed Tess's letter on her chest. Just like she'd pinned a note to June's chest once. Then she cleared all traces of herself out of that flat before leaving it for the final time. Not that there was anyone to clear away traces of. June Calloway did not exist. Neither did Mia Kelly. No one knew what name her birth mother had actually given her, so therefore, June was a real-life invisible woman. She didn't exist *anywhere*.

She dressed in her black leggings and jumper and packed away her bedding. Before leaving the shed, she opened the padded envelope and looked inside. She'd slept with her head on it, to make sure it would all still be there when she woke. Not that anyone was likely to break in there, but still. She shoved it back down to the bottom of the bag and covered it over again with her clothes. She zipped it up and let herself out into the cold morning air. This was the last time she'd wake up on the frigid concrete floor of the groundskeeper's shed. And no one would ever know that she'd been there at all.

It was only six-thirty when she let herself in through the staff door. She showered and changed quickly, but before going for breakfast, she went in search of Malcolm Levy. She found him in the first place she looked. He was sitting in his control room, fast asleep in his chair.

She knocked on the door and he woke with a start. She pretended that she hadn't been watching him through the small glass panel in the door.

'Yeah?' he called out, too lazy to get up and let her in.

June went inside and let the door close behind her. This was the part she was least looking forward to. The only part of her plan that she couldn't fully predict.

'What can I do for the maid today?' he said with a grin.

'Can you please turn the cameras off before you leave tonight?' This was not an unusual request. She'd made it many times before, as had most other staff. Always for laundry in her case.

'Hmmm, I don't know, maid. What's it worth to you?'

June put her hand in the pocket of her waistcoat.

His grin widened. 'Actually, I'm feeling a little uptight this morning.' He leaned back in his seat and looped his fingers through his belt. 'I'm thinking twenty quid might not cover it. But you could work off the rest?'

June pulled a fifty out of her pocket. Twenty was the going rate, but while she really needed the cameras off, she was not planning on touching Malcolm Levy. Offering him over and above was a risk in itself, though. It reeked of opportunity for someone like him. It pained her to do it, but it was a risk she had to take.

He raised his eyebrows. 'Oh! Looks like you *really* want those cameras off, eh? Got a lot of dirty knickers to wash?'

'Will you turn them off?'

He took the fifty, stretched it out and held it up to the light. Then he folded it and slotted it into the top pocket of his shirt. He waved her away and swivelled his chair so that his back was turned to her.

She left his office and headed back to the basement and the staff canteen.

'Early again?' Liz asked.

June was just putting bread in the toaster. 'Can I make you some?' she asked.

Liz shook her head. 'White bread will do you no favours, June.' She switched on the kettle. 'I can't eat until eleven. I'm doing intermittent fasting.'

June nodded but had no idea what she was talking about. Liz was always on some kind of food restriction, whereas June loved every pound she'd gained over the years. Even their rationed lifestyle was enough to make her so much heavier than she was. She was such a scrawny child.

Liz sat down heavily in her chair. While June waited for her toast to pop, she poured one cup of coffee with two scoops for Liz and a tea for herself.

'She's selling,' Liz said, as June placed the cup in front of her.

June stopped with her hand still on the handle.

'Isabelle called me last night. She's selling to Mrs Kelly with the stipulation that I'm to be kept on as manager for at least two more years.'

'Oh... well, that's something,' June said, not knowing what else to say to the woman.

'That's nothing, June,' Liz spat back. 'What good is two years to me? It'll be two years of that woman lording it over me. And I'll be two years older when I'm trying to get another job.'

'And what happens after two years?'

'What do you think?'

'Malcolm becomes manager.' June buttered her toast slowly with her back to Liz. 'Mrs Kelly is a businesswoman, isn't she? Deep down she'll know you're the best person to run this place. Besides, she doesn't want to come here to work. She wants to come here to...'

'Make everyone's life a living hell. That's what she wants. And it won't matter to her that no one can take care of this place like I can. She's not buying it because she wants it. She's buying it because she can. And maybe because she's bored. She could have a monkey run the Manor into the ground, but it won't matter. So long as her room is well-kept and her every need is met, she won't care about anything else.'

June didn't say anything, though she thought Erica was buying it because she wanted out of her home. Isn't that what her solicitor was fighting for? She could live here as a kept woman. It probably had nothing at all to do with Liz, but none of that mattered. Not to June.

'Anyway, why are you eating breakfast and showering here every day? Did Malcolm evict you from your flat or something? Have you been paying your rent?'

'No, I haven't been evicted. And yes, I've been paying my rent.'

'So, what then? This isn't your home, June. This is a five-star hotel. I hope you're not planning on treating it like some kind of halfway house.'

'I had a falling out with my flatmate.'

'You have a flatmate?'

June bobbed her head from side to side. 'Not so much a flat-mate, but a guest. She's leaving today, so this will be the last time you'll see me in here.'

'It'd better be.' Liz picked up her cup and walked towards the door. 'You know what's funny?' She stopped with her hand on the door handle.

'What?'

'Them.' She turned to look at June. 'They actually think I'll walk away with my tail between my legs.' She shook her head, then walked out, letting the door close behind her.

As June worked her way through the second-floor rooms that morning, she stood with her ear to the door of room 208, listening before she went in.

'Housekeeping,' she called, and knocked on the door.

'Come!' came Mrs Kelly's brusque voice from inside.

She was sitting in the chair, reading a newspaper when June stepped inside. She looked just like she had that day in the good room. The day she reminded Mia about all the thinking that went into Daddy's peanut allergies.

'Good morning, Mrs Kelly,' she said quietly, not expecting a response and not planning on saying anything else. Erica Kelly didn't like people in the service industry speaking to her. But June did find herself staring when she wasn't looking. She couldn't help it. How could she never have recognised her? Did Mia mean so little to her, that she'd erased her from her memory?

'Is there something I can do for you?' she asked, sounding annoyed as she lowered the newspaper onto her lap and glared at June.

That's when June realised that she was staring and not actually doing anything else. 'No, Mrs Kelly.' She jumped back to life and hurried into the bathroom, where she started cleaning, slowly and deliberately.

'I want new sheets today.'

'No problem,' June called back.

'I remember when standards used to be high in this place,' she huffed.

June didn't answer her that time. She could hear her folding up her newspaper and slapping it down on the table. She moved around the room for a bit and then the door opened and slammed shut. She had gone out without so much as a goodbye. Not that June expected one.

'You'll have the cleanest room in the hotel today,' June answered the dead air she left behind.

It was getting dark by the time Liz got to her car, as June watched. She was alone again, meaning that Malcolm no longer felt the need to accompany her through the darkened car park. She looked upset as she slid into the driver's seat. Angry even. That was good.

Once her car pulled away, June got up and wiped herself down. Taking a small backpack with her, she let herself back in through the Manor's basement door, through the corridor and into the hidden stone staircase. She walked quietly up to the control room and peered through the spyhole. The bank of monitors was all lit up, but that was okay. Nine pm was the designated time for power off. She moved upwards, away from his door, and sat down on one of the steps.

She opened her bag and took out some of the hotel's complimentary biscuits and a book. She leaned back against the stone wall and held it there in her lap. She let her hand roam gently over the tattered old cover, which was barely hanging on. She opened it to the first page and read, for the millionth time, the inscription there.

My very best friend, Tessie Calloway.
Thank you for minding me.
You will go home, too, someday,
and when you do, live, Tessie.
If not for you, live for your daughter.
Live believing that you'll hold little June in your arms again.

I love you, Tessie.
Your friend, always
Lorraine xxx

June patiently waited for the hours to tick by and when nine o'clock came, she moved quietly back down the steps to the control room. She looked through the peephole again and saw the monitors go dark. There was no sign of Malcolm. He controlled those things from his phone and June was aware that he could be hiding somewhere himself now, looking out for her. Looking to see what she was up to. He always liked to have something new to hold over those beneath him. But she wasn't worried about Malcolm. He'd be loitering somewhere near the laundry, if he wasn't up to something else to benefit himself.

June headed upwards again and exited through a door that was hidden at the back of a store cupboard on the second floor. She stood with her ear to the closed door, listening. It was quiet. No one was around, but just in case, she was wearing her maid's uniform. She stepped out, with her backpack in her hand, and walked to room 208. She looked up and down the deserted hall again and knocked quietly on the door.

'Who is it?' Erica barked from inside. June knew that she'd be after taking her sleeping tablet by now and wouldn't want to be disturbed. She knew the woman's routine as well as she did herself.

'I have an important message for you, Mrs Kelly,' June said. She had her key card with her, but she hoped not to have to use it. It would show on the system and that would lead the police to June as quickly as the cameras would have.

'What in the name of God can be so important that you're...'
'It's about Mia.'

There was a long silence then and June knew she was probably frozen to the spot in there, wondering what the maid could possibly have to tell her about the child she'd stolen. The child who'd killed her husband and stepson all those years ago.

The door swung open. Before she had a chance to say anything, June stepped inside, pushing her backwards, which was easy to do because she wasn't expecting it.

June closed the door and locked it. 'Hi, Mammy.'

THIRTY-FOUR

JUNE

She was glaring at June now, a hint of fear creeping over the confusion on her face. She stepped backwards away from her.

'Sit down.'

'How dare you? I'm going to have your job for this.' She moved towards the phone, but June got there first. She grabbed it and pulled the cable out of the wall.

'I said, sit down.'

Erica stumbled backwards into the chair in the corner of the room. Her eyes went wide with fear. 'Wh... who are you?'

June smiled. 'Who am I indeed?'

June Calloway was long gone. It seemed they both knew that. The woman standing over the grandiose Erica Kelly was unfamiliar in every way. She didn't have the same gentle suburban accent that the maid had. This woman's eyes were colder and harder, and impossible to escape from. She stood far taller than June, and unlike June, this woman brought with her a kind of power that seemed to fill the room.

June stepped back from her chair and sat down on the corner of the bed. She placed her bag on the floor beside her feet. She opened it slowly, keeping her eyes on Erica and the small smile on her face. She'd waited so long for this. She reached in and took out a knife. A boning knife that she'd taken from the kitchen while the chef was visiting a table of businessmen at lunchtime. She had a fine choice down there, but this one seemed fitting. She stood up again and stepped forward calmly so she towered over her again. She put the sharp blade to Erica's throat, which quietened her immediately. Not that she'd been saying anything worth listening to. Just a series of *buts* and *I... I* and *what*.

There was a half-drunk glass of her expensive red wine on the table, like June knew there would be. She drank a lot of wine. The more she drank, the meaner she got. But June wasn't afraid of her. She hadn't been for a long, long time.

'Wh... what do you want?' she stammered.

June smiled. 'You really don't recognise me, do you?'

Erica was pinned as far back in the chair as she could go, shaking her head. Maybe it was to say no. Or maybe it was in disbelief. June didn't know, nor did she care. But she was enjoying it, nonetheless.

'Why would you, I suppose?'

'Who are you? What do you want?' Her voice wavered. June had never heard fear in this woman's voice before and she loved the sound of it. It made her stomach fizz and pop with delight.

'What do I want?' She casually tapped the blade of the knife against her own chin and looked to the ceiling, as if thinking. 'Hmmm, I know what I want.' She pointed it at Erica again. 'I want to tell you a story.'

Erica frowned in confusion.

'And boy, what a story it is!' She was smiling more brightly that she ever had now. 'But first, I have a little something for you.'

She went and reached in her bag again. This time she took out a little foil wrapper. She'd got more pills from Tess's stash and added them to Heather's, and she'd crushed them all up into powder. She suspected there was enough in there to knock out a horse, but she didn't know for sure. She supposed she'd find out soon enough.

'Let me just pop this in here.' Still with a pleasant smile on her face, she poured the fine dust into Erica's wine. Then she sat back on the corner of the bed, and loosely clasped her hands together around the knife, on her lap. 'So, this is a story about two girls. One was called Tess Calloway, and the other was June Calloway. Do you know who they are?'

Erica shook her head.

'Oh, good!' June said. 'You'll enjoy this so. Well, people around here have come to know *me* as June. Perhaps you have, too, so this might be a bit confusing. But do you know who June Calloway *actually* is?'

Erica didn't budge, but the fine silk of her Coco Chanel blouse was trembling. The buttons were open halfway down, so she must have been getting ready for bed.

'It's you, Erica! *You're* June Calloway.' June held her hands out with a delighted expression, like she'd just yelled *surprise* to an unwitting birthday girl.

Erica's eyebrows folded in confusion, but her fear kept her from asking questions.

June held her hands up in surrender, the knife held loosely in one. 'Okay, okay. You're confused. I get it. Let me explain.' She reached in her bag for a third time and pulled out the plastic-wrapped package. A brand-new boiler suit. There was a pile of them in the groundskeeper's shed, which was really handy.

Erica's eyes widened as June opened the plastic and started putting the suit on over her uniform.

'See, there was this girl called Tess Calloway. Now, apparently, she always wanted to be a nun when she was younger.' June rolled her eyes. 'But I don't know how true that part is. Anyway, didn't her father's friend only go and make her pregnant and then she was shipped off to a Mother and Baby Home up in Galway. You've heard of that place, haven't you?'

Erica didn't budge. She was frozen to the spot. This spurred June on even more. She'd waited her whole life for this moment, and she planned to make the most of it.

'Of course you have. Who hasn't, am I right? Now as everyone knows, those places were not kind to girls like Tess. She was beaten and all that kind of stuff.' She stood to zip up the boiler suit and then sat back down. Sitting on the corner of the bed, she was close enough to Erica's chair that she could reach out and touch her. 'Now, there was this nun there called Sister Bridget. A horrible thing, she was.' June shook her head and frowned. But she felt her own anger bubble up at the thought of her. 'She delivered Tess's baby into the world in a very painful way, apparently.' She paused to calm herself. 'Tess died, of course. And then this Sister Bridget took the child away and handed it over to its new family.' She looked away and rolled her hand around the details. 'They paid for her, as far as I know. Are you with me so far?'

Erica was glaring at her now, but it was clear she had no idea where this was going. June wondered if she'd ever been told that she was adopted. Or bought. Whatever the case may be. She took so much pleasure in telling Mia every chance she got.

'I asked you a question. Are. You. With. Me?' She pointed the tip of the knife from herself to Erica and back again. Everything about her demeanour was casual, like she was chatting to a friend over a cup of tea. Aside from the boiler suit and the knife.

Erica nodded, her ridiculous hair bouncing on her head.

'Good. So, June was the name that Tess had picked out for her child. June Calloway. She told her best friend, Lorraine, that. Lorraine inscribed it in a book that she gave to Tess and voila! That's how we all know the name June

Calloway. The most misused name in the whole world.' She stroked the long, sharp blade of the knife absentmindedly. '*The Count of Monte Cristo*. That was the book. Did you ever read it?'

No movement from Erica.

June pointed the knife at her. 'I asked you another question. Did you ever read *The Count of Monte Cristo*?' Her voice rose slightly, and she frowned deeply. 'I'm sorry, have you gone deaf or something?' She smiled then. 'Or are you just stupid?' She leaned in closer and said, in a stage whisper, 'We don't really call people that anymore. In case you didn't know. But if the shoe fits, eh?'

Erica shook her head more rapidly this time. She looked like she might wee herself.

'Is that a no, to *The Count of Monte Cristo*?'

Erica nodded rapidly.

'Yes? Is that yes, you did read it, or yes, you didn't?' June was still smiling because she couldn't help it.

'I never read it.' Her voice had shrivelled up and was almost gone.

'Oh. Well, you should have. It's very good. It kind of reminds me of my childhood, you know?' She sighed. 'Anyway, back to the story. The child didn't get to be called June, like her mother wanted. Her *new* mother called her Erica instead.'

Erica's whole body shook, and she started to cry. They were silent tears, but her face contorted in such a way that she became almost unrecognisable.

'You're a very ugly crier.' June smiled. 'Did you know any of that?' She giggled a bit. 'Not the bit about being an ugly crier. I'm sure you knew that. I mean the bit about where you came from? That your grandfather's friend is your father? Did you know that you were bought and paid for? That your mother went through such awful things for you?' June frowned then as a thought occurred to her. 'I wonder what she would think if she knew that you grew up to be exactly like Bridget, sister of Satan?'

Erica looked sharply at her. June shrugged and returned her attention to the blade of her knife. Not so long ago, she would have felt an overwhelming urge to use that blade on herself. But that urge seemed to have vanished. It was like learning the truth of her life and slicing her wrists open had released all the pain inside her. Her old blood was replaced with new, and she felt the better of it all.

'I suppose that brings us to me, doesn't it?' She glanced up at the woman. She took a moment then to drink in the uncomfortable sight of her.

Her shaking stopped as suddenly as it started, but her face was a blotchy mess.

'Do you still not know who I am? Really?'

'I...' She shook her head in desperation.

June nodded. 'I've changed a lot, I know. See, when I left your house that night, I was found by...' She laughed then and shook her head. 'Of all people, it was Sister Bridget! Pretending to be Tess Calloway! Can you believe it? I mean, what are the chances?' She held her arms out wide. 'Actually, chances were good, as it turned out. Sister Bridget stayed very close to you all your life. I'll bet you didn't know that either.'

Erica looked confused again.

June pointed at her expression. 'Exactly!' she said. 'Turns out, no one in this bloody story is who they say they are!'

'But...' Erica shook her head, her eyes darting all around her. She was trying to make sense of any of it.

'Yeah. Turns out, old Sister Bridget felt so guilty about Tess, seeing as they'd been friends as kids or whatever, that she ran away from the nuns that night and spent the rest of her life keeping tabs on you! Can you believe that? She was making sure you were alright after killing your mother.' She laughed again. 'Wow. Saying all this out loud makes it sound like an episode of *Scooby-Doo*, doesn't it? You know the bit where they pull off the mask and they all gasp, because it was old Mister Withers from the fairground, the whole time!' She laughed a little louder. 'I loved *Scooby-Doo*.'

It was so worth waiting all these years for this. She knew now that she could never have done it this well at the age of ten.

'Did you know that she lived in that old farmhouse a mile down the road from your house? The one up on the mountain.'

Erica looked at her again. 'Tessie?' she whispered.

June pointed to her in triumph. 'Tessie. Yes! That's what Lorraine called her in her book. Little old Tessie. There you go! Are you seeing it now?'

She started crying again. 'Mia?' she asked, in a blubbery whisper.

'Bingo!' June pointed the knife at her this time.

'But... you...' She looked her up and down.

'Yes! I'm fatter.' She nodded enthusiastically. 'I eat absolutely everything that's given to me. I have short brown hair and look' – she cupped her breasts – 'I have boobs! I even have these.' With the knife still in her hand, she removed one of the brown contact lenses she'd been wearing every day for the past six years. 'All Tess's idea, would you believe! Or should I say, Sister Bridget's.'

June glanced at her reflection in the mirror opposite her. She hardly recognised herself, sitting there in the boiler suit with one brown eye and one green.

'She was getting a bit old to be chasing you around the place, you see. So, she thought she could use me to keep an eye on you instead.' June guffawed. 'She fixed me up, moved us up here, and helped me get the job here when I turned sixteen. She thought maybe I could be your confidante or something.' She laughed a little louder then. 'Well, that was just silly on all counts, wasn't it?' She stopped laughing then and leaned forward, resting her elbows on her knees. 'I wanted to come and see you that night. You were here then, too, weren't you?'

'You killed them,' she said, in a disbelieving whisper.

'I sent them away.' She bobbed the knife in front of her face, still grinning. 'And don't pretend you weren't glad that I did. You let everyone think that Kevin killed *him* and then killed himself. I read all about it.'

She shook her head. 'They came to that conclusion by themselves.'

'Oh, I think they had a little help. They didn't find my blood-soaked dress on your bedroom floor, did they? And I'm sure that wasn't all the evidence I left behind. I was only ten, after all. But they didn't seem to think they had a reason to look.'

They silently watched each other then. Erica's mind was racing, while June just drank her in.

'Of course, if they had found me... it would have raised a lot of questions for you, wouldn't it?'

Erica's face changed then and something like hope crept into her eyes. 'They were piggish men, Mia. I know what he was planning for you. Just like he groomed your mother, he was grooming you, too. Of course, that wasn't a word back then. *Grooming.* Did you know she was only just eighteen when he... and as for Kevin.' Her mouth turned down in disgust.

'Nope. I actually thought he'd decided to become my father there for a minute. But no. He was just doing the same thing you were. Using me to hurt you. And you used me to hurt him, and my mother, of course. I'm a professional hurter.' She half smiled at the look on the woman's face. 'That's what you made me. But what if he *had* done the same thing to me? What would you have done? Would you have taken my baby away? Would you have made *her* work day and night for you as well? Would you have told her every day how stupid she was? That she was retarded?' She looked to the floor then. 'What does that even mean?'

'I took no pleasure in that! I just... I... I knew no better.'

'I'm sorry, what?'

She was gripping the arms of the chair so tightly, that her knuckles were snow white.

'According to Tess, you were spoiled rotten by the couple who bought you.'

Erica looked down at her lap and cried some more.

'No answer for that, eh?'

'I took care of you better than your own mother could have. She was just a child herself. She was on drugs and... I educated you, I...'

'Oh! Did you send me to school? I must have forgotten that.'

'Homeschooling was the best thing for a girl of your...'

'Homeschooling?'

'I... I taught you a lot, Mia... I...'

'Oh, you taught me plenty. I read newspapers. That was my education. The rest I suppose you'd call home economics or something?'

Her blotchy face was destroyed from all the tears mixing with her make-up. 'He made me that way, Mia. Evan. He was awful to me. I knew no different when it came to rearing children—'

'Yeah, well.' June cut her off. 'You're about to make it all up to me.'

Erica's eyes widened. There was that hope again. 'What do you want?'

'Well, it's about what *you* want now.' She stood up and walked around the room, just to stretch her legs. And stretch out the moment. When she sat back down, she reached in her bag again. This time she took out her mobile phone. June's phone didn't have much by way of technology. But it did have the ability to record voice notes.

'I'm going to give you two choices.'

Erica started crying again. It seemed her hope was fading.

'You can let the world know that I, Mia Kelly, *did* exist. That I was a real child and that somebody cared about me.'

'But, Mia, I....'

'And somebody *did* care about me, *Erica*.' She spat the woman's name at her. 'My mother cared.'

'She...' She shook her head again, but June held her palm up to stop her.

'That's your first choice.'

She closed her mouth.

'Option two is that I can do to you what I did to Kevin.' She mimicked slicing her own, still-bandaged wrists and then stuck her tongue out and crossed her eyes in a childish death face. 'So, what's it to be, Mammy?'

THIRTY-FIVE

JUNE

'I'll do whatever you say.'

'I know you will.'

June reached in her bag again. She found the neatly folded sheet of paper, that she'd taken from the photocopying machine at reception earlier that day. She opened it up and held it in front of Erica.

'When I tell you, you're going to say exactly what's on this piece of paper. You will sound panicked and afraid. The less convincing you sound, the smaller your chance of survival will be. Do this, as if it was a very real thing, and I promise, you'll be long gone before they get here.'

Her eyes were moving as she read what June had written in clear capital letters. There was that look of panic again.

'I'm going to press record now.' June held the page closer to Erica's face and pressed record on her mobile phone.

Erica said nothing. She just stared at June.

She stopped the recording and let her hands go limp. Like a teenager who didn't get her way.

'You don't understand.' June stood up and went and sat on

the arm of her chair. 'Do it, or I'll kill you.' She pressed the knife against her neck again.

'Oh... okay... okay,' she cried.

And just like that, June had an idea. She pressed record and put a little bit more pressure on the knife against her throat. She started reading and she sounded perfect.

Hello? My daughter is missing!
I'm at the Cedarwood Manor Hotel and she was here with me.
She was right here! We both went to bed at ten o'clock and I
woke up and she was gone.

June smiled brightly. She sounded terrified. It was perfect.

Her name is Mia Kelly and she's only ten years old.
She has long, red hair and green eyes. She was wearing a white
jumper and black leggings. Her mother loves her so much!
Please help me!
Please find her!

June stopped the recording and lowered the knife. 'Well done. That was very good.'

'Please?' she said then. 'Please don't hurt me.'

'Did you like how I added the bit about my mother loving me?'

'Please, Mia.'

'I know it might sound strange when they listen back to the call. But I just wanted to hear one truth coming out of your mouth before you die.' She held up one finger. 'Just one.'

'Mia...' She started to cry louder now, like a child wailing.

She sounded so different. Not at all like the tyrant *Mammy* June remembered. She liked that things had turned around. And she liked to hear her begging. The woman who, until now, only knew how to *demand*. So, who was educating who now, eh?

June put the wine glass to the woman's lips and brought the blade back up to her throat. She pressed it against her flesh, so that a few drops of her blood ran over the smooth silvery surface.

'Come on now, you love this wine. Isn't that right, Mammy?'

Her eyes narrowed first, then widened. She started shaking her head, sinking backwards into the chair.

'Drink it. It won't kill you, but the knife will.'

There was no anger in June's voice, and she was proud of herself for that. Even though she never lost control, there were times when she worried that she still might. What if, at the crucial moment, she flew into a blind rage and killed her on sight? She could waste the whole thing. But she hadn't. Of course she hadn't. Erica needed to see this coming. She needed to go to her grave knowing that it was her own life that had caught up with her.

'Do you understand now?' June pushed the glass between her lips.

Her body kind of juddered and shook and she cried. But she did start drinking. For the first time in June's life, Erica Kelly was doing what *she* told her to do. *She* was in charge. She was the weapon again.

'Drink it all down now.'

She did, in one long gulp with her eyes clamped shut. Tears poured out of them and down her face.

'That's good, well done. Now, why don't you lie down on the bed? You may as well get comfy.'

'You said you'd let me go.'

'I *said* you'd be long gone before they get here.'

There must have been some powerful stuff in that powder because she was already so drowsy. Perhaps whatever she'd taken herself before June got there was kicking in as well.

'I always keep my promises, Erica.'

She was still crying as June took her by the arm and helped her out of the chair. She managed the few steps to the bed and then just kind of plopped onto it.

'What's my name?'

She wouldn't look at June and she didn't answer.

'I can't believe you never recognised me. All those times I was here in your room with you, and you never even looked at me. But why would you, I suppose?' June sat on the edge of the chair, with her elbows resting on her knees, watching. Savouring.

Erica didn't say anything, but she was looking at June now. Her head lolled to the side and her face sagged most of the way down to her shoulder.

'She wrote to me,' June said quietly. For the first time that night, her voice sounded truly menacing. She couldn't help it. She always felt anger when she thought about those letters. 'She begged for me back.'

'I...' Her eyes were drooping.

'You told her that I didn't want her.' June thumped her chest then, and through gritted teeth she hissed, 'She was my mother. I wanted her!'

Erica rolled onto her side and glanced at June. Her face changed then. Her lip curled and there was something like resignation in her slackened features. 'Fuck you,' she muttered.

June pounced off the chair and pulled her onto the floor. She sank the blade into her stomach and knelt down beside her. She brought her face right down to hers and looked her in the eye. Then she pulled the blade out and stuck it back in. Out and in. Out and in, until she saw the miserable life draining from her eyes.

Blood started to pool around her, and June stood up. She stepped backwards, away from it, and she sat back down in the chair, in the corner of the room. She watched the woman for a few minutes, hoping that somewhere, a raging fire was waiting to greet her. A small part of her was disappointed that she lost it at the end. But she achieved her goal. Erica Kelly knew exactly why she was dying and by whose hand. The last thing she saw as she exited the world, was the green eye of Mia Kelly and the brown eye of June Calloway. And after today, both would cease to exist.

THIRTY-SIX

JUNE

Before June left room 208, her bloody boiler suit was packed away and so was the knife. She was in her clean maid's uniform and the room, aside from the bloody mess on the floor, was perfect. Again, there was a pang of disappointment. She'd wanted to make it look like she slit her wrists after taking too many pills. This was somewhat messier, but she didn't dwell on it. It's not like it changed her plans in any major way. This would be June's last day at the Cedarwood Manor regardless.

But rather than leaving as soon as Erica was dead and the clean-up was done, June decided to stay for the morning. She wanted to be the one to find her. June wanted to see her like this one more time before she went. But more than that, she wanted to see the concern that a missing child would garner. She wanted to hear the name *Mia* on the lips of someone who cared what happened to her. Someone who desperately wanted her to be saved. She wanted that now almost as much as she'd wanted Erica Kelly dead.

. . .

It was four thirty in the morning when she left the room and headed back the way she had come, through the store cupboard on the second floor and into the stone staircase. She peeped into the control room as she passed. As expected, Malcolm was sleeping soundly inside. She continued down into the darkened basement and quietly into the laundry room, which, like the rest of the hotel, was also still sleeping. She quietly let herself into the junk room, pulling the door closed behind her.

The aga had been lit since very early yesterday morning and was sufficiently hot. June opened her bag and took out the knife. It wouldn't burn so there was no point in throwing that in. She set it down and started pulling each of the other items out of the bag. The overalls, the sheet of paper. The foil, which she knew wouldn't burn, but the traces of her left behind on it, would. One by one, she put them in and watched as flames flickered to life and licked up around each piece, making it crumple and burn. Her stomach clenched with excitement. It was done. All these years of planning and it was finally done! The timing had never been right until now. In a way, Sister Bridget forced her hand, but with Erica trying to buy the Manor, she created the perfect environment for June to finally act. All of the evidence would probably be found eventually. If the Gardaí were any good at their jobs, that is. But it didn't matter. She'd be long gone by the time they got to this room.

When everything had gone in, she rolled up the bag and put that in, too. Then she closed the aga again, picked up the knife and left the room, locking it behind her. The door to the junk room wasn't usually locked, and the key was kept on top of the door frame. But it was all invisible. Meaning that, when someone eventually noticed it, no one would know where to start looking for the key. Not even Liz. June smiled as she slipped it in her pocket and made her way quietly to the kitchen.

The night staff were milling around the hotel. June was aware of that, but none of them would venture into the laundry room or the kitchen. Everyone hated the laundry room. It was spooky at the best of times, but particularly at night. And the chef did *not* like visitors in his kitchen. That's why he placed enough food in the staff canteen daily, to negate any excuse for someone being in his sacred space. June knew where everyone would be. Rita would be sitting behind the reception desk, working on her knitting, while the night concierge would either be dozing somewhere out of sight, or lounging lazily at his post. They'd only venture downstairs for their canteen breaks, which were at midnight and three am.

However, the kitchen staff would be in before everyone else. Their morning shift started well before the sun came up. Still, she figured she had at least a half hour's grace. She poured bleach in the sink with some water and dropped the knife into the bubbly liquid. She put on the Marigold gloves that were draped over the edge of the sink and she washed every millimetre of the knife. She ran her gloved fingers slowly over the blade and smiled. She silently thanked it for its service. Once she was happy, she dried it off and returned it to the chef's block. It was time for a shower, some breakfast with Liz and then, back to work. For a short time at least.

'I don't know if I like this or not, June.' Liz joined her in the staff canteen a while later. June already had the kettle boiling. 'You promised me that I wouldn't see you here again and I like having the Manor to myself in the mornings.'

'I know. Last time. I'm sorry.'

June knew the real reason why Liz came to work so early. It was to see if Malcolm was where he was supposed to be. Still, she smiled at the woman. She couldn't help it today.

'Coffee?'

'Thanks.' Liz half smiled back. It didn't reach her eyes because it couldn't. Her Botox had been topped up.

They sat in silence drinking their coffee. Neither of them were eating this morning. Liz was probably still doing her inter-whatever fasting thing, but June's stomach was just too excitable. Her throat would close if anything tried to pass through.

'I need a quiet day today,' Liz groaned into her cup.

June nodded. 'Here's hoping.'

'I have a call with Isabelle at noon. I'm going to tell her that if she sells to that woman, I'll resign with immediate effect. Let's see how smoothly any handover will go without me.'

'You should be firmer, Liz. You should tell her that you won't go quietly.'

Liz shrugged. 'She's always said how much she values me. It's time to see if she meant any of it.' She tried to sound tough, but she was worried, June could tell.

Still, she nodded and got up. She couldn't sit still anymore.

Liz looked at her watch. 'It's only half seven.'

'I know.' June smiled. 'But remember what I said about getting my trolley done before the others get here?'

'No fear they'll be early.' Liz rolled her eyes and stood up as well. She took her cup with her to her office, while June headed for the storeroom.

With her trolley loaded, June pushed it to the lobby. She parked it up by the lifts, unhooked her bucket and brought it with her to the lobby table. She took out a small container of oil soap and two cloths.

'One last special clean for you today, pet.' Her voice was just above a whisper, between her and the table. 'You know, I think I might miss you.' She rubbed her hand over it and worked her way slowly all around.

She spent almost an hour on it that morning. Who knows when it would get the attention it deserved again? So, June would leave this under-appreciated thing of beauty in the best possible state she could. When she was done, she stood looking at it for a minute. Then she placed the palm of her hand on it one last time. 'Bye,' she whispered, turning slowly and walking back to her trolley.

She worked her way around the lobby and reception area, having similar conversations with each piece of furniture. June's purpose at the Manor had always been clear. But she had come to care for the place. And she truly believed that it cared for her, too. As she finished with the reception desk, she glanced at the clock behind Lauren's head.

'The morning is bloody dragging,' Lauren moaned.

'Isn't it, though?' June agreed. Though, really, it wasn't. She was living every second of it, her insides fizzing and popping with each movement. This was her last ever morning at the Manor. It was both the end and the beginning of everything.

She left Lauren and went back to her trolley again. She slotted her bucket in and stepped into the lift, pulling the beast in with her. As the reflective doors slid shut, she smiled at the brown eyes looking back at her. She pressed number two and waited for the ping. The doors slid open.

'Morning.' She smiled at the honeymoon couple from room 205.

The man gave June a curt nod. His new wife rolled her eyes and dropped her hands down by her sides. The woman was frustrated. She didn't want to have to stand aside to let the maid and her trolley out of the lift before they could get in. That's not what they were paying through the nose for.

'Sorry about that.' June smiled again. 'Have a lovely day.'

'Yeah, thanks,' said the man. The woman checked her reflection in the mirrored wall, like they all did.

When the door slid shut and the couple were gone, June

stood looking down the hall towards room 208. All was still. As it should be. She worked very quickly through the first five rooms. Then she wedged open the door to room 206 and parked her trolley outside. But rather than going in, she went to room 208. She didn't need to use her key card because she'd taped the lock before leaving earlier. She glanced up and down the corridor one more time, before pushing through the door.

She smelled the blood as soon as she stepped inside, so she closed the door quickly. She didn't want to let it out into the corridor. Then she stood in the entrance hall for a few seconds looking at the mess on the floor. Her face was grey now, and her skin had a waxy shine to it. She didn't look real anymore. But as much as she wanted to, June couldn't allow herself to get lost in the sight of her. She needed to work quickly now, so she knelt on the bed and reached for the phone. She had her own phone in her other hand with the recording lined up and ready to go. She plugged the room phone back into the socket and dialled 999.

'Emergency, which service do you require?'

June pressed play. 'Hello? My daughter is missing!' Stop.

'Putting you through to Gardaí now.'

June went back to the start of the recording.

'Gardaí, what's going on there?'

'Hello? My daughter is missing! I'm at the Cedarwood Manor Hotel and she was here with me. She was right here! We both went to bed at ten o'clock, and I woke up and she was gone.' Stop.

'Okay, so you last saw her at the Cedarwood Manor, that's in Cork? Is there anyone in the area that she might have gone to? Was anyone else with you?'

'Her name is Mia Kelly and she's only ten years old. She has long, red hair and green eyes. She was wearing a white jumper and black leggings.' Stop.

'Okay, ma'am, slow down a minute, Gardaí are on the way...'

'Her mother loves her so much!' Stop.

'I understand. Can you...'

'Please help me! Please find her!' Stop. June hung up the phone.

She smiled and crawled backwards off the bed. She straightened the covers, pulling them tightly across the mattress. As she deleted the recording off her phone, she resisted the urge to look at her again. She worried that if she did, she wouldn't be able to look away. Instead, she cast her eyes around the room itself, checking that everything was in order. She could still see Liz's handprint on the glass. Normally that would have bothered June immensely, but she'd purposely left it there. Not to frame Liz for her actions, or anything like that, but more for the sake of confusion. Everyone knew how angry Liz was at Erica. With some luck, the gossip and the handprint should give June enough of a head start. She left the room, pulling the tape off the lock as she closed the door gently behind her.

Room 206 was vacant and didn't require any attention, so June stood to the side of the picture window, looking down on the carpark below. As she stood there, she noticed the splash of blood on the cuff of her blouse. Her stomach leaped. Had that been there all morning? Had Liz seen it?

Surely, she would have said it if she had. Liz would not have let her work in a less than perfect uniform. Besides, given June's recent injuries, she would have assumed the blood was her own. It wasn't. But it could have been.

Her attention was pulled away from her sleeve by the arrival of the first Garda car. There were no flashing lights, which was disappointing. But it was moving relatively quickly up the long driveway.

June stepped back, away from the window, and watched for a few more seconds. Then she took a few deep breaths and left the room. She pulled her trolley past the unoccupied room 207 and parked it at the door of 208. Her stomach jumped and danced, and her skin pricked. But not in the way it used to. She breathed deeply, swiped her card, and stepped inside.

THIRTY-SEVEN

Six months later

Margaret Higgins was the best maid the Happy Days Aparthotel in Belfast City ever had. Laurence, the fat manager, both loved and hated her at the same time. He hated her, because she'd made a show of him in front of some guests, during her first week. He was trying to charge their credit card for a red-wine stain on the carpet in their room. The guests argued their defence but were about to concede to the extra charges, when Margaret, or Meg as she was known, interrupted them. She'd helpfully let them all know that the stain had been successfully removed. She was good with stains. But more than that, she actually cared whether or not the place was clean. And not just to an *acceptable standard,* which of course made the manager look good when his bosses were around. Hence his conflicting feelings towards her.

Meg stepped aside near the first-floor lifts to let the hen party out of their room. They looked sick, all of them, like they wanted to die. They each had sunglasses at the ready, even though they were still inside, and it was a dull grey day outside.

'Sorry about that lot.' One of them, the last one out of the room, thumbed over her shoulder. 'We're not normally that messy.'

Meg gave her a small smile and a shrug. The woman held the door open for her and Meg went inside. 'Thanks.'

'I hope your day is better than mine is going to be,' the woman groaned. Then she walked off to catch up with her friends.

Hen parties were always messy, but Meg didn't mind them. For the most part, they were nice. They nearly always said something friendly to her before they left. And not just that. They always left bags of crisps, and lots of unopened chocolate, scattered among the detritus in the rooms. Sunday was a feast day for Meg.

She let the door close behind her and looked around at the mess. It was bad, but she'd seen worse. Empty bottles of prosecco and dirty glasses. Those were standard. Probably some vomit in the bathroom, too. There were lipstick kisses on the long mirror and a sticky residue, like someone had taken aim with a bottle of fizz. She took a bottle and a cloth from her bucket and sprayed it. As she wiped it clean, she found herself making eye contact with the woman reflected back at her.

Her green eyes still caught her off guard at times, but she was getting used to them. Her natural red hair was tinted blonde, which was much easier to maintain than June's dark brown was. The roots didn't look so obvious as they grew out and it was longer now, too, almost down to her shoulders. She'd put on some more weight as well, thanks to the hen parties. Once again, she was a whole other person, aside from her hands. They were, and always would be, June Calloway's hands.

At times when she was alone, with her eyes closed and

when there was quiet all around her, she could still feel it. That sensation she got in the palm of her hand, through the handle of the knife that night. As its blade slid through all the layers of fat and muscle and whatever internal organs were in its way, June felt every sliver of it. Or at least, she imagined she had. She never felt that when she'd slit Kevin's wrists. Or her own. She never felt it when she sliced open the flesh on her thighs either. She was sorry to have wasted all those opportunities and she wondered if she'd ever get to experience that feeling again.

The thumb of her left hand circled the palm of her right. A subconscious act whenever she thought about it. Like an itch that needed to be scratched. She thought about that feeling now in the same way she used to think about cutting herself.

But despite the hands and the itch, June Calloway was gone away. Only Margaret Higgins remained. But she kept June's title – the hotel maid. A title that would always give her the invisibility that she craved. She didn't expect to have this new life for very long. She waited to be caught and when she was, she'd take herself off to meet Erica and Bridget and complete the vicious circle in Hell. Her whole life had been about killing Erica Kelly. But who knows? There was a ferry pilot called Jason who stayed there regularly. He actually drove the boat between Belfast and the Isle of Man and over there was where he lived. He liked to talk a lot during his stays. While she cleaned his room one morning, she'd told him the same story she'd told Liz when she first applied for a job at the Cedarwood Manor, and Laurence when she came here. A story about an abusive man called Kevin that she was hiding from. A man who controlled her life to the point where she had to leave without her passport. Meg was living in fear, terrified of him. Jason was nice. He worried for her. He'd mentioned his ferry and how nice the Isle of Man was, especially in summer. He lived in a place called Douglas, which sounded very nice. It had a really long beach, he said, and lots of hotels. One was even an ancient castle, right on the beach front. But that was closed for renovations now. Jason was due back next week. Meg thought maybe her fear of horrible, dead Kevin might intensify around that time. But who knows what might happen?

Sirens wailed somewhere in the distance, coming closer. Meg went and looked out the window, wondering if they were for her at last. The madness of Saturday night in the city had been replaced with the calm of a dull Sunday morning. The street below was quiet, aside from that siren. She stood there for a minute, waiting. Before long, a single police car rushed by and didn't stop. It would someday. It had to, and that was okay.

She'd enjoyed the newspaper coverage the Cedarwood Manor Murder had got in the weeks following Erica's comeuppance. One catchy headline said *Murder at the Manor*. She particularly liked that one. Malcolm was first to be brought in as a suspect. Of course he was. He'd been having an affair with the victim and the security cameras had been switched off at the time of the murder. It turned out he had an alibi, though. Liz had had a camera installed in the control room that he knew nothing about. Proof that theirs wasn't such a one-way relationship. They liked to keep tabs on each other, just as June had come to suspect. Anyway, Malcolm was asleep in his chair at the time of the murder, which put him in the clear.

Liz was next to be thrust into the spotlight. The victim had had an affair with her boyfriend and was threatening her job. Everyone happily testified to her state of mind on the matter. Plus, there was that handprint on the glass, right above the woman's dead body. She laughed when she read that. Meg liked that all those little details were made public. Not only that, but they were trawled over and picked apart in the media. But it was the pages and pages of concerned words about poor Mia Kelly that made Meg's heart sing. The whole country was looking for her now, when not one single person had looked when she actually went missing. Aside from her poor, stupid mother, that is.

Meg cut out every article that was written about Mia and had almost a full scrapbook after a couple of weeks.

It took them a full day to realise that the maid was missing. Then, of course, in their search for her, they found good old Sister Bridget. News of her suicide and her history with the victim went viral. The Mother and Baby Homes were back on the front page of every paper and on everyone's lips again. Victims talked of their memories of the vile Sister Bridget and how she had stalked the child of one of her victims, right up until the end. *Could she have been the one who killed Erica Kelly?* the world asked.

Meg particularly enjoyed that line of enquiry. There were still those who thought the evil nun did it. But there were details that didn't add up to her. For example, the only DNA found at the scene matched the swabs taken from the maid. But she *had* stumbled around the room in her shocked haze. Or did she do it intentionally? Either way, they didn't match anyone in any system. Also, the remains of burned clothing were found in a disused kitchen in the Manor's basement and the murder weapon was found having been bleached and returned to its block in the kitchen. How could the old nun have accessed either of those areas? But the maid could have. All the evidence pointed to the hotel maid and now she was missing. What's more, there was no record of the woman anywhere. It was as if June Calloway never existed.

The online world had started to compare the Erica Kelly murder to an unsolved murder that took place in West Cork in the nineties.

Meg smiled as she worked her way through the room, preparing it for the next budget city-breakers or businessperson to pass through it. There was a steady stream and very few of them complained about anything. She did miss the Manor. She thought about it often as she worked her way around the nondescript rooms of this particular three-star. But more and more now she found herself wondering about a place she'd never heard of before recently. Douglas. The Isle of Man. What would it be like there? Was it big enough for her to get lost in? Big enough to lose the pilot Jason in after he got her there? Sometimes she even wondered if perhaps June might be over there, somewhere waiting for her.

She closed her eyes as her thumb circled her palm again. She pictured that castle hotel near the sandy beach. She smiled, returning a small wave to a brown-haired maid waving at her through an upstairs window. The itch in her palm grew stronger and she pressed her thumb deep into it. 'I'm coming,' she said, opening her eyes. June Calloway looked back at her now from the streak-free mirror. On the cuff of her white sleeve, a dash of red shone out. She smiled at Meg and Meg smiled back. Then she picked up her bucket and got to work.

A LETTER FROM THE AUTHOR

Dear Reader,

Thank you for reading *The Hotel Maid*. If you would like to join other readers in keeping in touch, stay in the loop with my new releases by signing up to my email newsletter here.

www.stormpublishing.co/michelle-dunne

If you enjoyed it and could spare a few moments to leave a review that would be hugely appreciated. Even a short review can make all the difference in encouraging a reader to discover my books for the first time. Thank you so much!

I find inspiration in absolutely everything. But the all-important setting for my books is usually inspired by my beautiful hometown and the city that I love, Cork. In keeping with this, the Cedarwood Manor Hotel is inspired by the fabulous Fota House – once the private home of the Smith-Barry family, but for the past 200 years or so, it's been in the care of the Irish Heritage Trust. I've been visiting Fota House and Gardens for years. It's a stunning example of regency architecture, filled with history and amazing stories. Seeing the contrast between the grand décor of the formal rooms and the servants' wing – it's hard not to be inspired! There is a much more modern hotel on the vast grounds of Fota Island now as well, which, like the Cedarwood Manor, is surrounded by beautiful woodland with a stunning Chinese garden out front. But it is *far* more welcoming than the Manor. And I suspected it's a lot safer, too!

Thank you so much for reading, and if you'd like to join me on our ongoing journey, please do!

facebook.com/MichelleDunneAuthor

x.com/NotDunneYet

instagram.com/michelledunneauthor

ACKNOWLEDGMENTS

I've really enjoyed writing this book and am incredibly grateful to everyone who has supported and encouraged me along the way. I'm especially grateful to the brilliant team at Storm Publishing. Anna, Elke and Alexandra for their passion and attention to detail. And a very special thank you to Claire Bord, who is the kind of editor that all authors dream of working with. Thank you for your patience and guidance and for your belief in this story.

A massive thank-you to all at WGM Atlantic Talent & Literary Group, especially my lovely agent, Nicky Lovick, who has championed my work since the day we met. You are genuinely the most encouraging person I know. Thank you.

To the amazing community of Irish crime writers, whose friendship and support means the world, especially Cork author Amy Jordan who's always up for a coffee and some plotting.

To my family, beautiful Emily, Dominic and the long list of outlaws and in-laws. But a special mention to the driving forces behind us all – our formidable mothers, Ann McNamara and Kathleen Dunne – their strength knows no bounds.

Finally, to all the bookish people out there. Readers, book-sellers, bloggers and the rest, without whom no one would ever hear about any of us writers! From the bottom of my heart, thank you.

Made in United States
North Haven, CT
02 September 2024

56839312R10157